M000221544

BEST
LESBIAN EROTICA
OF THE YEAR

VOLUME FOUR

BEST
LESBIAN EROTICA
OF THE YEAR

VOLUME FOUR

Edited by
SINCLAIR SEXSMITH

CLEiS
PRESS

Copyright © 2019 by Sinclair Sexsmith.

All rights reserved. Except for brief passages quoted in newspaper, magazine, radio, television or online reviews, no part of this book may be reproduced in any form or by any means, electronic or mechanical, including photocopying, recording, or information storage or retrieval system, without permission in writing from the Publisher.

Published in the United States by Cleis Press, an imprint of Start Midnight, LLC, 221 River Street, 9th Floor, Hoboken, NJ 07030.

Cover design: Allyson Fields
Cover photograph: iStock
Text design: Frank Wiedemann

First Edition.
10 9 8 7 6 5 4 3 2 1

Trade paper ISBN: 978-1-62778-295-1
E-book ISBN: 978-1-62778-508-2

For my boy, of course.

CONTENTS

ix   Introduction

1   Do Tell • FOSTER JOY
15   My Sweet Femme Nightmare • JUNE AMELIA ROSE
27   Of Sword and Sorcery • MARIA CHIARA FERRO
35   Pinked • AVERY CASSELL
45   Pleasure with Her Pain • ADA LOWELL
60   Leviathan • CATHERINE COLLINSWORTH
74   Good Girls Do • MARIE CARLSON
87   Here Comes the Sun • Mx. NILLIN FUCHS
93   Gina, Across the Tracks • FALLEN MATTHEWS
101   Adventure in Palm Springs • DOROTHY FREED
110   The Strip • J. MORK
123   The Butler, the Flapper, and the Stable Boy •
     GIGI FROST
134   All Dolled Up • OLIVIA DROMEN
141   What I Want • LAUREL ISAAC
148   Brunch Service • TOBI HILL-MEYER
160   Pay Me No Mind • R. MAGDALEN
166   Modern Lovers (You Probably Haven't Heard of
     Them) • T.R. VERTEN
179   Because Today Has Been the Most Beautiful Day •
     BD SWAIN
190   Crave • XAN WEST
201   Love Remembers • ANGORA SHADE

213   About the Authors
219   About the Editor

INTRODUCTION

Have you ever written erotica?

You probably have. Maybe you've written an email describing what you wanted to do that night, or reminiscing over the weekend's sexcapades. Or maybe you wrote a love letter on rose-scented gold paper, with a declaration of love and lust. Or, at the least, you have probably texted something dirty out into the eager hands of someone at the other end of the screen.

Even if it was just a few sentences, it counts.

While some erotica is fanciful literary writing, much of it is the simple dirty notes we send each other, the manifestation of our longings and wants and hopes and hormones.

When we put words to our desire, we make it real. We make it powerful. We make it relatable. We put it in a form where other people can also interact with it, relate to it, revel in it. And while I do not advocate for erotica as a form of sex education—it is too full of fantastical, flawed human wants—when we read others' desires put into words, we can learn.

The *Best Lesbian Erotica* series is the reason I write erotica.

Finding a tattered copy of *Best Lesbian Erotica 1997* in the secondhand bookstore on Capitol Hill in Seattle as a college student in 2000 was a significant event, and I continued to devour each new edition when they came out, studying them like a treasure map to my own desire.

Finding language for the things I was feeling, for the things I wanted, was always significant. I wanted to know who I was, how I fit in the world, how to find the love and closeness I wanted, and how to have the mind-blowing sex I knew was possible. Devouring erotica became one of my major sources. Descriptions of first dates, of first-time kink experiences, of dark and sexy dungeons, of long-lasting lovers, of long-distance relationships, of breakup sex—each time I read stories like those, I found a piece of myself.

Unlike heterosexual desire, queer desire isn't pasted on the walls of pop culture for us all to consume, consciously or unconsciously. Unlike heterosexuals and their versions of desire, we don't see hundreds of models of queer desire in advertisements, films, shows, and music.

I put my queer self together piece by piece. I made myself from scratch after pulling apart the societally constructed version of myself and knowing I needed something different. I did not find my queer desire out in the world: I had to dig for it. I had to pull scenes and sentences from hundreds of different media.

Writing erotica has been the way I created my sex life. I write what I want to feel, what I want to witness, what I am curious to do. I write what I think other people would like to read. I write what I want to read. I write things I have never published, and never will, for fear (and educated guess) that they will be harshly judged. I write for inspiration, for erotic energy, to turn on my partner, to entertain, or just because I'm bored.

Identifying what it is that turns me on, writing it down, and sharing it has been one of the biggest steps to looking my own sexual shame in the eye.

While the queer representation continues to grow and become increasingly common and accepted, queer communities and the erotica representing queer folks are still a microcosm of the larger culture, not a safe haven. It is still dominated by images of cis, white, thin, able-bodied, and neurotypical people. It is still full of stereotypes and much-repeated (and much-loved) common tropes.

And this is why I think everyone should write erotica: it has the potential to be transformative. "Write the erotica you wish to read in the world"—to paraphrase Mahatma Gandhi.

I'm honored to have been asked to edit this edition of *Best Lesbian Erotica*. I'm honored by all of the writers who sent me their beautiful stories. I am including as many as I can—I pushed the limits of what this book could hold, stuffing in every one possible. I have chosen stories that break away from the stereotypes, that challenge preconceived notions, and go beyond what one would usually think of as lesbian erotica.

I hope you read it and enjoy. Even more so, I hope you write your own story, and submit it to the next edition—or, at the very least, share it with someone, even just one other person.

Let our desires be written and witnessed. Let our desires be real.

Sinclair Sexsmith
Oakland, California

DO TELL

Foster Joy

At the bar entrance, Leona, a hulking leather butch, gives me a thumbs-up. From my seat, I catch Wanda's eye and she nods before taking the stage. Six-six in heels, miniskirt, fake nails, and a bouffant. I'm still conflicted about whether a drag queen was the right choice. Oh well—I'm sure I'll hear about it from someone tomorrow. I scan the venue. Decent turnout, multiple genders, many ages and ethnicities. Good-looking crowd . . . except for the beard/man-bun combo.

"Good evening, friends, my name is Wanda Bite and I am your emcee and timekeeper for this glorious event, Do Tell!" Applause and a few wolf whistles. Wanda growls like a cougar and paws at the air. "I'm not on the menu tonight, honey." Laughter. "But look at all of you—gorgeous! Thank you all for being here. I have a good feeling about this." She crowd-whispers, conspiratorially, "I think some of you are gonna get laid tonight." More laughter and hoots from the crowd. "Let's all thank our hosts, the Dapper Den!"

As the crowd cheers, I scan the setup. Everyone has a name

tag. Stanchions with dark-green braided ropes sequester the line of tables snaking around the crowded mahogany oval bar, three bartenders working a section from the center. Each table has a black tablecloth with one flickering small fake candle, one empty chair, and one seated guest. Others stand or sit at the bar. Some look shy and nervous, others eager. Everyone is eyeing everyone else.

"Keep drinking, folks, you'll all look sexier as the night goes on, and remember to tip your bartenders!" Wanda waves her drink in salute to the bar crew who wave back. She turns her attention back to the crowd. "You ready to do this?" Cheers. "I can't hear you! I said are you all ready to do this?" Louder cheers. "That's more like it! You all chose the right night. I am thrilled to officially welcome you all to Do Tell, bringing the sex to pansexual speed dating!"

Hoots and hollers, whistles and cheers.

"Yes! Here are the rules: Temptees are already seated and waiting to be seduced. Tempters will have one minute to make a great first impression with a one-line sexual fantasy. Naughty, naughty minxes! Temptees will either invite you to Round Two or release you. That is your cue to immediately skedaddle to the next table. Rejection is part of the game folks so put on your thickest skins—clearly some masochists up in this bitch!—and have fun. Remember, any uninvited touching, name-calling, threats, or violence and Leona will be thrilled to escort you out." Wanda waves to Leona, still seated at the entrance. Leona blows a kiss and the crowd hollers again.

"All right you sexy beasts, Do Tell!"

I smile as my first tempter approaches and sits across from me. White, nonbinary, buzz cut, bright blue eyes, midthirties. Name tag reads *Em, she/they*.

"Em. Do Tell."

"Hi, Grace. Great earrings, by the way."

I touch the beaded hoops I'm wearing. "Thanks, they're from Ghana."

"Really? Do you have family there?" Here we go. "Oh, I didn't mean just because you're black. Shit. Do you identify as black? Or African-American? Or Caribbean-American? God, I'm really sorry. I'm just super nervous."

"Take a deep breath. They were a gift. African-American, thanks. Also, tick tock, Em."

"Huh? Oh, right. Sorry. Okay, may I hold your hand?"

I extend my right hand. Em sits up straighter, takes my hand and turns it palm up placing slight pressure at the center. "First, I would blindfold you and lay you down on my massage table." They pull out a small bottle of oil. "May I?" I nod. "I would start with your hands." I watch as two drops fall from the bottle into my palm and Em begins to massage. I close my eyes and take a deep breath as relaxation takes over. Their fingers entwine with mine, pinching lightly, and I feel my nipples harden which leads me to a self-conscious grin. "You have a beautiful smile."

I open my eyes and focus on Em's mouth. Is it too soon to kiss them? The time bell dings and Wanda calls out, "That went fast, huh? Move along, move along!"

Sigh. "See you in Round Two."

Em smiles widely. I watch them approach the next table. Damn, if they can do that by just touching my hand!

I am pulled back to the present as my next tempter—African-American; early forties? Hard to tell—sits down. *Ronald, he/him.* Tailored suit, ruby stud, dazzling smile.

"Hello, my beautiful, ebony sister! May I say you are looking stunning tonight?" He takes my hand without asking and kisses it gently.

"Thank you, Ronald. Do Tell."

He leans in and whispers, "May I call you Mommy?"

"You may not. Feel free to advance to the next table."

Ronald's face falls. "Your loss. My cock looks great in a diaper."

"You do you. Good night."

When my next temptress sits down, she crosses her long legs in my view, the high slit in her velvet aubergine dress placed just so. *Anastacia, she/her, trans woman.* Forties, long, flowing black hair, brown eyes, burnt sienna skin, high femme, great décolletage, long nails. Yikes, no fisting with those, please! I smell lavender as she reaches out her hand.

"Grace, so lovely to meet you."

"The pleasure is mine. Do tell."

"We would spend a secluded weekend in my lake house, stopping along the way to pick up your favorite wine and any other delicacies you desire. After a light, gourmet dinner, we would enjoy a drink on my enclosed porch. For dessert, strawberries dipped in chocolate...while I slowly undress you."

"That's more than one sentence."

"Ooooh, a rule follower! Shall I stop?"

"You certainly paint an intriguing picture." The timer dings. "See you in Round Two."

"I can't wait."

Anastacia unlocks the door then opens it and steps aside so that I may enter first. "Welcome."

She turns on the lights and moves behind me. "Let me take that." I feel her breasts as she leans into my back and removes my jacket. I turn, hoping to kiss her, but she has stepped away. She slides out of her own coat to reveal a teal satin dress beneath. Her turquoise jewelry pieces are a perfect complement. As she brings our groceries to the kitchen, I take in the lavish surroundings: light hardwood floors, exposed beam ceiling, fireplace, plush furniture, large, framed black-and-white nude photography, abstract sculpture bathed by a carefully placed light source, and huge almost floor-to-ceiling window. Outside, the lake shimmers in moonlight surrounded by majestic redwood trees. I turn to Anastacia who's unpacking our treats. "I've never known anyone who actually had a lake house. I figured it was just an extravagant pickup line."

"And yet you said yes anyway! Glad to know you're not just after my architect."

"Well, I would love to see more of his work. Is he local?"

"*She* is. I'd be happy to introduce you."

Wince. "Oh no! She!" I pump my fist in the air. "Screw you, societal conditioning!"

She laughs. "I'll drink to that!" She holds up a bottle. "Champagne?"

"Always." We lock eyes. "Also, dessert first."

On the porch, I sit in a rocking chair by the window listening to her movements in the kitchen, glasses clinking, while looking out at the water. I hear her stop in the doorway: she's watching me. She puts the champagne and two flutes on the bedside table then turns on the fireplace and slinks slowly around the room, lighting candles. She's shoeless and I can see her perfectly pedicured toenails through her nylons. Thank god I got mine done, too. When the candles are done, she walks to me and reaches for my hand, pulling me up gently. She tucks my hair behind my ear before leaning in and whispering, "I think you'll be more comfortable on the bed." I feel myself blush as she leads me there.

We stand, facing each other. "I'm so glad you're here," she whispers and leans in for our first kiss. She tastes like honey and I feel my skin explode with goose bumps as her tongue explores mine. She whispers, "*Tu eres una persona bellisima o guapisima.*" Our mouths are warm and wet, tongues gentle at first then more eager. I run my hands over her sides and waist then enjoy the curve of her ass. She pulls me to her, pressing her breasts to mine. This feels amazing—but we're wearing too many clothes.

She stops suddenly, sits me down on the bed, and kneels to remove my shoes. I watch her hands and am relieved to notice her fingernails are much shorter this evening. I feel a tightening in my vagina, an ache, as she runs her hands up my calves and the sides of my thighs as she stands.

She kisses me again then whispers, "Sit back. I'll get dessert." As I prop myself up on the extravagant pillows, she hands me a champagne flute before lifting her own. "Cheers . . . to pansexual speed dating."

I laugh and clink glasses. "Pansexual speed dating!"

She returns to the kitchen, calling, "I can't believe no one's ever done that before."

"Well, they have, but my twist was the fantasy one-liner intros."

She returns with a tray of cut fruit and a lit fondue pot. "Yes! Cut through the bullshit and get to the good stuff. I don't care where you grew up if our fetishes are incompatible."

"Exactly!"

She dips a strawberry in the pot and removes it drenched in dripping dark chocolate. "Hungry?" I open my mouth invitingly and she brings the strawberry to my lips. I lock eyes with her as I take a bite. She smiles then eats the other half. "I think I'll start with . . ." She kisses me deeply as her hands work deftly, unbuckling my belt. She kneels over me as she slowly drags it through the loops and lets it plunk to the high-pile throw rug beneath us. "Mango?"

"Yes, please." She lets the mango dance over my tongue making me stretch to take it in. She returns to kiss me before gently biting and licking my ear. I feel an electric shiver from my head to my thighs. Her tongue glides over my neck to my clavicle and then she kisses her way lower. I arch my back as her hands slide over my breasts straining toward her touch. She buries her lips between my cleavage and looks up at me as her fingers encircle my nipples. I gasp at the jolt that vibrates from my breasts to my clit.

"You like that?" she teases. She sits up and begins unbuttoning my blouse from the bottom as I watch, breathing rapidly. She nods to the tray. "Which one next?"

Who cares about fruit? I want her to fuck me! I look at the tray then back at her, bite my lower lip. "Grapefruit?"

"Excellent choice." She finishes with the final button and spreads open my blouse, easing me out of it before letting it join my long-forgotten belt. She selects a section, dips it in the chocolate, and feeds me half. The second half she dips again then paints small chocolate dots from my belly button to my neck before feeding me the second half as she licks each dot clean, and then our mouths meet once again. My hands travel to her breasts, but she sits up. I moan and reach for her.

She entwines her hand in mine, and smiles. "Patience, *mi amor*. Choose."

"This is torture, you know?"

She kisses me gently and smiles. "*Si*, I know."

I glance at the tray. "Fine. Banana."

"Pants first." She unbuttons then slowly unzips my pants. I help ease them over my hips and watch as she walks backward sliding off my pants slowly, so slowly, until they fall from my bare feet. "Nice toes! Are you warm enough?"

"So far, so good."

"Okay, let me know. The fireplace has a remote." She points to the nightstand where I see a slender platinum device.

"Good to know. I'm okay for now."

"*Perfecto*." She returns to the fondue pot. "Banana, was it?"

"Yes." I watch her lift the dipped fruit to her mouth. She then leans down and kisses me. I taste her mixed deliciously with the fruit and fondue. "I'm in heaven."

"*Bienvenido! Que otro*? What's next?"

"Umm, first I think you have far too many clothes on. This does not seem fair at all. May I help you?" I reach for her knotted belt. Instead, she stands. I prop myself on my elbows for a better view as she unties her belt and allows her dress to fall open to reveal matching bra, garter, and bikini briefs in teal-and-black lace. God, she's beautiful! The fireplace light flickers over her skin as she slips the dress from her shoulders. She poses with a foot on the fireplace ledge as she unhooks her garters and slides out of her hose. "You are exquisite."

She smiles and returns to stand with her back to me. She sweeps aside her hair and looks at me over her shoulder. "Help me with the clasps?"

Behind her, I kiss her shoulders, neck, and spine, as I unhook her garter belt. I embrace her with one arm around her waist, the other hand between her breasts, and breathe her in, relishing our skin-to-skin connection. She leans her head back as I kiss her ear and neck. I free her bra with one hand and smile. Still got it.

She turns to me, holding her bra in place. "We're uneven again."

I unclasp my bra, holding mine in place to mirror her. "Better?"

"Much."

We kiss and toss our bras to the floor as we lie back on the bed, intertwined. I seek out her breasts, enveloping each nipple with my tongue. I return to her mouth. "Does that feel good?"

"Incredible." My tongue seeks hers again.

"Oh my god, I need to fuck you very soon. Any special requests? Areas off limits?"

"You're sweet." She reaches out to open a nightstand drawer

and removes lube, dental dams, a dildo, pink fuzzy handcuffs, nipple clamps, and a Polaroid camera. Hello! "Thanks for asking, but my guests always come first. Anything here you like?"

"Wow, so much to choose from!"

"That's not even all of it."

"Do tell!"

"So clever. Let's just see where the night takes us." She picks up the fondue tray and sets it on the window seat.

"May I turn up the fireplace?"

"Of course!" She kisses my shoulders as I play with the functions, watching the faux flames intensify. I get a chill down my back. "Oh, you *are* cold."

I turn to her. "No, that was from you." I get lost in her mouth again, wanting to drink her in. Everywhere she touches me makes me want more. Her hand slinks down the small of my back, a finger grazes my asscrack then lingers at my bikini line, running under the elastic. I realize I'm holding my breath and finally exhale. Her hand continues across my pubic bone, through my hair, and between my labia. I open my legs wider as she strokes me slowly.

"You're so wet." I close my eyes and bite her shoulder. "Look at me." We lock eyes as she slides one finger inside me, then two. I gasp and close my eyes again. "Look at me." I open my eyes and look at her. She continues to plunge her hand inside me, holding my gaze, and I rock my pelvis in rhythm with her fingers.

"Deeper."

She pushes in deeper, watching me. "Is this what you want?"

"Yes, yes."

She stops moving her hand. "Tell me."

"I want you. Don't stop." I feel her slide inside me again. "Yes . . . Yes."

Her mouth hovers over my breast. "Tell me to fuck you." She starts sucking my nipple.

"Fuck me. Fuck me."

"Again."

"Fuck me, fuck me. Anastacia." She pulls her hand out and kisses me while we pull off my underwear. I reach for hers. "Let me touch you."

She smiles while moving out of reach, between my legs. "I want to taste you." Her face disappears and suddenly she licks me deeply. I fall back on the bed, waves of pleasure spreading through me with every movement of her tongue. My clit is throbbing as she lays her tongue against it, unmoving. I touch her head and freeze. "Wait."

Pulse.

Pulse.

Pulse.

My mind is racing. If she keeps going (please!), I'm going to come, but I also don't want this to end yet. "Wait. Come here." I feel her tongue lift gently and another jolt runs through me. She crawls closer and I feel her breasts glide across my body. As she kisses me, I smell and taste myself, musky and slightly sweet.

"I was so close. You're incredible."

"You're delicious."

I slip her underwear off one hip. "Take these off. Let me touch you." She lies back on the pillows and allows me to undress her. We make eye contact as she slowly spreads her thighs. I finally look: she's beautiful. Her gorgeous brown labia make my mouth water. I kiss her inner thigh. "May I?"

She nods and hands me the lube. I slick my fingers and scooch in closer to her vulva. With my lubed fingers, I begin to explore, spreading her gently apart. I slip in with my tongue and hear her breathe in sharply. She tenses then relaxes as I massage her hips while I lick her inside and out. I focus on her clit and hear her moan as I lick it slowly, then firmly, then barely with the tip of my tongue. As I suck on it, I slide one finger inside of her, feeling her warmth.

"Oh my god, oh my god. Yes! Grace! Grace!" She whimpers and tangles her fingers in my hair, pushing my face into her while I continue to suck and lick her pussy. I feel myself start to drip down my thighs as I devour her.

I can hear her gasps subside to contented moans and whispers of "Yes. That's so good." I emerge to kiss and gently bite her inner thighs, then lick and kiss my way up her body, lingering at her breasts, then move up to her neck and ear before whispering, "Thank you."

She kisses me and laughs. "No, thank *you*." She drapes a hand on her forehead.

I kiss her cheek. "I'm so glad you liked it."

She kisses me deeply. "Very much."

"But you didn't come. Do you . . . ?"

"Usually alone, with a vibrator."

"Sounds fun. Where is it? Your drawer of fun?" She smiles, nods, and gets up to refill our champagne. I root around in the drawer and find a small egg attached to a remote. "This?" She nods again while she drinks. I turn it on and it starts to tingle in my fingers. I reach for her and run the egg around her breasts and across her nipples while she squirms.

"Do you have a favorite setting?" I ask.

"I usually just play around until I get it right."

"What if . . . ?" I scoot closer to her and wrap my leg around her thigh while tucking the egg clit level between us. I hand her the remote. "Wanna turn it on?" She puts down her glass, takes the remote, and pulls me closer, kissing me more and more intensely. I can taste the champagne and am lost in her mouth when suddenly I feel a steady vibration between us. We continue to kiss and maneuver ourselves for optimal positioning.

"I get why you like it."

She nods with a grin then asks more seriously, "Will you come for me?"

"No doubt, but you first." I hand her the egg. "Hold this." I stand and grab the dildo and the lube and position myself between her legs, watching her enjoy herself with the egg, smiling at me. I lube up the dildo along with my fingers again. "Tell me what you like best." I guide one finger inside of her and she arches her back. I stroke her inside and out slowly. "Or . . ." I insert two and hear her gasp and moan my name. "Is that better?"

"Yes, yes, don't stop."

"Okay, you don't stop either. God, you are so fucking hot right now." I continue to fuck her with my fingers while I watch her writhe on the egg and twist free the sheets. I see the dildo glistening on the bed. "Do you wanna try . . . ?"

"No, don't stop! That's perfect. Don't. Stop. Don't. Stop."

I navigate the dildo so I can rub my pussy against it. Yes, that works. Wow. I look up at her. "Are you gonna come for me?"

"Yes, yes, make me come." I push into her deeply then slide out almost all the way before gliding slowly back in. "Oh my god, yes." I continue this pace while I watch her face contort in ecstasy. I stroke my other hand up her body and begin to lightly twist her right nipple.

"Oh my god, Grace. Grace. Yes," she says. I ever-so-lightly and repeatedly flick the tip of her nipple and see her mouth drop open before she begins again. "Yes, yes, oh my god, fuck me, fuck me. Grace, I'm gonna come. Don't stop. Don't stop. Yes . . . Yes . . . Yes!" she cries out, guttural and loud. I wonder if her neighbors heard that.

I feel her shiver, then collapse in surrender, shutting off the egg. She reaches for me and pulls me to her mouth. She is so warm and wet and open. She entwines her legs in mine and pulls me closer. I hold her and listen to her breath slow down and then catch. She's crying. I hold her closer.

She takes a deep breath. "I have no words. *Tu eres increible.*"

"You don't need words. Just feel." Soon, I feel her fingertips gliding across my back, down to my ass, up my hip and waist, circling my breasts, then moving up my neck to my mouth. I kiss her fingertips and snuggle in closer. Her skin is warm and smooth. We kiss and her hands embrace me more firmly, squeezing and grasping until she finally reaches down for me. I open my legs to her fingers and she easily slips inside me. I rock on her hand, moving her deeper into me, pushing against her, moaning with each plunge.

"You feel so good." She kisses my neck while she fucks me with her hand. I wish I could come like this, but I know I never will.

"I need you to lick me," I whisper. "And use the dildo." I spread my legs wider in anticipation.

She moves lower and I feel her tongue lick my clit as she slowly inserts the dildo into my waiting pussy. As she pushes it in deeper, I am overwhelmed with the waves of pleasure that reverberate through every pore of my body. I have never felt so electric or so alive. She fucks me slowly and I thrust my hips for more. Her mouth and tongue never leave me.

I call out loudly, "Yes, that's perfect. You're perfect!"

I clench her free hand and hold it tightly as she fucks me and sucks my clit. I never want it to stop. I can't focus on one sensation because the next feels just as good, only different. She begins to tongue my clit in quick flicks and I feel warmth spreading through my back and in my toes.

"Don't stop," I moan. "Slow down the dildo." She moves it more slowly in and out of me and the warmth begins to spread farther, and tingle, and build in intensity. "Don't stop, don't stop, please don't stop. I'm gonna come in your mouth. Make me come in your mouth." And then I'm coming and the world falls away and all I feel is waves of ecstasy and joy, again and again and again.

Suddenly, it's too much. "Stop!" I yell and close my legs although I can still feel an incredible glow and steady pulsing. She crawls behind me and spoons me close. I snuggle farther into her body and stretch my neck to kiss her slow and deep and long. "You are magic," I whisper.

She kisses me gently then whispers back, "Do tell."

MY SWEET FEMME NIGHTMARE

June Amelia Rose

Darby hooked a slender, black acrylic–lengthened finger through the loop of the O-ring on the leather collar around my neck, the sweet, beautiful, pungent sweaty crust of the bodies around us filling the Legion Hall to capacity. It was a moment of hurt-filled friction, so many bodies in botched tattoo jobs launching up and over and around us, trying to catch a glimpse of the band.

She heaved me closer to her and wrapped me in a kiss, her serpent's tongue dominating my face. Darby bit my lip until the skin began to break, a bite much harder than vanilla. She gripped me around the neck. I was dripping with the wealth of my desire and the perspiration of the dehydrated bodies that wouldn't stop rubbing up against us in motion to the music. Moments earlier, someone had accidentally dumped an entire beer over my head after being thrown back from the mosh pit. A whole pint glass of stale beer went pouring down my face, soaking the length of my hair, seeping into my clothes, lubricating me further.

The band, Sister Salvation, were more waterlogged than the crowd, all decked out in various amounts of bondage gear. Jane, the prowling and preying singer, was the hard femme Latina babe everyone wanted to know. She was all wrapped and plump in a corset and thigh-high boots, her dyed crayon-red hair progressively reaching upward into a nest of frizz. She gripped the microphone like a bomb.

"I want to fucking hurt you, Jessie, you little bitch!" Darby shouted at me with a smile. She bared her teeth, unsheathing them like little swords, possessing my heart.

Darby owned me, and in a sense I *was* her property. It was all in this anarchist sense of a mutual ownership, a consensual erotic arrangement. I bargained away parts of myself when we were together, and she gave me gifts and grasps at beauty, at love, at purpose. She would take her power over my body and use pain to bring the flesh a new meaning.

Darby was my femme Daddy, the dominant to my submissive. A few months ago, she had come out as genderqueer and started injecting testosterone. It was a low dose, an idea she had told me she had first gotten from Masha Gessen. To alter her body but retain her dykehood and her femme identity. It worked well for her. Her body hair had grown in more pronounced and her body began to give off this muskier smell. I first noticed the changes one time when she had locked me in her armpit, making me beg for mercy.

I felt so lucky to be a part of that dyke community. The trans girls I knew out West, the ones who lived in small rural towns without even support groups, they didn't have the privilege of inclusion. They had to fight tooth and nail, day and night. Brooklyn had enough progressive dykes if you knew where to look, trans-inclusionary lovers who fucked trans women without a second thought. I was proud of my lesbian comrades.

The hall obscured the music into a cataclysm of poetic noise. Scar, the butch of our household and guitarist of the band, was decked out in a leather chest harness with her tits out, weathered black boots on her feet. Her guitar ripped across walls of sound at a blitzkrieg speed, the notes jumping and chugging over each other so fast that you couldn't grab a single one. Her fretwork was a pure frenzy.

Trixie was Scar's girlfriend and the keyboard player of Sister Salvation, the femme in lingerie, her tattooed ass hanging out in a striking thong as she bounced and twirled to the music, yet never missed a note. Each press of the piano rang out like a twinkling music box that haunts you until death—it swirled to fuck the sounds of Scar's careening guitar work into a jangling church chime, a religious declaration of maudlin filth and glory. The two of them shared a room together in our kinky punk house, the Coven.

Jane was screaming into the mic, which was pressed up against her lips and smearing black lipstick all over her face. With her other hand she threw handfuls of dark gothic glitter into the crowd that transmuted into the sweat, morphing into a glue that engulfed the room from floor to ceiling.

A year ago, Jane had posted a wanted ad for some new members for a punk band, and Trixie and Scar had answered. To round out their trio they used a drum machine, adding a hint of gothic industrial flair. We had been happy to invite Jane as a new addition to our friend group.

Darby wrapped her fingers around mine, softly guiding my hand under her dress. To my surprise, under the comforting lace of her panties, she was wearing a dildo strapped to a harness. A hefty one that bulged just like a dick, in all the right places. I let out a whimper as she inched closer toward my ears.

"To give any boys in this crowd with wandering hands a nice little surprise." Her eyes lit up with perversion and malice. "And to remind you who's boss here, bitch."

"Haaaaaah," I moaned.

"That's my girl. So good. So wet. You'd better stay wet for me until after the show. I have a surprise for your slutty ass."

With that, Darby pulled away from me, the O-ring on my collar clanging as it dropped. As she backed away she became engulfed in the arms of the crowd. I couldn't stop thinking about how turned on I was. Next thing I knew, Darby was up in the air atop the hands of ten or so queers, crowd-surfing around toward the front of the room. Her panties flipped down as her dress flipped up to reveal the harness around her pelvis, the deep-red dildo pointing toward the heavens as the crowd roared and gawked. She had certainly fucked with them.

The hands carried Darby to the front and she clumsily planted her feet on stage as the band played on. Jane wrapped her arm around Darby to invite her to scream into the mic, a proposition that Darby fully indulged. We'd fucked to this album so many times that she knew all of the words.

She cut off mid-verse to run over to Trixie and Scar, shredding away on the other side of the stage. Darby quickly wrapped an arm around each of their backs for love and support, then turned her gaze back to the mess of bodies going wild in front of the stage.

I saw her step backward to get a bit more of a running start, and then she sprinted forward to the front of the stage, leaping with faith off the end. She twisted as she dropped into the waiting hands of the crowd, falling in time with the peaking crescendo of the music, exploding into the sounds of crushing fire.

I was handcuffed to Darby, the key hanging on a chain around her neck as we walked down the street after leaving the show. We were holding hands to stay inconspicuous.

"Where are we going?" I stammered out, feeling weak and

vulnerable. Technically, we were cuffed to each other, but we both knew I was actually cuffed to her.

"Oh, I'm gonna punish you for that one. We've discussed this so many times. Don't be so curious. It's unbecoming of your submission. Trust me to surprise you."

"I'm sorry, Daddy, I won't do it again. I promise I trust you."

"Good girl. To indulge your question—where we're going is down to the basement."

Darby blindfolded me outside our house.

"Trust is key. I want you to always remember that. I love you. Now, are you ready? Enjoy yourself tonight."

"Yes, Daddy. I will."

"Thank you, sweetie. Follow my lead, I don't want you to trip."

She led me inside, and we stopped at the foot of the basement stairs. Darby made me strip all of my clothes off, then guided my feet into what I assumed were my usual black Pleaser heels. She walked me carefully down the stairs, then stepped me forward a bit. With her hands, she put a pressure on both of my shoulders that meant: Kneel for me.

My knees dug into the mildewed concrete of the floor. Despite the blindfold, I tried to sniff out what was going on around me. I thought I felt another presence, but I couldn't be sure. I'd been fucked up and dominated in our basement dungeon a hundred times, but this was the first time it had truly felt foreign to me.

As the blindfold was removed, I got my answer.

Jane, Trixie, and Scar were all in front of me, decked out in the bondage gear they had worn onstage, makeup smeared and runny, perched in stances that said, *We're ready for the after-party.*

"Oh fuck," I blurted out, immediately regretting it.

Trixie stepped forward, sizing up my body from head to toe. She bent down to squeeze my face between her thumb and index finger, hard enough so that my cheek began to throb with the rush of blood. She moved my head back and forth, examining every inch of me as I held my breath.

"May I have permission to slap you?"

I tried to answer, "Yes," but as soon as Trixie saw the beginnings of the syllable, the first sound of the letter Y, she cracked her hand like a leather strap against my cheek, echoing throughout the basement as the others giggled and jumped at the shift of intensity.

"No cursing. Bad girl, filthy mouth. That's no way to greet your dominant femmes for the evening," she sneered.

"I . . . I'm sorry Trixie," I gasped.

"Ma'am. You will be addressing us all as 'Ma'am' tonight."

"Yes, Ma'am."

Scar, Jane, and Darby began to circle us, surveying their prey, their prize for the night. They walked with calculated steps, opening up the circle of a spell that was soon to become my own personal hurt. I was the eye of the hurricane.

Jane stopped in front of me, staring.

"I've wanted a crack at this one since I saw her from the stage. You were looking way too arrogant tonight, hon. A submissive out of line. To be honest, it pissed me off," she spat through her asphalt lipstick. "I heard you like to be tortured. I'll be sure to make you regret that."

Scar left the circle. She had a black ball gag in her hand. She knelt down to face me, with Trixie, her girlfriend, snickering next to her. Darby was still creeping around us, her boots stomping hard, making my heart race. Scar held the ball gag up to my face.

"May I please have permission to ask a question, Ma'am? Before you place the gag in?" I asked. Her eyebrow raised.

"Yes, slut, you may. Go on, ask it," she said.

"If you're a butch, how is this a night of femmes?"

Her eyes lit up, almost as if she had known I was going to ask that exact question, almost as if she had wanted, no, maliciously planned, for me to ask. Knowing I couldn't help but bring the pain of a punishment on myself, simply to have the gift of clarity. Scar, my housemate who had played with me so many times, had picked up on my curiosities. She had found a way to use them against me.

"She's an honorary femme for tonight," Darby spoke out from behind me. "I let her borrow a pair of my heels." My eyes turned to the bright-red heels, shimmering out in front of me, making my mouth water. "Just for you, because I know you love them so much. Trixie and I did her eyeliner and helped her put on mascara too. Bitch didn't know which was which." I smiled at Darby's wit.

"Who told you to smile?" she snapped, peeking out from over my shoulder. "Scar, honey, would you please do the honors?"

Scar didn't hesitate to place the ball gag in my mouth, shoving it between my teeth, then tightly adjusting the strap against the back of my head. The drool started to pool in my mouth.

"Thank god. Now we can get started!" Trixie said.

I was taken by two sets of hands and pushed down on all fours, my ass curling up into the air. I didn't dare look up, but I heard a rustling behind me, then a few throws of what I guessed was a leather flogger, the ends flapping as they flew. When it finally landed on my ass with a warm sting I knew I had guessed correctly. The hits continued.

I wasn't sure which one of them was hitting me, as I was quickly losing track of my own thoughts. My eyes rolled back in my head, as I sank further and further into submission with every strike. I was approaching that docile state of acceptance, that breathless feeling of giving myself over to another person, except this time the person was a dungeon full of femmes. The flogging stopped.

Next was a plastic paddle with holes in it. Darby's black acrylic nails had brought it up in front of my face for me to survey the implement. She tapped it lightly on my face, tormenting me. I felt her nails on the back of my head and the gag popped down, hanging down around my neck. They were taking the gag out so quickly. Why?

She brought the plastic paddle up to my mouth, dangling it once again in front of my face.

"Lick," she commanded.

She was fucking with me.

Obediently, I began to run my tongue across the length of the plastic, blessing the paddle with my spit as she ran it in the opposite direction.

"Good girl. Making such good use of that filthy mouth," she said.

Darby brought the gag back up into my mouth and I took it back between the teeth without hesitation. Once again, I was forbidden to speak.

She turned to my ass.

The paddle hurt like a bitch. It swung hard and fast, and each time it slapped into me, I yelped into the ball gag. I could feel my asscheeks buckling under the lightweight implement. They sang with a red-hot fire of pain. The sensation was beat into my head until it was the only thought I could focus on.

My mind had gone so blank it took me a few seconds to realize the strikes had stopped. I was drooling onto the floor in front of me. I looked up.

Darby had her cock out and so did Trixie. They both had their cocks affixed to smooth leather harnesses. They were stroking their dicks, rubbing them with lube. Trixie came over. Their cocks swung with each movement.

"Now we're gonna gag that mouth in a different way, slut," she said. She walked behind me and popped the clasp of the gag once more, the spit heavy and pouring down my front and over my tits.

Darby took her shining red silicone cock and rammed it into my waiting mouth, grabbing my hair and making pigtails for leverage. As she bucked into my face, she tightened her fists around the strands, using them as sissy schoolgirl handles to guide my mouth as I choked and slobbered on her cock.

I felt a pressure on my ass and knew it was Trixie's finger, prying me open, wet and sloppy. Next came the head of her dick as it slid in so easily.

The burning submission of desire overtook me as Trixie pushed in and out, Darby fucking my face, smashing me between the two pressures. I was being spit-roasted by two gorgeous femmes, fucked into oblivion. The clit between my legs was throbbing, but I didn't dare touch it without permission. If I was allowed to have a rub, they'd let me.

Trixie was the first to pull out, then Darby. I was ready to take the breather they had given me, but as Scar and Trixie's hands grabbed my armpits, yanking me into the air, I knew they had much more in store for me. I could smell the sadism in the air.

I was pushed up against the wall, the side of my face digging into the cold concrete. My hands were up, covering the back of my neck. Trixie was pushing one of my elbows up against the wall, and Scar had her grip on the other one.

A single-tail whip cracked inches away from my ear like a bullet shot. I tensed up by instinct, the sinews of my back flexing in antici- pation of a pain I couldn't wait to feel against me, the validating snaps of broken skin putting me in my place as I whimpered.

I looked out the corner of my eye to see Jane wielding the whip, and felt the first tear run down my cheek due to the sheer wonder of fear.

Jane flung the whip at me and it landed with an echo boom throughout the basement. I squealed and my leg lifted slightly with the successive hits. The femmes cheered each one. I was the post-gig entertainment. They kept coming, leaving streaking hard lines of wonderful red across my back.

The single-tail furled and unfurled, flexed and extended and shot against my back again and again, each time pushing me closer to the edge. Jane kept the intervals between the hits completely random. Some were in rapid succession, some fell in between spaces of time that felt like hours.

One huge knifing slash hit me across the back and that was when I finally buckled, my legs giving out. Trixie and Scar loosened their grips as I fell to the ground in a puddle of thankful submission. I was gasping at the dirt and grime of the floor as tears began to pour down my face.

My mouth found the tip of Trixie's red heels, her toes painted black and poking out the front. I ran my tongue in desperate, submissive licks across the bottom of the platform, then up and down the stiletto heel, tasting my helplessness on her footwear. I was begging, pleading, for the four of them to hurt me more.

Darby stepped in, reading my mind, her faux-leather Doc Martens stomping down right in front of my face. I didn't wait for her to order me to lick; I knew what I was meant to do. I extended my tongue, my hair falling down in front of my face and mixing with the spit and dirt. As I shined her boot, she brought her other leg up into the air and began kicking my ass, kicks hard like knuckle punches. I could feel the ridges of her boots digging into my ass with each thrust of her foot.

Scar lay down on the bed in front of us, the one with the latex sheets. She rubbed her legs and ankles, obviously not used to the strain that high heels put on the body. Her muscles flexed as she removed both heels with little grace, dropping them to the floor.

"Ahhhhh, I've wanted those heels off since the minute you bitches made me put them on." She looked over at us. I was on the floor licking Darby's boots, while Trixie giggled above and Jane watched. "Slut, get over here, now," she said.

Darby grabbed my hair roughly with her fist and yanked me over to Scar like a dog as I crawled across the room on hands and knees. She shoved my head right up to her bare feet, pushing my face humiliatingly into the soles.

"Lick, slut!" they shouted in unison.

"Thank you, Ma'am," I said. I flexed my tongue once more, running it along the soles, then up and over and around the toes. I lapped and lapped, massaging her with my tongue.

"You can use your hands too." I added my hands to the mix, kneading and rubbing as Scar flexed her back in an arch. "Yes, that's it. That's a good girl," she said. "I'm quite pleased with you. Come here, up on the bed with me." She motioned for me to crawl up onto the bed and I obeyed.

That was when I collapsed.

We were all curled up on the latex bed, body parts sprawled and spilled out over one another. Someone was scratching my head like a dog's while someone else was rubbing my thigh and yet another was rubbing my throbbing, sensitive ass.

I was lying with my head on Darby's thigh, curled into the corner of her legs as I came down from the adrenaline high.

I was blessed to be on that latex-covered bed, surrounded by the energy of four fierce hot femmes, the woman among them who had fought the hardest just to comfortably carry the gift of womanhood on my wet and wanting lips. It had taken years of clenched fists, fire-soaked teeth spitting ash from my mouth, sweating sacrifice and turmoil and heartbreak.

I am blessed to have lived out my own sweet femme nightmare, I thought, as I kissed Darby on her exposed thigh, submissive as always.

OF SWORD AND SORCERY

Maria Chiara Ferro

I had lost my warrior.

As I turned back from five minutes of conversation with my girlfriends, ze was gone. I quickly scanned the venue, where people had started to scatter away after the concert: no sign of hir, not even behind the beer counter, where I had last seen hir.

Unlike my friends, this was my first time at the three-day folk/medieval/pagan festival, and my expectations didn't go beyond good music, beer, and marijuana: I surely didn't foresee encountering such a queer beauty as soon as I set foot inside the festival, the afternoon before. Ze was very good looking, with an outfit that screamed, "I can survive in a forest with my bare hands," which, I confess, is kinda my weakness. Ze had a Viking haircut, just a hint of chest, and a jawline to die for. My girlfriends had to remind me to collect what was left of my dignity and go set up our tent, luckily before ze noticed my staring.

The following day went by fine; the place was big and there was much to enjoy, so I only saw hir again in the evening, during the concert: there ze was, cocky and handsome, with hir dark hair and chestplate. During my fangirl-meets-stalker observations, all conducted with extreme stealth and skill, I could see that ze was the easygoing type, had a swaggering walk, and knew almost everyone, including some of the organizers of the weekend. At some point ze was serving beers, which I clearly had to take advantage of. While ze was pouring my pint, I was thoroughly blushing, trying not to stare too obviously at those naked, muscular arms, and huge hands. But, as I walked away, I was almost sure that hir gaze was following me, lingering on my steps, on the motion of my hips; after all, I'm quite a catch, if I dare say so myself. I had pinned my copper curls in a messy half updo, always a win, had a decent cat-eye makeup, and, as usual, wore a black dress, which I hoped had enough tulle layers to make me look like a sorcerer in a short gown, given the occasion.

But it seemed I had lost my warrior. My girlfriends were telling me that some people were gathering elsewhere to play music around a fire, or something like it, and they were planning on going. I was a bit disappointed that the evening was rushing to its conclusion, and I had not managed to talk to the warrior, so I needed a moment alone to rebuild a good mood.

I assured my friends that I would meet them later, and wandered off to someplace quiet. The sky was beginning to darken when I found a nice patch in the trees, finally away from the noise. I sat and rolled a cigarette, already starting to feel better. If I was meant to meet the warrior, we would surely bump into each other the next day. Otherwise, why shouldn't I have fun nonetheless?

"Do you need a light?" I turn, startled, and fuck, there ze is. Actually, ze seems to have been here longer than me. Smiling mischievously, ze looks at me like I'm something exquisite to eat and the most interesting person in the galaxy, all at the same time.

I try to regain myself and stop looking like a fish. "Thank you. Actually, I'm sure I have a lighter in my bag." Pathetic attempts to find it follow, while the object lies complacently hidden at the very bottom. "Maybe it would take a while to find it . . . Thank you."

I try moving toward hir, but ze is faster, gets seated near me, and chivalrously proceeds to light my cigarette.

"I needed to escape from the crowd. After a while it can be pretty overwhelming," ze says, stretching those well-built arms like we are on hir couch, and I'm not a total stranger. I don't have such confidence, even when I'm in flirtatious mode, which at this point has not fully kicked in yet. But I can manage a conversation, and smoke seductively enough; as for the cat eye, I didn't have time to check my mirror, so I can only rely on its resilience.

Ze already knows, but I reiterate: "I saw you in the beer stand, so I reckon this is not your first time here."

After that, we have a pleasant conversation: awkward, like all first conversations between people who like each other, but in a nice way. We exchange names and preferred pronouns. We speak about music, people, a bit about ourselves, and discover that we share many thoughts on life, the universe, and everything.

At last, after a not-so-brief silence, ze gets up. "Would you like to get away for a while?"

"Oh sure, yes." We both know on which slope we are standing: the talking was just foreplay.

Ze leads the way in a different direction than I was expecting, toward a blocked path in the trees, closed with a barrier.

"Where . . . ?" I say.

Ze pushes the barrier aside, signaling me to pass, with a half-crooked half-gallant smile. Then I remember: "Right, you know the management . . . you can sneak wherever you like!"

"Actually, I even helped set these up the other day."

I surely won't say it out loud, but I would have loved to watch hir do just that.

While we walk through the trees and up the hill, the air

OF SWORD AND SORCERY

between us is growing thick, and static electricity seems to spark every time our hands or limbs touch. Our bodies are being pulled together, and I'm tingling with anticipation, and a bit of uncertainty. We reach a pretty clearing in the trees, almost on top of the hill; some stars are already glimmering above us, but there is still light in the summer sky. My warrior looks satisfied and smiles at me, while gesturing as if to encompass the beautiful view with hir whole self. Smiling and enjoying the spectacle, both human and natural, I extract a crumpled throw from my bag and place it on the ground.

Now, ze only has to sit next to me, and I will start melting.

And of course ze does.

The warrior places a hand on the side of my face, dragging me close; I'm bracing for the kiss, drowning in hir warmth, but ze just stares into my eyes and, cherry on top, asks, "Would a bit of roughness be okay?"

"Mm, it would surely be okay."

What a good kisser my warrior is. Ze puts one hand behind my neck, holding me firmly enough, while the other one starts to climb its way up my side, toward my breasts. We are pretty entangled, still half sitting, and ze kisses me with hunger. I start moaning even before placing my hands on hir biceps, absorbing the feeling of hir skin. Our breaths accelerate between deepening kisses, and I'm briefly thankful for not wearing lipstick, one of my last rational thoughts. I lustfully explore hir back, tracing with my fingers the pattern of hir muscles from above the chestplate, but I'm interrupted, shivering and whimpering, by hir touch. The warrior effortlessly holds my whole breast in hir big hand, gently and not so gently squeezing it, weighing it, while playing with my nipple through the dress, teasing it with hir thumb until I shudder.

Ze is so good. I'm already completely lost, squirming in hir arms. I want it all, I want to feel my warrior's strength and firmness. Ze is probably thinking the same, only in reverse, as I'm pushed to the ground on my back, and ze crawls on top of me. My legs are as open as they can get, my pussy feels like it's about to explode under the pressure of hir body, stroking and pushing, pinning me into the soil. My warrior weighs on me as heavily as I had fantasized: being crushed by hir body makes me feel safe and whole.

Ze places hir hands on my thighs, looking very serious, as if ze is both elsewhere and right here, studying my body, breathing all of myself in. Brushing aside my dress, ze starts to lower hir head, disappearing between my legs, while I run my fingers through hir shaved hair, enjoying the sight of hir perfect jawline resting on the junction between my thigh and pussy.

But the warrior has something different in mind than what I was expecting, as I discover when hir teeth dig into the softness of my right inner thigh. I whimper, surely scream a little, and instinctively try to lift my chest from the ground; ze is swift and sure in pinning me down again with hir right arm, all without releasing a bit of flesh from the grip of hir mouth. Deeply satisfying pain stings, as ze is seemingly ripping me out. Deliciously shuddering, I endure; by now I'm wet beyond repair, and my pussy is throbbing in an almost painful way.

Finally, ze releases my thigh and climbs on top of me, kissing me hard, while I squirm trying to press myself against hir body. I want more, I need to feel more of my warrior. I swap our places, or rather, ze lets me, so that I end up on top of hir, free at last to push my pussy on hir crotch as much as I like. Ze is quick to lower my dress, grabbing my breasts in hir hands and brushing my hair behind my shoulders, while I manage to remove my panties.

Ze flickers hir tongue on one hardened nipple, teasing the other with hir fingers, staring as if spellbound at my breasts, smelling, tasting my skin. Moaning, I bend down to kiss hir, exploring hir nape, hir upper chest, the contours of hir face with my fingertips. Ze goes for my pussy: as soon as hir hand brushes me, I can feel my wetness slip between my thighs, dripping on hir fingers. Ze is ecstatic yet serious, and starts stroking my clit slowly, building up even more combustion in me. Half blinded by pleasure, I reach between hir legs and slide inside hir pants, tentatively feeling hir above hir briefs. Ze pushes toward me, while I lightly enclose hir with my whole hand.

When I overcome even that last layer, I find that my warrior is definitely happy to see me; the mere act of brushing my fingertips over hir flesh, feeling every crease and fold, finding how swollen and engorged ze is, sends me over the edge. I keep touching hir, shuddering and rubbing my nipples against hir chestplate, our legs intertwined on the grass.

My warrior is merciful and looks knowingly at me. "All good?"

"Mm, yes . . ."

"May I . . . ?"

"Please, do."

We understand each other, no doubt. Pure chemistry at work here. Ze enters slowly, and I savor every inch. It feels as if I can perceive every detail on the surface, every vein under the skin. Two fingers is the perfect amount, we discover. Ze starts pushing and pulling, inside and out.

With hir left hand ze finds mine, almost forgotten in hir pants, and pushes it out, growling, "Later." Ze is right, we have no attention left for anything else now. Our bodies click like cogs. I feel myself tighten around hir stiffness, while ze pushes inside, up to the knuckles, hammering me. My warrior is relentless, and pins me down on hir body, hard, blocking me with hir left arm. Hir low growls on my neck are melting me; my back is arched, following every thrust. We are embedded together, shuddering in this rhythmic dance: inside and outside, up and down, push and pull.

I didn't realize it, but I must be moaning, or screaming, too loudly, because my warrior tightens hir grip around my chest, and whispers, a bit harshly, "Shhh."

"Sorry."

I push my head on hir shoulder, trying to be less noisy, while ze changes hir pace inside me, and reprises stroking my clit with hir thumb; this time the motion is not playful, but decisive. At this point, fulfilled and used up, I need very little to come, and ze feels it. My warrior holds me firmly, crushing my face into hir neck, and sinks hir teeth into my shoulder. I feel my flesh swelling inside hir mouth, and ze bites harder as I tremble and moan, finally coming in hir hand. Ze keeps pushing inside me, landing some more deep thrusts before we both collapse, panting and sweating, on the ground.

My warrior looks content, but I still want hir, and I guess ze won't object to some more playing. I crawl back on top of hir, grasp hir hand, and start licking hir fingers, swollen and coated in my taste. Just one last kiss, and I'm off trying to lower hir pants, an endeavor in which ze is eager to help. I can't wait to feel hir deep in my mouth, but I try to go slow, enjoying my warrior bit by bit, tracing the landscape of hir flesh with just the tip of my tongue. Ze moans lowly, and I drown happily in hir flavor, hir texture. At last, I take hir all in my mouth, savoring hir swollen flesh, hir hunger for release, sucking and rubbing hard.

My hair starts getting in the way, and I try to push back the fugitive curls without stopping, when my warrior lifts up and smiles: ze removes a band from hir left wrist and hands it to me. I smile back, a bit stunned by the intimacy of the gesture, and lift my hair up.

Now I can return to where I was, this time fully focused. I can feel that ze is truly enjoying my mouth, as ze grabs my head and starts pushing hir body toward me. Holding my hair, ze forces me to take even more flesh in my mouth, making me gasp for air. I'm wet and throbbing again, moaning as much as I can with my mouth so lusciously full, my head buried so deep between hir legs. Intoxicated, I keep a fast pace, lost in hir taste.

Hir growls become louder, and ze starts pulling my hair really hard, while thrusting hir body against the pressure of my tongue. When ze comes shuddering in my mouth, I'm delighted and breathless, equally satisfied by hir pleasure and my uncomfortable position.

Now we really have no more energy, and collapse for good on the ground. The sky is almost completely dark, dotted with stars; the feeble sounds and lights from the festival below are the only reminders of reality we have. But we are back, and I start wondering what comes next, while trying to recompose myself a little.

My warrior pulls up hir pants and crashes again on what is left of the throw, looking pretty at ease. Ze smiles at me and puts hir arm on my shoulders, gently pushing us on the ground.

"Look how many stars," ze says.

"Yes. I like them too."

Ze manages to extract a spliff from hir pocket, slightly crinkled but not crushed, lights and passes it to me first, always charming.

We just lie smoking, comfortable near each other, and I'm starting to forget about what comes next, when ze looks at me. "I was thinking . . . will you come to my tent later? I like you, and I would love to get to know you more."

It's unbelievable how blunt my warrior is.

"I would love to get to know you too. And to come to your tent. And I like you too."

Smiling, ze holds me tightly, and we keep staring at the sky. I never would have expected it, but maybe this is just the beginning.

PINKED

Avery Cassell

Scout and I had been shacking up for over a year now, but the bloom was not off the blossom, so to speak, and we were still crazy for each other. Scout liked to rib me that I was a cradle-robber; I'd turned seventy-two last October and Scout was a relatively rambunctious sixty-one. Scout was my sweet service top and I was her greedy little bottom. We were both cantankerous, randy butches and despite the twitches, aches, and pains that came from having older bodies, we had a hot sex life full of intrigue and mystery. I'd been a happy-go-lucky bottom for decades, so imagine my surprise when I discovered that I was a switch. It was all Scout's fault and it happened early on in our relationship. We were sexting one dreary Monday afternoon, when Scout confided that she loved having her hair pulled during sex. Hard. I filed that information away under things-that-turn-Scout-on, and one night reached over casually, yanked her curly disheveled pompadour, her eyes got all soft and misty, she went down, and the next thing I knew I was caning her tender inner thighs until she wept, then fisting her until she couldn't come anymore. Afterward, we cuddled and she gazed at me, stunned. It looked like Scout had neglected to mention that the slightest tug of her silver pompadour sent her directly into subspace. Do not pass Go, do not collect two-hundred dollars. And the way her eyes got all dreamy and she went limp when I pulled her hair turned me into a top. I felt pretty stunned myself!

"I don't understand!" Scout's blue eyes got rounder and rounder as we snuggled together in bed. She looked so sweetly vulnerable. That lost small-animal look in her eyes combined with her come drying on my wrist made me fall even more in love. I felt like a paternal, ferocious mountain lion protecting a fawn from the big, bad wolf.

"What's there to understand?" I kissed her forehead, inhaling the musky scent of our sweat. "Did you like it?"

"I loved it," she whimpered. "But I'm the service top! I'm supposed to be topping you, not you topping me," she blurted in a worried whisper.

"I wanted you to bottom. If it's what I want, then aren't you being my service top after all?" She groaned as I rolled her nipple between my fingers.

"Oh, I don't know . . ." Scout said. "I was going to beat and fist you tonight. It's my job!" she whined plaintively.

I squeezed her ass and held her closer. "This is what I like. For real." I tugged her hair for good measure, then licked the tip of her nose. "You turn me on."

The truth was that I was more than a little nervous about topping. I was an experienced bottom and masochist, but insecure about topping and sadism. I'd only tried topping a couple of times before and not very successfully. At least, my ex had complained that they didn't like it when I tried topping them, and who wants to fuck someone and have them bitch about your technique afterward? Although beating Scout for the first time had been incredibly sexy, intoxicating, and nerve-wracking all at once, I'd been worried that I would be inadequate and clumsy, and that Scout would only tolerate my efforts.

Things had settled since that night. We'd discovered that we were both switches. She swooned when I topped her and, being eager to please, I was always looking for new ways to torture her. Little did I dream that one of my beautiful plans and an implement of doom would reveal itself a year later as we talked one Sunday morning over hot tea and omelets.

It was raining that morning, dismal sheets of sooty gray rain that whipped the leaves of the trees in front of our second-floor apartment into a frenzy. I watched, mesmerized, as the trees blew in the wind, the branches looking like seaweed fronds swaying in the ocean. I'd just set the table, and Scout was in the kitchen cooking our breakfast. I heard her pad down the hall to our dining room, and I sat down at the table as she placed an oval platter laden with breakfast on the tabletop. There was a fat goat cheese and wild mushroom omelet, strips of crispy peppered bacon, and buttered English muffins topped with homemade ruby-colored quince jam. I poured her a fresh cup of Earl Grey, and we started eating.

This particular Sunday morning conversation started with Rachel Maddow and politics, segued to Lulu and hairballs, then to the likelihood of finding Arts and Crafts–style stained glass at the Alameda Flea Market, before finally meandering toward sewing projects. Scout had a pile of mending and I wanted to make her some shirts. Somehow, between moving in together, writing books, our day jobs, and life, I hadn't yet made Scout anything, and I yearned to dress her up like my own wee butch paper doll. Maybe that didn't come out right. The truth was that she was a delightfully stocky pocket butch and, as such, had a hard time finding clothing that fit. I was determined to make her a stack of the bowling shirts of her dreams. I started planning the first shirt in my head as I crunched into a slice of bacon. I had a length of periwinkle and cobalt striped linen and some coordinating azure linen that would be perfect for a color blocked bowling shirt. Pair that with a set of blue buttons, and she would be the hottest butch on the block.

As I was planning the project in my head, I was brought up short when I hit a possible snag. Although she and I were similar in many ways, she had a strong streak of the stern and meticulous German hausfrau in her, whereas I was considerably more lackadaisical. Lazy, even. This extended to my sewing habits, and I rarely finished my seams. I figured that they were on the inside, so who the hell cares? But I knew that Scout finished her seams when she sewed. All of them. Every fucking time. This could be a problem.

"Baby, do you know that I don't finish my seams?" I asked, cocking my head and trying to sound casual, but with my stomach fluttering with nervousness. I nibbled a corner of my omelet.

Scout raised one eyebrow sternly and snorted in derision. "I always finish my seams," she intoned decisively as she buttered a toast triangle.

"Umm, I was going to make you a shirt, and would you wear it even if the seams were unfinished?"

Now it was Scout's turn to look nervous. She pushed her toast around on her plate. "No," she said abashedly. "I'm sorry."

"I could pink them for you. Would that work?" I was hopeful. In my world of careless unfinished seams, pinked seams were fancy-pants.

"My mother always said pinked seams were tawdry and the lazy woman's seam!" Scout huffed, as she took a dainty sip of tea, pinky up. Dainty butches get me every time, and I sighed.

I glared at Scout, trying to hide my laughter. "I love you too.

Well, maybe I'm just tawdry. That's it. I'm tawdry." I ate my last bite of omelet.

Scout chuckled, gathered the empty serving platter to take into the kitchen, and nuzzled my neck. "I forgive you for being tawdry, but don't expect me to wear anything with pinked seams. I have my limits, and pinked seams is a hard limit!" I admired her ass as she sauntered off to the kitchen to wash up our breakfast dishes.

I was amused by Scout's reaction to pinked edges. She was normally easygoing but, like all of us, some things inexplicably set her off. In my case, it was rubber bands; they cause my soul to seize up and shiver in revulsion. It was something about their shape and their stretchiness that I abhorred. I had an ex that was triggered by irregularly shaped holes and so avoided Ethiopian restaurants with their bread baskets full of injera. There was even a word for that last one, trypophobia. I adored Scout and found her aversion to pinked seams endearing, even if it made sewing for her infinitely more complicated. After all, French seams were prissy and a bear to make. Fuck French seams!

We'd decided to stay in that day since the weather was so ghastly. We turned on some music, Scout wrote out a list of home projects for the day, and I laid out the pattern pieces for Scout's new bowling shirt on the dining room table. I brooded over seams as I pinned the sleeves, and cursed Scout's mother's aversion to pinked edges as I cut out the shirt facing.

I could hear Scout whistling and the clank of metal as she sharpened our kitchen knives. I finished cutting out the shirt and rummaged in my bobbin case for azure thread. I threaded my sewing machine, and started sewing. I was attaching the contrasting front pieces together and had started pinking the edges of the remaining shirt pieces in preparation for sewing when Scout strolled back into the room.

Scout shuddered as she walked past the table. "I love that

color of linen, but must you pink the seams?" she asked queru-lously.

"I didn't feel like making French seams," I mumbled, then plucked a glass-headed pin from between my teeth and pinned the freshly pinked side seam. "Really, you won't wear it?"

Scout sighed, and with a hangdog look said, "All right, I'll wear it even though it pains me."

I rolled my eyes and laughed through my pins. "You!"

I knew right then that Scout needed to be taught a lesson, and that lesson was to never look a gift seam in the mouth. I started developing my devious plan.

By the time Scout had moved on to re-oiling the cutting boards and had started chopping vegetables for a lunchtime pot of tom kha gai, I was ready for her. I figured that a little Sunday after-noon delight, along with a lesson in gratitude, was in order. I laid out another length of fabric, this one a red and gray ombre plaid cotton-and-wool blend. This was my lure, my butch bait. I knew that Scout would be drawn to it like a moth to a flame, and this time, I was going to boldly use the pinking shears directly as I cut out the pattern. I giggled as I picked up my shears, leaned my yardstick against the table, well within reach, and called out for Scout: "Baby, could you come in here? I need to measure your neck for this shirt pattern."

Scout walked into the room, drying her hands on a dish-towel, and froze at the sight of the yellow tape measure dangling from one arm and the pinking shears in my other hand. I smiled slyly.

"Love, come over here." I tried to look casual, but I was getting turned on thinking about my plans. My cunt was already wet, and my clit hard and throbbing.

Scout came over, eyeing my shears nervously.

"Turn around so I can get your neck measurement,"

I demanded, holding the tape measure up to her neck for emphasis.

"Why do I have the feeling you're up to no good?"

Scout turned around to face the sewing table and I wrapped my arms around her, hugging her close. "Who, me? I'm just making my girlfriend a couple of shirts."

I wrapped the tape measure loosely around her neck and pressed my groin against her ass. "Baby, do you think it was nice of you to demand French seams?" I murmured into her ear. "Don't you think you should be more grateful when someone offers to sew for you?" I pulled the tape measure a little tighter and reached around to untuck her flannel shirt, slip my hand under her sports bra, and pinch her right nipple.

"Oh god," Scout groaned as her nipple hardened between my fingers. "I'm sorry. I won't do it again!" she stammered.

"I think that you're way too picky about gifts and need to learn to appreciate the beauty of pinked seams." I nibbled her earlobe until her knees started to buckle, then placed the pinking shears on the table in front of her. "Pick them up."

Scout squirmed to get away, but I had her pressed firmly against the table. I tightened the tape measure around her neck. "Do it."

"I can't!" Scout panted. "Really, this is hard."

I reached around, unbuttoned her jeans, and pulled them down to her knees. "Baby, you can do it. Be a good boi." I pulled her plaid shorts down too. Her ass lifted toward me as I undressed her.

Scout shuddered and picked up the shears, her hand trembling.

"Now, I want you to cut out the pattern with the pinking shears." I hissed the word "pinking" into her ear as I stroked her slippery cunt. "Just think, as you're cutting out the pattern, you'll be pinking its edges. Maybe after you do that you'll appreciate all my hard work." I thrust three fingers into her cunt at the word 'hard.' "Bend over."

I picked up the yardstick, holding it by its center for balance, eyed her delightfully meaty ass as she bent over the cutting board, and smacked her dead center.

"Ow! What are you doing?" Scout yelled.

"This is what you get for complaining when I offer to sew for you. Start cutting, my little horndog." I smacked her again, trying to stifle my giggles.

"This isn't fair!"

"Now!"

Scout started cutting out the shirt pattern as I spanked her with the yardstick.

"Fuck, fuck, fuckety fuck," Scout muttered as she cut out the sleeves.

"'Thank you, Sir' would be more appropriate than curses, don't you think?"

"Yes, Sir," Scout grumbled as she started cutting the second sleeve.

"Good job. See how pretty those pinked edges are? Go on. Unpin the sleeve that you just finished so that you can admire it. Lickety-split!" I whacked her hard on the left buttock. "And make an effort to sound grateful. No more curses under your breath, my little dog."

Scout started unpinning the sleeve slowly and hesitantly. "I can't do this! Please don't make me."

I hit her harder, reddening her cheeks with each stroke of the yardstick. I could hear her breath catch. Then I heard the tiniest sob. That was exactly what I was waiting for, that little break, that crack that would let her heart tumble out, shining and sweet. "It's all right, baby. You can do it. I know you can."

At that, Scout started crying as she unpinned the sleeve, tears falling on the tissue pattern paper, staining it. Each shiny silver pin that she removed brought out another sob, until she had the entire sleeve unpinned, with the pins stored neatly in the tomato pincushion.

"Now look at your pinked edges. Go on. Touch them." I commanded as I caressed Scout's swelling ass, her ass that was now the same shade of tomato red as the pincushion.

Scout continued to cry. "I can't touch it."

I reached down to grab her cunt. There was precome dripping down her thighs and she thrust her hips up, back at me. I ran one slippery finger along her cunt, parting her swollen labia, and jerking off her hard clit. Then I slid two fingers inside of her and started to fuck her. "Baby, touch the pinked edges. You can do it." I added a third finger. "Do you want my hand inside of you?"

Scout groaned, "You know I do."

"Then touch it. Now," I said in my deepest, sternest Daddy voice, as I continued to fuck her, pressing deep into her and hitting her cervix, the way she liked it.

Scout hesitantly let the tip of her forefinger graze the pinked edge of the plaid fabric and I rewarded her with another finger.

"Tell me you like it." I twisted my hand inside of her cunt.

"Fuck me, Birdie." Scout started to come and I pulled out.

"No, baby. I know you want me to fuck you. Tell me how pretty your pinked edges are." I grabbed a hunk of her sweet, hot, red ass and squeezed her bruising flesh.

"Please fuck me, please," Scout whimpered pitifully.

"Not until you tell me how much you love pinked seams. No fucking for you until then!" I thrust one finger inside of her cunt and out again quickly for good measure.

"I love it, really!" Scout pleaded.

"I don't believe you. Kiss it and say, 'I love pinked seams'! Hip hop!" Teasing Scout had me close to coming myself.

"Fuck."

I slapped her ass with my palm. Hard. "What did I tell you? No cursing. Remember your manners and express your gratitude!"

"Yes, Sir. I love pinked seams, Sir."

"That's better." I slid my fist inside of her eager cunt. Her cunt clenched my hand and we started fucking.

Within minutes, Scout became a messy babble of broken sentences and come. "I love pinked seams, Sir. Oh god. Pinked... yes! Fuck me." The pincushion toppled off the table and the bobbin case rattled.

I was fucking her hard and deep, my other hand tightening the tape measure around her neck like reins. "Say it!"

"I love pinked seams, Sir," she shouted as she started coming hard for the third time around my hand. "Pinked seams!!!" she yelled, still clenching the shears in her right hand and her knuckles white. Her body collapsed, her pink, sweaty face resting on the pattern tissue and a puddle of drool darkening the paper.

"Oh god," Scout moaned into the crumpled pattern. "Thank you, baby."

"Now, will you ever tease me about pinked seams again?" I kissed her shoulder gently as I snuggled her close to me.

"Never. I love pinked seams. Really, I do," Scout smiled wickedly and ground her ass and hips against my groin, "except maybe sometimes French seams are neater, don't you think?"

"Bad puppy." I nuzzled Scout's neck and grinned.

PLEASURE WITH HER PAIN

Ada Lowell

It had been one of those nights. Kate relaxed into the plastic bus seat with a sigh; she was so glad to be off her feet after a twelve-hour shift that she didn't care that the plastic pressed into her aching muscles, or that the bus jolted seemingly with every turn. She longed to take off her shoes. She longed more for sleep, and even more for the sharp sting of Nina's eyes and hands as she gave her orders. It was the only time her mind could really relax.

Anxiety made Kate a better nurse: she was always preparing for the worst, for a seemingly stable patient to code or for there to be a problem with the latest order from the pharmacy. Yet it made it hard for her when she was off the clock. She could never stop planning for contingencies. Except when Nina was there, shocking Kate back into her body, and the moments they stole together.

Sometimes Kate stayed up after her shift to sneak some time with Nina, pushing herself past the early dawn hours. She considered detouring to the Spinning Jenny Diner now, even though she was tired. She needed that woman's reassuring smile over the diner counter. Something about Nina's eyes grounded her; most peoples' eyes burned when she looked at them. There was her voice, too; the way she winked mischievously when Kate was there and called out completed orders in the same domme voice that made Kate quiver. Nina knew it, too; she knew how to tease Kate until she was begging, and then some.

Impulsively, Kate pushed the button on the bus wall to take the transfer to Nina's restaurant. It would mean more standing, and it was starting to drizzle, but her body ached more for Nina than it did from all her hours of standing.

She arrived just as Nina was clocking out and hanging up her apron for the night. Nina's mouth quirked slightly at Kate's arrival, her eyes going up and down Kate's body like a promise.

"Did you still want a coffee?" Nina asked. "I can whip up some of those hash browns you like."

"At your place," Kate replied, blushing. What was it about Nina that made her blush like a schoolgirl?

Nina grinned and grabbed her jacket, then gently took Kate's hand in hers as they walked out into the awakening city.

There was something about the fresh dawn hours that drew the two of them together, enlivened them even after the graveyard shift. It was as though the world belonged only to them in that liminal space before the rest of the world woke up. There was something about the silence, stretching between them, and the anticipation of what was to come.

"I thought you wouldn't come," Nina said, her voice husky with lack of sleep in a way that made Kate purr.

"I, uh . . ." was all she could stutter in reply.

"What was that?" Nina asked.

"I needed to see you."

"When's the last time you slept?" Nina asked, pulling her car keys off the carabiner she kept on the left side of the waistband of her jeans.

Kate waved her hand absently. "You know, yesterday. But I needed to see you."

"Sleep first," Nina said.

Kate opened her mouth to argue, but Nina stopped her with one look. "Sleep first. I'm worried about how tired you look."

"Fine," Kate said, struggling to contain a yawn.

As she settled into the lumpy passenger seat of Nina's ancient Corolla, she was too tired to argue.

When she woke up the sun streamed through the window, and Kate was still just as tired as when she'd gone to sleep. More tired, even, because the various aches and pains from her shift had somehow multiplied on Nina's lumpy mattress. She tried to surreptitiously massage her body back together, but Nina was just beginning to stir.

"I'm going to make that coffee," Kate said, before Nina could see the pain in her eyes. Nina always knew how to see the pain in her eyes.

"Make it two," Nina groaned from the bed. "I'm not awake yet."

That was probably all it was, Kate thought. She just wasn't awake yet, or maybe it was the night shift catching up to her. This sense that she just couldn't wake up had been plaguing her for the past few months. There was no reason it needed to stop her today, or any other day. She sighed as the coffee hit her throat, hoping the caffeine would help her survive her last shift of the week.

"It's nice to sleep next to you," Nina said. "I could get used to this."

Kate's heart raced with the compliment; surely that was all it was. None of her serious relationships ever seemed to work out.

There was no reason this thing she had with Nina should be any different, but she'd enjoy it while it lasted. Until she was back to loneliness and tweaking her Fet profile, looking for someone else to help stop her brain from its eternal spinning.

"Me too," Kate said.

"Are you sure you're okay?" Nina asked.

"Yes, I'm fine. I just really can't wait for uh…well. Whatever you have in mind for me."

"Why don't you tell me about it while I make pancakes," Nina replied.

Kate mocked a pout, but this was all part of their game. The more Kate wanted Nina's palms against her thighs, the more Nina teased her by going slowly. It was glorious agony.

"You get two choices," Nina said from behind her.

Kate gulped. She had already chosen to be facedown on the bed, hips arched over Nina's wedge.

A flogger and a spatula thudded in front of her. "First, choose between those."

Kate squirmed. In truth, she wanted both, she wanted everything. She had tested Nina before on her choices, trying to answer, "Both," or "Everything," or "You choose." But Nina always held firm that Kate had to choose, and in truth the choosing helped her drop ever closer to subspace.

"Flogger," Kate finally squirmed. She loved the sting of the spatula, the anticipation of it, and the way it sang across her body. Today, though, she wanted the satisfaction of the flogger's thud to calm her mind.

"Good," Nina said. "Now, do you want to be blindfolded or not?"

Part of why Nina's choices were so delicious was because they tantalized Kate into thinking about the possibilities, the possibilities of what Nina could do to her while she was wearing a blindfold or not. Did she want to be able to see what Nina was planning to do to her, or did she want the anticipation of not knowing? Did she want Nina's eyes to meet hers, to hold her in her vulnerability, or did she want to be held there instead by the low purr of Nina's voice?

Ultimately, her position made the choice for her. "Blindfold," Kate said.

"Good," Nina said. "Now I don't want to hear anything from you but pleasure or some sort of safeword, you understand? You can answer my question."

"Yes, Sir." Kate gasped, already slipping toward subspace. The nagging pain in her hip and her exhaustion were holding her back, holding her in the wrong kind of pain. Soon, though, soon, Nina would take care of everything. She would take care of her, and Kate could forget about juggling all her worries at once.

Kate sighed as Nina tied the blindfold around her eyes, trailing the flogger suggestively down her back.

With the first thud against her thighs, Kate quivered. With the second, she wriggled uncomfortably. The thud was more pain than she was expecting.

"Yellow," she said. They used a traffic-light safeword system, where red meant stop and leave the scene, and yellow meant pause and check in. She never needed to yell green for go, because Nina could always tell by her moans and muffled begging.

"You are so good for safewording when you need to," Nina said.

Kate blushed. "It's uh, it's right on the edge of what I can tolerate. Maybe work up to it?"

"I think that can be arranged. Do you need a longer break or—"

"No," Kate said quickly. "I mean, I'm fine to try again."

"Eager, are we?" Nina asked. "I like that."

In response, Kate could only gasp as the flogger hit her ass. The pain arced up her body, and she bit back a curse. Tears welled behind her eyes. She needed this release so badly. Why wasn't her body cooperating?

"Are you okay?" Nina asked. Tears were not uncommon in their sessions together, but they were usually a form of release. Kate bit her lip to hold back a sob, but Nina was onto her tricks.

"That isn't a safeword," Nina reminded her. "You may speak."

"I just really want this today," Kate said.

"Hey, I know that," Nina said. "You don't have to protect my feelings. But I'm not getting the vibe that you're into this today, so maybe we should stop for tonight."

Not for the first time, Kate wished she were dating someone who wasn't such a mind reader. A part of her knew Nina was right, that this was not a normal amount of pain, that she should stop for safety and her own mental health. But she didn't want to stop.

"I don't want to stop," Kate found herself pouting.

"I know, love," Nina said, untying her blindfold. "But you're already bruising, and I didn't even hit you that hard. You know I love a good bruise, but I'm concerned."

"You're right, of course," Kate said. She loved Nina for how she could balance concern for Kate's safety and a firm hand on the flogger, and most of all for the way she held the safety of their shared headspace so Kate could finally let go. But there was no use forcing it if her body had decided not to let go today.

When it happened again the next time they were together, Kate let out a string of curses. Nina held her while she cried and praised her for letting her feelings out, and it was as close as they could get to kink for a month. Meanwhile at work, Kate was tired beyond belief. She kept hoping it was simply the lack of subspace making her so out of sorts. Surely everything would be fine once she worked through whatever this was. They tried all sorts of toys: floggers and a soft foam bat and a host of pervertables and even a cane, to see if sting would be better. It was, briefly, and for a while Kate thrummed with happiness at the matching line of cane marks running down her ass. Yet even that did not make the tiredness better.

It was after Kate complained about how much her hands hurt that Nina suggested she go to a doctor for a checkup. Kate had been dreading this, because somehow it made everything much more real. She was sure it was just a little cold or a touch of flu or anything temporary.

The rheumatologist her doctor referred her to drew vial after vial of blood that showed nothing. Then he had pressed, gently, on her body and Kate had screamed more than she did in any dungeon.

"Fibromyalgia," he'd said. "I'll write you a prescription for physical therapy."

Kate didn't know how she was going to work at the hospital and find time for physical therapy three times a week. She didn't know how she was going to keep working; night shifts had been her refuge but now it was hard to stay awake, to walk the long hallways of the hospital. At least the medicine had started helping with the pain that constantly screeched through her body.

She didn't call Nina. She dialed her number and hung up before the ring, composed text messages, but she didn't know how to tell her. It seemed like the cruelest thing about this diagnosis was how it interfered with her subspace. She was so stressed and tired now, all the time, and she just wanted a little relief. Just something to take her mind off the pressing worry and pain. Kate wanted a different kind of pain, one that she chose rather than one forced upon her. But she didn't know how and was afraid it was lost forever. It wasn't fair to Nina, she told herself, and deleted another text message.

So she was surprised when the lobby door buzzed and Nina was on the other side.

"Can I come up?" she asked.

"Of course," Kate said.

When she arrived, Nina opened her arms with a questioning look and Kate found herself walking into the embrace.

"I was so worried," Nina said, her chin resting above Kate's head. "I thought, maybe she's ghosted me, and I should stay away. Or maybe she's like in a coma and can't tell me, or really sick—"

Kate fought with herself, but the floodgates opened. It all came rushing out, the fears and the diagnosis and everything.

"So I have chronic pain and fatigue from the fibromyalgia, and I just don't think I'm the sub you want because I don't know how to make this work anymore."

"Are you breaking up with me?" Nina asked. "Or are you telling me about a problem you want help fixing?"

"No I mean, I don't want you to leave," Kate said. "But I feel like you should. I mean, what good am I—"

"Stop," Nina said, using her domme voice. Then her voice wavered as she said, "Let me worry about what's good for me. Let me figure this out."

That night she slept curved in the circle of Nina's body, and for a while she felt safe until she remembered that Nina would be better off without her. She woke with her body on fire yet again, but didn't tell Nina, and she hid her eyes as she drank her coffee. Nina could always see what she was hiding in her eyes, and she didn't have the energy to explain this pit of sadness in her stomach. Nina was leaving her someday, Kate knew, and that was that.

* * *

The next night there was no Nina at the door, and Kate was convinced that she was right. The night after, she resigned herself to another night tossing and turning with pain, and sleep that didn't make her feel any less tired.

She was in a pain-filled stupor in front of the television when the apartment buzzer startled her.

"It's me," Nina said, and Kate buzzed her up, and then she was there with her arms full of packages. Kate felt a pang, sure that this was it. Nina was returning everything she'd left at her apartment, telling her it was over, ending it and moving on to a simpler sub.

"Hey," Nina said, dumping her packages on the sofa in one swift move and stepping toward Kate. "Hey, what's wrong?"

Kate found herself babbling all of her worries, and Nina was only pacing quietly. "I'm sorry," Kate said again. She knew she should hold them in but she couldn't help herself. Then she was sobbing and blowing her nose on Nina's shirt, and Nina was rubbing her back.

"I don't know why you thought I'd leave. It's just groceries, love," Nina said, gesturing to the packages. "Give me a little credit."

"But why would you want me now?" Kate asked. Nina only smiled that mischievous smile of hers.

"Oh, love," Nina said. "You're going to have to do a lot worse than get a chronic illness to keep me away."

"Are you sure?" Kate asked. She hated how vulnerable she sounded, so dependent. It wasn't the kind of vulnerability she craved, the kind where she chose to expose her soft underbelly to Nina.

"Hey," Nina said again softly, her finger under Kate's chin. "I'm sure. But if I ever change my mind about being part of us,

I'll let you know. And I can tell you now, it won't be because of fibromyalgia."

"Okay," Kate said dubiously.

"Can you be a good one and try to believe me?" Nina asked.

"I'll try," Kate said, sniffling.

"I'm sorry I was working late yesterday," Nina said. "But I have some ideas, if you're interested. I've been doing some reading."

"Reading?" Kate asked.

"On fibromyalgia and kink," Nina said. "Because it seems like you need something kinky to help stop your brain from spinning out with anxiety."

"Yes," Kate said, and it was the first thing she really felt certain of all evening. "I just, I'm sorry I'm such a mess but I haven't had—"

"I know," Nina said. "I'm sorry I haven't been able to get you into subspace."

"But that's not your fault," Kate said.

In answer, Nina simply raised an eyebrow at her.

"Oh, I see what you did there," Kate responded. "I just feel like this is all my fault."

"I know," Nina said. "Now can I show you what I found, or do you want it to be a surprise?"

"Surprise," Kate said. She loved Nina's surprises.

"First I have to ask you one thing," Nina said. "How do you feel about wax play?"

"Oh," Kate said. "That sounds nice."

"You have two choices," Nina said. "First off, where is the most comfortable spot for you to sit?"

"The armchair by the window," Kate said.

"Blindfold on or off?" Nina asked, deftly closing the blinds.

Kate considered. Her eyes were puffy, and a voice in her head said they were ugly. But she craved the look in Nina's eyes as she dommed.

"No blindfold," Kate said.

"Good," Nina said. "Now please sit down and make yourself comfortable."

Kate felt awkward making herself comfortable for a kink session; wasn't the whole point to enjoy the discomfort?

"Is there a problem?" Nina asked, the steel of domme voice edging her words.

"No, Sir." Kate sat rigidly in the chair.

"I said comfortably," Nina said. "Are you comfortable?"

"No, but—"

"Comfortable," Nina said. "Unless but is a safeword?"

Kate was being a brat and she knew it, but she just didn't see how this was going to work. Still, she did enjoy surprises, especially when Nina had already broken out the domme voice. She grabbed a couple of extra pillows and settled into the chair.

"I like this skirt on you," Nina said. "It gives me such lovely access. But I think these panties need to go."

Kate moved to remove them, but Nina gently caught her wrist.

"Let me take care of that," Nina said with a growl.

"Yes, Sir." Kate lay back in the chair.

Nina's hands on her thighs were gentle, flitting over her skin with the lightest of touches. It was almost a tickle, but not quite. Pleasure rippled down Kate's thighs, and she stopped wondering if Nina knew what she was doing and moaned. She arched her hips to help Nina remove her black panties—no lace since the pain had started—and leaned into Nina's touch.

Yet all too soon Nina had removed her hands from around Kate's waist, and returned with tantalizing touches around her thighs and down to her calves.

Nina knelt in front of her and Kate gasped at the implications.

Usually it was Kate who knelt, Kate who serviced. Yet Nina was topping her with those light touches from her knees, and Kate wriggled in pleasure at the thought. There was something she'd always loved about flipping the expected scripts, and Nina knew it.

"I've been reading up on massage," Nina said. "For you. So please let me know if the pressure is good, or if I need to change it."

Kate's eyes went wide as Nina found a spot on the back of her calves that ached, not with desire but with pain. Under her deft hands the pain lessened, transformed. It hurt so good to be touched like this. The pain had been this daunting, unrelenting wall and now her body was becoming all tingles again. She couldn't even moan, just met Nina's eyes as her own went soft and yearning.

"Please," she moaned.

"Please what?" Nina asked, a pleased smile teasing the corners of her lips.

"Don't stop," Kate said, moaning as Nina found a spot between her toes that she didn't even know was on fire with pain until Nina massaged it away.

For the first time in months, her nerves were singing with pleasure instead of with torment. Kate found herself slipping into subspace at the experience. She moaned as Nina removed her hands and left the room, only to return a moment later with the wax bath Kate's occupational therapist had recommended. She set it before Kate's feet like an offering before some ancient goddess.

"Do you still want to try some wax play?" Nina asked again.

Kate was genuinely torn. She wanted the massage to never stop, but Nina hadn't been wrong yet. "Yes," she said.

"Good," Nina said. "You'll let me know if there's a problem with the temperature."

With the gentleness that Cinderella must have used to handle her glass slippers, Nina gently lowered Kate's foot into the wax bath, dipping it so several layers of wax formed.

Kate gasped at the sting of the heat, then moaned as it began to penetrate into the ropey layers of pain still lingering in her foot. She offered her other foot to Nina without hesitation, whimpering a little in anticipation as Nina dipped her foot in wax.

Carefully, Nina wrapped Kate's feet in towels to keep the heat in.

Kate's body was singing, and she found herself crying at the relief. She had thought she would never experience this again. Thought she would forever be in pain. Even though she knew the pain would be back later, today or tomorrow, the relief was so palpable she found herself almost writhing under the unfamiliar sensation of having less pain coursing through her body.

Her eyes were soft and pleading as they met Nina's. "Please," she said, whimpering. "Fuck me. Please."

Her hands fumbled toward the hard pecker bulging under Nina's jeans.

"Not yet," Nina said, playfully slapping her hands away. Then she gently lifted the wax bath to a nearby table, and dipped Kate's hands one by one into the delicious warmth. Kate thought she might come from the ripples of unfamiliar pleasure alone.

"Now you are bound with wax," Nina said, and she quivered in anticipation.

Nina flipped her skirt up over her belly, leaving her exposed and whimpering on the chair.

"That's my good girl," Nina said, surveying her soft and vulnerable flesh. But instead of picking up a cane or a flogger, she ran her nails down Kate's thighs. The sting of pain mixed with the heat of pleasure filling her body, and Kate thought she might burst then and there.

"How attached are you to that shirt?" Nina asked.

"It's old," Kate said. "I'm not."

Nina produced a pair of sharp steel scissors from a nearby table and cut a nick in the front of Kate's shirt collar. Then with a wink, she ripped the fabric down to Kate's waist. She had stopped wearing bras at home because of the pain, so her breasts were at Nina's mercy. Kate's nipples hardened in the cold air and her eyes begged Nina to touch her.

"Good girl," Nina said. "Now if you want to take me, you have to tell me if you're hurting."

Kate nodded obediently.

"I want to hear it," Nina said.

"Yes," Kate said. "I'll tell you if I'm hurting."

"Good," Nina said, as her jeans hit the floor. She adjusted the straps of her harness, moved the wax bath to a different table, and carefully rolled a condom down over her cock. Kate waited, the cold air caressing her cunt and her tits, contrasting with the warmth pleasantly filling her hands and feet.

Nina cupped her tits as Kate spread her legs, and then Nina was edging inside her and filling her. Kate gasped at the sensation, but she couldn't wrap her arms and legs around Nina because of the wax on her hands and feet. She wriggled with frustration, and Nina chose that moment to slip one hand from her nipple down to her clit.

There was a fire running through Kate's body now, a fire of pleasure and yearning running from her feet to her calf muscles to her clit, and out to her hands and up her spine and around to her tits. She came, the orgasm bursting through her body, made all the more sweet by the months of waiting.

She lay spent on the chair as Nina pulled out and surveyed her.

"Please," Kate said. "Let me fuck you."

Nina was already replacing the condom on her cock. "One condition," she said.

"Please," was all Kate could reply.

"Two actually," Nina said. "You let me help you to the bed, and you don't open your mouth too wide. It's not allowed."

"But —" Kate protested.

"I don't want you to hurt your jaw," Nina said firmly. "Do you want to fuck me or not?"

"Fine," Kate said. "You're probably right."

It was only a few wobbling waxy steps across the studio apartment to Kate's bed, where Nina helped her prop herself up on her favorite pillow.

Then she was in front of her, grabbing her hair and growling, "Fuck me," before releasing her head back to the bed.

Kate whimpered at the restrictions placed on her. No touching with her hands, no straining her jaw. She wanted to show just how grateful she was for today.

She began to lick the head of Nina's cock, as Nina knelt straddling over her. Nina braced herself against the headboard and held remarkably still, letting Kate set the pace of how deep she would take her.

"I want you to remember this," Nina said. "I want you to remember that I'm not going to leave you over something so silly as having chronic pain. You're a good girl, and you're my good girl."

Kate found her eyes welling with tears, both from the sweet vulnerability of Nina's cock in her mouth and Nina's words of reassurance. They split her wide open like Nina's cock in her cunt. She was pinned down yet utterly vulnerable and open, and she felt so seen Nina's eyes on her burned.

With enough repetitions of this, she might believe Nina; she might believe that she wasn't some useless burden. She rolled her tongue over Nina's cock as Nina came moaning in her mouth, and thought how she could get used to this.

LEVIATHAN

Catherine Collinsworth

1

Standing at the bar at Leviathan, Kay wondered how she'd gotten from Randi's dinner party last Saturday night to this gay men's leather club tonight. Over a particularly good beef Wellington and a 2004 Château Laforge Merlot, her friends had been discussing the affairs all their mutual friends were having. Kay was preoccupied with how best to handle her new boss, who'd turned out to be an imperious bitch after the terrific interviews the publishing imprint had with her, when she'd felt a hand on her arm and glanced up, startled. Laura was looking at her with those chocolate eyes that always melted her.

"Kay? Yes or no?"

"To what?" Apparently, when Kay hadn't been paying attention, Randi and Georgia had confessed that they'd been going to Ladies' Night at Leviathan for a year now. After Randi described their experiences, Janice and Yumi wanted to try it. So when Randi looked at Laura and Kay to extend the invitation . . .

"I want to go," Laura had said, excitement lighting her eyes.

"You want to tie me up naked and whip me in front of a room full of strange women, don't you?" Kay had teased, unsure of what Laura really wanted.

"We'll just watch, honey. We don't have to do anything. Unless you want to."

2

That's how Kay found herself surrounded by hot-looking women in leather and scanty costumes, women of all shapes and sizes nearly naked, and women under the spotlights on the club's intimate performance stage at the back of the main room doing things to each other with ropes, collars, and paddles that left her staring slack jawed. Kay hardly knew where to look, on sensory overload not five minutes after walking into the place, holding on to Laura's arm as if it were the last life preserver on the *Titanic*. *It's not that I'm a prude,* she thought, looking at all the tits brushing by her, *but I have everything I want in Laura, and she has everything she wants in me.* She'd found it amusing that Laura had ransacked her closet for the tight black jeans, the sleeveless black T-shirt that accentuated her toned biceps, her steel-tipped black cowboy boots; had slicked back her lustrous short black hair, and looked like the delectable Puerto Rican butch she was instead of the business-suited marketing executive of indeterminate background she let everyone in her professional life think she was. Then, she'd opened Kay's closet and carefully dressed her. Several women, Kay noticed, had already scanned Laura.

"I told you they'd eat you right up in that suit," Laura leaned in to say over the bass of the music.

"They're looking at you, babe."

"No, no—" Laura flashed her index finger in a zigzag down Kay's body. "They lookin' for a mommy to spank them or a boss to tie them up. Somebody gonna come for you tonight and I'm gonna have to fight *la perra*." Laura only turned on the accent or used that kind of vernacular when she was hunting. But after Kay had landed her, the only place Laura hunted anymore was in their bed. She smiled at her wife's posturing. As Laura waded into the crowd at the bar to flag a bartender, Kay wondered if she was right. Looking down at her black suit, the jacket buttoned over a lacy red bra, the little red leather bows on the backs of her black stilettos, she'd sighed—this so wasn't her, but she knew she looked damn good. What would the other editors at the imprint think if they knew how she was inhabiting this suit tonight? In the mirror behind the bar, she checked her hair, a mass of auburn curls she'd tamed into a tight twist. Her green eyes shone like emeralds in a mask of flawless makeup. Even the lipstick and her manicured nails matched the red bra.

Her reflection was met by that of a handsome woman with intense blue eyes. The set of her shoulders, the tilt of her head, the way her eyelids closed just a little as she regarded Kay—it was how her cat Benito studied his prey, still as a statue. One errant brown curl rested in the middle of her forehead giving her that naughty-boy look. Her mother had warned her about such boys when she was thirteen. But it was the naughty girls a young Kay had wanted. Still did.

She was drawn to the woman's long elegant neck, and the harness on bare skin underneath her jacket. As she turned to—what? Say something to her?—Laura grabbed her hand.

"Come on, Randi and Georgia are already in the back room." She shoved an icy glass of Johnnie Walker Black at Kay. "You're never gonna believe this. Yumi says Georgia's naked, Randi's got her breasts in a pair of giant handcuffs, and there's a crowd gathering for whatever they're gonna do."

Kay turned to look for the blue-eyed butch but she was gone.

Despite the muted lighting, it was still easy to see women engaged in play around the back room. As Laura edged them closer to Randi and Georgia, Kay's eyes darted everywhere. She was fascinated and frightened by what she saw: crosses freestanding on the floor, hanging on the walls; cuffs, chains, paddles, belts, and other paraphernalia dotting the walls; all sorts of benches, chairs, and wooden horses here and there. Almost everything was in use. The scent of female arousal hit her and as she stood on her tiptoes to see over the other women, a hand on Laura's shoulders for balance, Kay suspected it wasn't just the women being tied up, spanked, or kneeling obediently in front of their doms who were perfuming the air.

She watched a topless Randi cuff Georgia's wrists to a bar above her head, her brown skin glistening with sweat under the lights. Georgia was, indeed, stark naked, her ample breasts protruding through a pair of enormous handcuffs that were also chained to the bar. A flush rose up Kay's throat and her clitoris hardened, the sight of the cuffed breasts provoking an unfamiliar excitement in her.

Taking a large gulp of her scotch, she realized she'd never considered her friends without their clothes on, but now her gaze slid down the rest of the petite blonde's voluptuous body, coming to rest on her completely shaved pubic mound. It was small, adorable, and reminded her of a stuffed bear's sewn smile. Kay saw the dewy coating on Georgia's pussy as Randi secured her feet to a spreader bar. She wondered at the Pavlovian response, at her own uncontrollable physical reactions as she looked at the scenes around her—certain pictures of bondage had excited her whenever she'd seen them, but she'd never thought watching the actual act would be titillating.

Randi turned to the crowd, a half-naked Vanna White, and Kay admired her large full breasts with their chocolate-drop nipples, one of which she'd never realized before was pierced with a little bar. Kay's clit pulsed.

Randi kissed Georgia's kewpie-doll mouth, lavished her pink nipples with her tongue, and picked up a flat cat-o'-nine-tails.

Kay nearly lost her next mouthful of scotch when she gasped at the sound of the whip lashing Georgia's breasts. Georgia grimaced and arched her back, her breasts jutting out, red blossoming across them. A moment later, one nipple turned darker red, a Bing cherry on her breast. Randi swung the whip again, leaving marks across Georgia's stomach; she struggled against the restraints. Kay drained her glass as Randi swung the whip right up into Georgia's wet pussy and as Georgia's head fell back and she moaned, the onlookers murmuring appreciatively.

Kay turned away, unsure she could continue watching even as the pulsing between her legs notched up to a throb. She needed to get to the bar. There, not ten feet away, the blue-eyed butch watched her instead of any of the many floor shows. She hesitated, the woman's eyes traveled down her body approvingly, and Kay blushed. *I can't just stand here,* she thought. She wanted to reach out and run her hand through the woman's curls.

Working her way around the crush of bodies, Kay headed for the bar and ordered another scotch. When the bartender put the glass in front of her, a hand with two sharply creased bills caught between the index and middle fingers blocked her from paying. She turned to see the intense blue eyes studying her.

"I've never seen you here before." The woman smiled, the warmth of it reaching her eyes, but Kay didn't feel she could let her guard down. The woman thanked the bartender as he took the bills.

"No, really, you shouldn't—I can't let you—"

"Do you always dictate to people how they should treat you?"

"I, uh—" Kay became flustered. Glancing around for Laura, she realized her wife didn't know where she'd gone.

"If you're looking for Romeo, she's still watching the show she dragged you to. You didn't seem as interested."

Kay deflated. "They're friends of ours. I couldn't really . . . It was hard to..."

"So you *haven't* been here before. But you know Randi and Georgia."

"You *know* them?"

"Everyone here knows them. They put on good shows. Randi's become quite a talented dom. And Georgia's a very sought-after submissive, when Randi decides to lend her out."

"She . . . lets other women *have* Georgia? And Georgia lets her . . . ?"

"Some of us are very generous with our women. As we are with teaching others how to be responsible dominants. I taught Randi almost everything she knows. Georgia—she was a natural. She only needed to give herself permission to be who she really wanted to be with Randi."

Kay studied the woman, trying to read anything about her in her eyes, hoping the woman couldn't discern the desire and curiosity fighting the fear in hers. *But what do I want? This woman? Laura to use me in the back room?*

"I'm Teddy Winston." She held out her hand.

Kay hesitated, but then she shook Teddy's hand. "Kay Connors." The hand was rough, calloused, as cool as Teddy's beautiful blue eyes.

"Romeo in there your date?"

"My wife."

Teddy smiled. "Two for the price of one."

"We're not here to . . ."

"No one ever is the first time. Does Romeo have a name?"

"Laura. But we're—"

"Why don't you go get her. I could bring the two of you back to my place, away from all this, and begin to teach you, if you're interested. It can be overwhelming here."

"Oh, I—"

"That's how Randi and Georgia got started. With me. The rooms upstairs only rent by the half hour and you can't learn anything in that amount of time. Or in that setting."

"Oh—here you are. You got away from me."

Laura's arm encircled Kay's waist and relief flooded her. Then she sensed Laura pulling herself up to her full height, expanding.

"Hi." Laura held out her hand to Teddy. "Laura Fontaine."

Any other night, Kay might've laughed at Laura's peacock presentation.

"Teddy Winston. Nice to meet Kay's Romeo." There was a teasing edge to her voice.

Kay knew without looking that Laura's eyebrows rose in that quirk they did when she was moving into confrontational mode.

"Wait—are you the Teddy who took Randi and Georgia under her wing?"

"I am, yes. I was just telling Kay I'd love to do the same for you."

Kay saw the fire in Laura's eyes when she turned to look at her. *Oh dear god, she wants it. . . . What is this place doing to us?*

"My apartment is a short walk from here," Teddy said.

3

Kay stood by a floor-to-ceiling window in Teddy's loft. The street below was deserted, only a few lights on in other apartments at this hour. She caught her reflection in the window, *Alice Through the Looking Glass,* and wondered how the night had taken this turn.

"Thank you for coming here, babe." Laura kissed the back of her neck, ran a hand underneath her jacket to cup and palm one of her breasts. Kay let her head fall back onto Laura's shoulder, let Laura kiss her. "We'll just talk with Teddy. We don't have to do anything . . . unless you want to."

A pang of guilt. *I want to.*

And that was how she found herself here, wanting to please her wife, fulfill a fantasy, albeit one Laura never realized she'd had until tonight. But Kay also had a fantasy, long-harbored, one she was perhaps so afraid of that she'd never examined it until it was facing her tonight at Leviathan, all around her, women fucking other women in full view of everyone in a . . . public space. The whips, cuffs, and chains weren't part of that fantasy, but if that's what it took to get her a step closer to fucking another woman in front of her wife.

Suddenly Kay understood what Leviathan had laid open in her.

Teddy displayed several sets of handcuffs, and various whips and dildos on a wooden plank table that had placemats and a centerpiece on it, obviously her dining room table, but Kay was certain it served another purpose when she spotted small metal handles on all four sides of it. Laura inspected everything, feeling the fluffy sheepskin inside one pair of cuffs, running the flat, supple straps of a short leather whip through her fingers.

"Where do we begin?" Laura asked.

"With Kay's permission."

Kay turned to look at the two of them, apprehensive. Teddy had shed her jacket and Kay dropped her gaze to the small round breasts, their dark nipples hard. She wanted to touch one. Teddy's leather pants sat low on her hips exposing another harness. The room suddenly became warmer.

"Permission?" Kay asked.

"I want to work with you first." Teddy approached her

slowly, gracefully, moving like Benito did when he was stalking the occasional water bug in their apartment. "Laura can watch. Find out what you like, what you want, what you need. What you crave."

Oh. She almost moaned. *And I want to work with you.*

"May I touch you?" Teddy asked. She unbuttoned Kay's jacket and ran a finger over her cleavage. Kay tried not to shiver. Kissing her throat down to the rise of her breasts, Teddy slipped the jacket off and let it fall to the floor. Laura sank against the couch, a look of surprise on her face, and excitement roiled in Kay's chest. Teddy's tongue teased her nipples through the lace; she unhooked the clasp of the bra and let it join the jacket.

"We're in the window." Kay glanced over her shoulder. Could anyone see them from another apartment, from the street below?

"Yes, we are," Teddy whispered. "Laura, turn off everything but the lamp on my right."

Kay inhaled as Teddy's lips closed over one of her nipples, sucked it in, her fingers circling the other nipple. Kay had to steady herself against the window frame to stay upright.

"I haven't said yes yet."

"You haven't said no."

Kay let Teddy unbutton her skirt. She could hardly breathe, her mind a tangled mess of desire, lust, fear; the skirt dropped to her feet. Teddy crouched down, ran her hands up Kay's legs, pulled the lace panties down them. Kay was wetter than she'd ever been before, her clitoris involuntarily responding to what it wasn't even sure was coming, betraying her. Teddy's tongue pressed into her soaked vulva, delved into her. Kay didn't know she was capable of moaning from a place so deep in her throat. A corresponding moan from Laura intoxicated Kay and she reached for her, but Teddy caught her hand.

"I'll take that as a yes from both of you." Teddy stood and

undid her pants, sliding them down her slim hips, stepping out of them and tossing them aside.

Kay was breathing hard but when she saw the harness around Teddy's waist and thighs, the crisscrossed straps with the dildo hole, the pair of handcuffs draped over the strap at her right hip, her breath caught in her throat. Teddy asked Laura to hand her the dildo of her choice and Kay looked at Teddy, astonished.

"Shouldn't that be Kay's choice?"

"Your submissive acquiesces to *your* desires."

Kay bit her tongue to keep from saying anything. Laura smiled, handed Teddy the largest phallus, small bubbles all over it, big balls at its base. They had never engaged in penetrative sex because Kay wasn't sure she liked it. Had Laura wanted to and simply given it up for her? Would Kay let Teddy be the first? Fear and excitement tightened inside her chest. Teddy fastened the cock into her harness, took Kay's hand, and helped her step out of the pile of clothes, kicking them aside. She ran a hand down the front of Kay's body and between her legs, a promise.

"Anything you don't want, just tell me 'red light.'"

Teddy placed Kay's hands on the handles on either side of the window frame, her back to the window, and began trailing the leather tails of the whip over every inch of her skin. Kay closed her eyes. The leather was soft, Teddy's touch deft. She arched toward the tails, wanting more.

"That's it—give me those tits." Teddy whipped them and Kay gasped.

Teddy traced the whip's braided handle under Kay's jaw, down her neck, her torso, between her legs, pushed the tip inside Kay, swirled it, withdrew it and put it in Kay's mouth, slowly moving it in and out. Laura reached her hand into her jeans as she watched Kay suck the hard leather farther into her mouth. Teddy again caressed Kay with the whip, swinging the straps in a wider arc, landing them harder, Kay closing her eyes to bathe in the sensation until the sting of it between her legs seized her attention. Laura whimpered. Teddy told Kay to turn around. She bent to take off her heels but the whip's tails blistering the heel near her fingers stopped her dead.

"I like those on you. Don't touch."

Kay stood and braced herself as ordered. Being told what to do by this woman aroused her. And now she knew it inflamed Laura, too.

Oh my god . . . there are people on the street . . . watching. She tensed.

Before she could focus or say "red light," the whip was crossing her back, a sharper tempo that left a definite warmth in its wake, the dildo rubbing in and out between her legs, probing, the tip penetrating her, missing her, finding her again, pushing in deeper, Teddy fondling her buttocks, urges flooding her body and she wanted more, wanted those people down there to see her getting it.

"You have an audience outside," Teddy whispered in her ear. "Strangers. Perform for them."

Excitement fluttered into her chest like a bird landing on a tree branch. Kay ground into Teddy, squeezed the dildo, bent to try and catch it in her dripping hole as it moved back and forth, her breasts now swinging with the rhythm of her hips. Teddy increased the pressure of the whip, lightly stinging blows landing on Kay's back, her thighs, and she winced.

Teddy took Kay's hair down and ran her fingers through the long curls. "Give them a show," she growled. The order electrified Kay and she pressed her breasts to the window. The strokes of the whip became sharper, Teddy's cock probed faster, spearing Kay, and she gulped in air, moaned. Teddy wrapped her hair in her fist, yanked Kay's head back and kissed her, her tongue invading Kay's mouth in concert with the thrusts of her cock in Kay's pussy. Laura, unable to contain herself any longer, shed her jeans and panties, penetrated herself with her fingers.

Kay trembled, at the edge.

"Not yet, my beauty." Teddy pulled out. "I want you to show them those beautiful big tits first. Make their mouths water. And then I'll reward you. Laura, open this window."

Startled, Laura obeyed, pulling the handles and swinging the window wide. "Are you okay?" she whispered. "This is...not you."

Kay looked at Laura, reached between her legs and found her as wet as she was. Teddy snapped the whip against Kay's ass and Laura backed off, a hunger in her eyes. Teddy bent Kay over the iron rail of the tiny balcony and several people below clapped and whistled. She leaned into her, skin on skin, scooped Kay's breasts into her hands, moving against her, pulling Kay's nipples until they were hard, nosing the big cock into her wet, open pussy. Kay wriggled to find it, an elemental lust at her core, her breasts dancing back and forth bringing another round of whistles and catcalls from below.

"Please . . ." Kay whispered.

"Please what, my beauty?"

"Inside . . ." Kay had never been so close to senseless in another woman's arms that she couldn't form a sentence, but now she could barely stand.

"You want what inside you?" Teddy was right at her ear.

"Cock . . ."

"Just inside you?" the voice teased. Teddy's hips moved, the dildo easily sliding all the way in. Teddy held herself there. Like it had a mind of its own, Kay's pussy clenched around the cock, sucking it in. Kay had never known such fullness, or that her cunt could split so wide open, but it was Laura who groaned, a guttural noise, and Kay's pussy convulsed in response.

Teddy fingered her clitoris. "Is this for me? For Laura? Or are you so wet for them?" Teddy's nose traced Kay's neck, she inhaled her scent. "Look at how many people have gathered to see you. Naked. In my window. Getting whipped. Getting fucked." She pinched Kay's nipples, and Kay squirmed, whimpered, squeezed the cock, thrust back against Teddy.

"Fuck me . . . please," she whispered, afraid Laura would hear, wanting her to hear.

"Tell me what you want. Tell Laura what you want."

Heat spread up from her nipples. "Fuck me. In front of her. In front of all those people." She heard a small sound from Laura.

Teddy shoved her cock into Kay right up to the balls and set a blistering pace. Again, whistles and catcalls arose from the street.

"I want them to *see* you getting impaled on my cock."

Just when Kay thought her legs would give out, Teddy reached for her wrists, cuffed them behind her back and turned, profiling them both in the window, her cock still buried inside Kay. Teddy put her hands on Kay's hips and began moving in and out of her, slowly, deliberately, and Kay rutted against Teddy like an animal, embarrassed by that need, the blind craving, out of control and nearly crazed to reach orgasm. *In front of all those people.*

"Laura—" Teddy pointed to the floor in front of Kay and instantly Laura was on her knees in front of her, her tongue lapping in every direction on Kay's stiff clit, fighting Teddy's cock to get inside her, slurping against her juices, bracing Kay's thighs as Teddy's thrusts quickened, banged into her with piston-like precision. Applause, hoots, and shrill whistles came from the street below. *In front of all those people . . . In front of Laura.* With one last thrust, Teddy stilled, and Kay's clitoris exploded on Laura's tongue, her knees buckling, Teddy wrapping her in her arms to keep her from falling, Laura reaching up to kiss her, juices all over her chin, kissing them into Kay's mouth.

Teddy slowly withdrew and Laura stood and took Kay into her arms.

"Why didn't you ever say anything to me?"

"I didn't know." Several men still stood below whistling. "It was a fantasy. *You* wanted things, too."

Teddy brought Kay a scotch. Between the smile and the cock still gleaming, wet, she looked like the cat who'd eaten the canary.

"Now that you know what *you* like," she said to Kay, "let's find out what Laura wants."

GOOD GIRLS DO

Marie Carlson

Angie's in the tack room the hot August evening it begins, wearing cutoff jean shorts and an old tank top worn thin; her short twists are covered by a pink kerchief. There's a storm brewing, but it hasn't hit yet, the air muggy and flat.

She's cleaning tack. It keeps her hands busy and lets her mind wander. She's hoping it'll wander right over to a plan for wooing Mag, the hottest stable hand Angie's ever seen.

Four months ago, Mag turned up with her funny name and her slow smirk and her hat tipped so it shadowed her eyes. Angie'd been wearing ancient jeans, shit-kicker boots that would never be free of the smell of manure, and a ratty T-shirt. She was dressed to work, not flirt. Mag was dressed to work, too, but she looked competent and smoking hot. Angie'd felt like a grubby little kid even though she's closing in on forty.

Still, Mag tipped her hat as Angie stumbled through introducing herself and then flashed a smile that sent heat shooting straight through her.

These days, Angie makes a point of swinging by the stables

when she looks good. She wears work clothes when she's with the horses, but when she's not, she slips into flirty little sundresses and fancy red leather boots—but nothing catches Mag's eye, and Angie's not sure what to do next.

She's never had to do the pursuing before. There've always been farm girls who'd come around to kiss and canoodle up in the hayloft or in the bed of their truck out in the middle of the fields, girls who wore T-shirts with the sleeves cut off and heavy boots, girls with short nails and blunt fingers that felt so good inside. She likes women who come after her for no more than a skirt flip and a smile.

She's deep into the rhythm of cleaning when Mag walks into the tack room and pushes the door shut. Angie's too caught up in what she's doing to see what's happening at first; then all she can do is stare. Mag's wearing a crisp black sleeveless shirt, dark-wash jeans that look nearly brand new, and shiny red boots. That's the detail Angie catches on, of course.

"You're not supposed to be here," Angie says without meaning to.

"Oh yeah?" Mag raises her eyebrows and smiles, one side of her mouth curving higher than the other. She has a dimple on that side Angie's never noticed before, no matter how many times she's sneaked a look, and there are wrinkles at the corners of her eyes and mouth and freckles across her brown cheeks. "I can leave."

"No!" Angie spits that out fast, and her cheeks burn. "No, that's okay. I'm just surprised. You aren't usually around on your days off." She wants to smack herself, because she sounds sillier than ever and now she's let Mag know she's paying attention.

Mag smiles wider and starts toward her, leading with her hips.

Then again, maybe being obvious is a good thing.

Angie sets down the bridle and wipes her hands on her shorts. With the door shut, the air feels hotter and closer than ever. The exhaust fans run, but all they do is move warm air around. Sweat gathers along Angie's hairline, under her breasts, in the creases of her thighs.

"You know," Mag says, easy as anything, "passing time with the boss's daughter's generally a bad idea. What would your mama say if she saw you here with me now?"

Sadly, they're not doing anything at all, and even if they were, the last thing Angie wants to think about is her parents, and it's not like they're ever around, not since they bought that place down in Texas where it's warm and put Angie in charge up here, but she tosses her chin up anyway.

"She'd be proud of me for catching your eye," Angie tells her. "Mama and Daddy met working stables." Back when they were young and hungry and horse wild.

Mag laughs. "You sure about that, princess?"

Angie leans back, resting her weight on one hand behind her on the bench so her breasts thrust out and her shirt rides up. "Do I look like a princess?" she teases. "I'm over here doing chores."

"Chores, huh?" Mag takes a few more steps closer. "Looks to me like you're sitting around baring all that skin and hoping someone comes by to take you up on it."

"Not just anyone," Angie says.

"Someone specific?"

Angie shrugs, embarrassed by how blunt she's already been, but that discomfort sends heat throbbing between her legs. "Just what is someone taking me up on?" she asks instead. "Guess I could use some help with the tack."

"I'm sure I can think of something to do with all those reins," Mag says. She flexes her broad hands, fingers thick, blunt, then hooks her thumbs into her belt loops and lets her hands fall against the front of her jeans. Angie can't stop staring, and the more she looks, the more convinced she is that Mag is packing.

Angie very nearly swoons.

"Is that why you're lurking?" she asks. "Trying to catch someone unaware?"

"Not just anyone," Mag echoes, and from the lilt in her voice, she knows exactly what she's doing. "And not unaware."

Angie wants to say something else flirty, but her throat is tight, her mouth dry. She blinks up at Mag, breathless. Angie's straddling the bench, and with one slow step, Mag is, too, close enough that her legs push Angie's farther apart. It leaves her feeling exposed, and wet.

Mag gives Angie a long once-over. Angie's nipples are hard and visible through the thin tank top and old sports bra. She's sweaty, and probably smells disgusting, and she's ninety-nine-percent sure she's got dirt everywhere.

Still Mag looks at her like she wants to eat Angie alive.

When she brushes her thumb along Angie's cheek, it comes back with a streak of dirt on it. Angie wants to bury her face in her hands, but that'd just smear things around worse.

"I'm a mess." All those times she came around looking beautiful, and this is when she finally gets a minute alone with Mag.

"I like it. Oh, you're pretty enough all dressed up." Mag's voice is low in the quiet room, rough, and heat curls between Angie's legs. She opens her mouth, and Mag touches her lower lip with her thumb. Angie smells Lava soap and musky cologne. "But I like you like this, dirty and open."

Mag reaches down and puts her other hand on Angie's bare thigh, far enough up that her fingers touch the edge of Angie's cutoffs. Mag's palm is hot, her fingers calloused.

"I didn't"—Angie barely gets the words out, her breath catches so much—"think you noticed."

"How could I miss it?" Mag asks. "How could anyone miss the way you walk around here flashing those thighs in your pretty little skirts?" She angles her leg until her knee presses against Angie's leg, shoving her legs even wider. "Watching me when you think I'm not looking. I noticed. I noticed it all." Her tone is dry, but she smiles down at Angie.

"Oh," Angie says, breathless. She grabs Mag's shoulders and tugs her down so they can kiss, so Angie can press her mouth against Mag's and run her tongue along Mag's lips and push it inside when Mag opens her mouth. Mag lets her lead the kiss, and Angie's smug about it for half a second before Mag slides her hand up so she can push the flat of her palm between Angie's legs, rubbing her through shorts and panties. Angie rips her mouth away to cry out. She's dizzy from the heat and Mag's closeness and how good it feels to finally be touched after wanting it for so long. Dizzy, and desperately horny.

Mag's hand keeps working against her while she talks, but her tone is casual and light. It's a terrible combination, in the very best way. "Every time you sashayed through here, I wanted to bend you over a hay bale, flip up those little skirts of yours, and tan your hide. Only bad girls try to distract me from my work."

Angie moans and leans back so she can push her hips up, trying to force Mag's hand closer, trying to up the speed or the pressure or anything, anything at all.

But every time she thrusts, Mag lightens her touch until Angie stops and then goes back to the exact same pressure and pace as before.

"I want to tie you up," Mag tells her. "I want to lay you down and eat you out until you're a shaking mess, then upend you over that bench and ride you for hours. I want to blindfold you and fuck you until you can't say anything but my name, and then can't say anything at all."

Angie moans.

Mag curls her fingers under the edge of Angie's shorts, under the edge of her panties, and strokes through the wetness there. "Oh god," Angie says.

"What was that?" Mag teases. "You want all those things too?"

"Yes," Angie groans, nodding. "Yes, please, anything. Everything."

"So eager." Mag circles her fingers around Angie's clit, then pulls away completely. Angie's eyes lock on her hand as Mag licks wetness from her fingers. Mag laughs at her and takes a couple steps away from the bench. "On your feet."

Angie scrambles up, nearly dumping herself onto the floor. She wipes her palms on her shorts, then forces her hands down so she won't pick at the fraying hem. Mag watches her, silently, until she's still.

"Put away the bridle," she tells Angie. That's not at all what Angie expects, but she grabs it up and sticks it back on its peg as fast as she can.

Mag's on her before she can turn back around, hustling Angie into a corner. There's just enough room for Angie to catch herself before she face-plants against the wall, palms flat. Mag kicks at Angie's feet until they are spread far apart, puts one hand on Angie's hip and tugs until she's angled, ass pushed out, back arched.

Mag runs one hand down the dip of her spine then walks away. Angie starts to turn, but Mag catches her. "Stay put," she orders. Angie shudders and obeys.

First thing Mag does is wrap a kerchief across her eyes. It's thicker than normal and doesn't let much light in at all. Then she peels off Angie's shorts and panties, but not the bra and tank top. Mag leaves her alone again after that. Probably for the exact same amount of time, but now that Angie can't see, it feels longer, each second stretching out.

Her pussy clenches, clit aching, and each slow stir of warm air makes her twitch. She's left alone, legs wide, ass out, presenting herself, and the more she thinks about how anyone could open the door and see her like this, half naked and needy, the hotter it feels.

"Hard to choose where to start," Mag murmurs, close enough her warm breath touches Angie's ear. "So many things I want to do to you." She drags her nails up the back of Angie's thigh; Angie twitches and jerks away, a shriek of laughter torn out of her.

"Anything," Angie pants. "Please, Mag, touch me."

Sharp bite of nails into her bare skin. "I am touching you," Mag says, but then she stops and pulls away. Angie tries to follow, shoving her ass out farther, chasing body heat.

There's a snap and a sharp line lights up across the meatiest part of her ass. She shouts in pain this time, and before it's even died off, Mag hits her again and again. Each one lands at a different angle, until her entire ass is covered with welts, and she's wet enough she feels it smear on her thighs.

"Mag." That's all she can say. "Mag."

"Good girl likes her crop," Mag says. She taps Angie's cheek with the end of what must be a riding crop. They don't actually use them on the ranch. Mag must have brought one with her.

"More," Angie says. "Please."

Mag makes a pleased hum, and the pain starts again, sharp, steady snaps that make her scream and jerk and scramble into the wall, but as soon as the pain eases, she pushes her ass out again, begging for another. Mag drags them out, stroking her warm hand across Angie's ass and thighs between each hit, teasing her fingers along hot skin, pushing her hand tight between Angie's legs.

"Such a good girl," Mag says. She taps the crop against Angie's cheek again. Angie turns her head, lips pursed, and Mag touches it there next, letting Angie kiss it. "Five more." She draws the tip down Angie's side. "Count them this time."

Angie can barely remember to breathe, much less how numbers work, but she does her best. Mag keeps one hand pressed against the small of her back, thumb curled under the edge of Angie's shirt, and brings the crop down hard with the other. The first one burns. The second one makes her shout. The third and fourth light her up from the outside in and leave her squirming and crying, tears soaking into the blindfold.

"Good girl," Mag whispers when Angie manages to stutter out the fourth count. Her fingers tease Angie's bare skin and there's a pause long enough for Angie to start catching her breath.

Then Mag brings that crop down harder still, right across the top of her thighs, where they meet the curve of her ass, hard enough it feels like Angie's skin splits open, fire spilling straight into her, and she screams, wordless, at first, but ending in a strangled, "Five."

"Good girl," Mag says. The crop is gone and both hands settle on Angie, rubbing her back, reaching around to stroke the front of her thighs. Her ass burns, each line a distinct pain, and when Mag brings their bodies together tight, Angie almost asks her to stop, because the pressure is agony.

But she feels the hard press of a strap-on, and Angie wants that more than she wants the pain to stop.

"You took that so pretty," Mag tells her. Angie nods, head hanging down between her arms, which are braced against the wall still. Sniffs, hard. Sort of wants to wipe her face with the bottom of her tank top, make sure there's not tears and snot everywhere. "You're such a good girl, Angie."

"Thank you." It takes a couple of tries, but Angie finally manages to get it out.

"Thank you," Mag says. "You were so good for me." Her hand slides down Angie's stomach, fingers teasing along the top of her pubic hair. "Can you be good again, or do you need to stop?"

Angie's breath shudders through her. "More," she says, then, when Mag's nails dig in, she adds, "Please, Mag, more. I can be good."

"I know you can." Mag presses a quick kiss to the center of her back and steps away. Air stirs against Angie's overheated, sweat-slick skin, and she trembles and leans into the wall, struggling to breathe.

She hears a zipper, jeans dragging over skin, and Mag is back. Angie can't take her hands off the wall for fear of falling face-first into it; as Mag rubs against her, she feels hard plastic and the scratch of what might be a harness.

"God, Mag, please," she mumbles. The pain is still there, but it's fading into something warm and deep, and she wants to fall into it, but the ache of desire tightening her pussy keeps her from reaching it. "Fuck me."

"Oh, princess, that mouth." Mag laughs, and strokes Angie's back, then rolls her hips forward so that her dick prods against the welt from that last stroke, the sharpest, most painful one. Angie shrieks, and Mag does it again. "Ask nicely."

Somehow, Angie manages to pop off, "I said please."

"And I said nicely." Mag grabs Angie with both hands, thumbs pushed hard into all the painful spots. "Real shame you chose to be a bad girl this time."

Angie snorts and opens her mouth, though she doesn't actually have anything else smart to say. It doesn't matter, because Mag drags Angie's hips down, thrusting up at the same time so that she slides right inside Angie with one hard, fast stroke.

That fake cock is wider than it has any right to be, and she burns as it forces her open. She's wet enough it doesn't hurt, exactly, but it's been a while, and this is bigger than she uses on herself.

She tries to buck away, but Mag holds hard to her; Mag has

the leverage, especially when she kicks Angie's feet even farther apart, and there's not much Angie can do but grit and bear it. Five strokes like that, deep and fast, and Mag stops, dick filling Angie.

"Ready to try again?" she asks, breathing fast, voice steady.

"What, you got more than that?" Angie asks. "Something I'll feel, maybe?"

"Oh, princess." Mag smacks her left asscheek. "You are a treat."

Angie squirms. "Thought you'd be less chatty than this."

"Hmmm." Mag's hands leave her a second, and then the damn dick starts vibrating.

"Oh god," Angie cries, and Mag spanks her again. "Please!"

"Too late." Mag presses her chest into Angie's back. "You had your chance. This is for me now."

She rolls her hips, pulling out of Angie and then thrusting back inside, each stroke slow and steady and deep. The buzz of the vibrator isn't loud enough to cover the wet slap of their bodies. Mag shifts the angle, catching that spot just behind Angie's clit, and Angie chokes on her next breath, twitching and mewling in need.

It doesn't take long until Mag's groaning with each thrust, driving inside and then grinding down for a second before thrusting again. Angie keeps up a wordless babble, rising up onto her toes with one thrust, shoving back into the next. She's close. She's so damn close, and from the sound of it, Mag is too.

"Mag," Angie says. "Oh, god, Mag, plea—"

Right at the edge of her orgasm, Mag stops.

Mag stumbles back away from her, footsteps heavy, and Angie shouts in frustration. "What the hell?"

There's a thump behind her, and Angie spins, tearing at the blindfold, not caring that she's half naked and well fucked and breathing hard enough to power a steam engine. Nothing's wrong, though, and she has to take a second to come off that adrenaline rush of terror.

The thump was Mag flopping onto the bench. Her jeans are tangled around her ankles, she's still wearing her boots, and that damn strap-on is double ended, one side curled up into Mag's pussy. Mag has a hand wrapped around the other end and grinds it down as she drives it inside hard and fast, short, choppy thrusts. Her other hand works at her clit.

Angie's anger dies on her lips, and she wastes far too long staring, mouth open, eyes wide.

Mag whines, and it shakes something loose inside Angie. She stumbles to her knees, puts one thumb against Mag's clit, works her fingers along the edge of the dildo.

"You're so hot," Angie says. "Show me, Mag. Please."

Mag bites her lower lip and closes her eyes. Angie drops her head, licks a warm wet stripe across the jut of Mag's hip bone, digs her nail in a little on the next sweep of her thumb across Mag's clit, and pushes her fingertips inside along the line of the dick.

Mag shouts her name when she comes, and it's almost, almost enough to make Angie come too—but not quite.

"That's a good girl," Mag says. She touches sticky fingers to Angie's cheek; Angie turns her head and sucks them into her mouth, licking them clean.

"I'll stay good," Angie promises. "Please fuck me, Mag. Please."

Mag sits up. "No, you lost your chance at that." She's smiling, though. "Still, you're a good girl."

She grabs Angie's arm and tugs her down over the bench, ass in the air. Angie wiggles it at her, but stays put even when Mag waits, not touching her further.

"Good girl," Mag says again. She fiddles with the strap-on

for a second, and then it comes free and she pushes it back inside Angie, vibrating just as hard as ever. It's not the same, the angle's different, and she misses the feel of Mag's body against her, pressed in a warm, sweaty line along her back, but this is good too.

Especially when Mag works her other hand between Angie and the bench and presses fingers against her clit.

Angie thrusts once, then forces herself still, waiting. Mag does nothing. The vibrator buzzes inside, pleasure building until it starts to cross the line into real, terrible pain because she's close, she's so close, but it's not enough to make her come, not without more.

"Mag!"

"Oh, did you think I was going to take care of this?" Mag asks. She swats Angie's ass, quick and light, then grips the dildo again. "Nope. You're on your own, and you're lucky I'm giving you this much." Her fingers stroke across Angie's clit once.

It takes a second for that to work its way through Angie's lust-blurred thoughts, but her body starts thrusting even before she figures it out. Mag holds still, keeps her fingers angled against Angie's clit and the dildo pressed inside, but it's on Angie to do all the work.

The angle is hard, and it's harder than it should be, but Angie thrusts and rocks and listens to Mag's breathing. The whole room smells like sweat and sex, and she tastes Mag on her tongue, and each roll of her hips makes every single one of those stripes on her ass burn.

Angie grinds down against Mag's hand, breathing hard, and comes. Another shout tears out of her sore throat, and she freezes as the pleasure rips through her. When it's gone, she collapses onto the bench, a puddle of sweat and come and pain.

"Good girl." Mag kisses her shoulder and withdraws the dildo. She doesn't take back her hand, though, until Angie finds the strength to sit up.

This is where things could get awkward, Angie knows. She starts to straddle the bench again, but that puts pressure on all the wrong places and she rockets to her feet.

"You'll be sore for a while," Mag tells her. She's got the dildo back in the harness and closes her jeans. "I've got some salve that'll help it, if you want."

"Here?" Angie asks.

Mag's smile is soft. "Back at my cabin. I was hoping you'd let me make you dinner." Thunder crashes outside. She scoops Angie's shorts off the floor and holds them out.

"Where's my underwear?"

"Not yours anymore." Mag touches her pocket, and her smug look nearly does Angie in. "If we hurry, we can beat the storm."

Angie tugs her shorts up. "You scared of getting wet?"

"Counting on it." Mag brings her hand to her mouth and breathes in deep.

"Next time, please fuck me all the way through," Angie begs.

"Next time, be a good girl," Mag counters. She slings her arm across Angie's shoulder and leads her out to the truck. Opens the door for her. As soon as Mag is behind the wheel, Angie slides along the bench seat. She kisses Mag, soft and slow, and before she knows it, she's straddling Mag's thigh, rocking in careful circles, and Mag's hand is up her shirt, fingers on her nipple.

They don't make it to Mag's place before the storm hits.

HERE COMES THE SUN

Mx. Nillin Fuchs

I sigh, opening my eyes yet again to the light-red glow of the alarm clock sitting next to me on Kate's nightstand, showing 3:00 A.M.

She lies behind me, with my other partner, Max, curled up on the other side of the bed.

Sometimes I still find it surreal to be with Kate like this. She'd been our best friend for years and while Max and I certainly always found her attractive, and we cared about her a lot, we never would have thought she would be our partner someday.

Yet here the three of us are, lying in bed completely naked together after a great night out for drinks and karaoke.

I'm sure that I'm the only one awake until I feel Kate nuzzle her head into my back, right between my shoulder blades. She kisses me there, then lifts her head so it's right next to mine.

A soft whisper pours into my ear. "Can't sleep either?"

I turn my head slightly to make sure she can hear me. "Nope. Wide awake."

She shifts her body closer. I feel her smooth, warm skin and perky breasts against me, and all I can think about is how erect her nipples are.

She teases her fingers along my arm then lays her hand flat, slowly caressing me down my side.

"Same. We should make out for a bit and see if it tires us out."

I chuckle as I turn toward her and lie flat on my back.

Almost immediately, she begins rubbing my chest. Her fingers quickly find their way to circling my areola, knowing that it doesn't take a lot to make my sensitive nipples rise. My breath quivers and a pleasurable groan escapes me.

Kate, never one to miss a moment like that, quietly laughs. "I take that as a yes?"

I turn again, this time so I'm propped up on my elbow and facing her directly. All I can make out in the dark is her silhouette, but I'm so familiar with her form that I know exactly where to touch. I reach out, my arm wrapping around her waist, pulling her right against me again so that I can rub the small of her back.

"That's definitely a yes," I say.

Kate moans as she leans in to kiss me. Her lips are so goddamn supple and full. I feel her body come to rest in my embrace as she slides her smooth, wet tongue over mine.

My girl cock twitches in excitement between my hot thighs, each little pulse making it thicker and firmer. Kate's hand reaches out and finds it immediately. Her breathing quickens as soon as she realizes how hard I am and begins teasing my perineum with her fingers.

"God, I love feeling you throb in my hand," she whispers.

I slide my hand between Kate's legs, pushing gently through her soft pubic hair until I feel her warm, already wet pussy lips. She lifts her leg up so that I can tease my fingers between her labia more freely. I don't waste the opportunity, taking my time to explore every part of her before slowly sliding my pointer inside her tight wet hole.

This elicits a deep, pleasurable moan as she begins grinding her clit against the palm of my hand while I curl my fingers to probe her deeper, brushing up against her G-spot. She pushes her head right against mine so that we are forehead to forehead and for a moment we both just lie there playing with each other, panting excitedly, quivering with each exhale.

Suddenly, she pushes her lips against mine, kissing me deeply once again while she tightens her grip on my rock-hard girl cock and strokes me faster. I can feel myself edging closer to an orgasm with each firm jerk of her soft hand along my shaft, and I know that she is getting close too as she grabs my wrist with her free hand so that she can use my fingers and palm as a sex toy.

Just as we're both about to come, Max stirs awake behind Kate, no doubt because of our intense shuffling and groaning. Kate, still holding on to my girl cock, cranes her head to look over her shoulder just as Max places their hand on her bare side.

"Mmm, and what are you two doing?" they playfully ask before softly kissing Kate's shoulder.

I let my finger slide out of Kate as she rolls on her back and Max catches the glimmer of my soaking wet hand in the moon-light, little strings of thin fluid webbing between the knuckles of my middle and pointer fingers. Max reaches out and grabs my hand, bringing it close to their face just above Kate so that she can see them lap up her juices. Once they are satisfied they lick their lips and happily moan.

"God you taste amazing."

"Yeah?" Kate says as she laughs a little.

Max sits up more and leans right over her.

"Yeah, here. See for yourself."

With that, they grab her by the back of the head and pull her in for a passionate kiss. I watch as the two caress each other, Kate slowly leaning into Max so that she can climb on top of them.

"Now I want to taste you," Kate says before she begins to

slowly kiss Max's neck, working her lips and hand down their body toward their tight blue boxers, which she promptly slides down their hips to expose their pussy. Max looks over at me, glancing down at my girl cock dripping with precum, and opens their mouth, then motions with their head for me to come over to them.

I don't hesitate.

Before I know it, I'm at their mouth. I hold my girl cock so that the head of it is just out of reach of their tongue. You'd never hear them admit it in the moment but they loved a little playful denial. So, I make sure to let them squirm a bit while taking a moment to appreciate the view of Kate with her face buried in Max's pussy, loudly lapping her tongue over their clit. It was an especially exciting sight knowing that I was witnessing the first time Kate had ever gone down on somebody with a vulva.

Max, always impatient, doesn't play my game for long. While I'm distracted they grab me by my waist and pull me to their mouth so that they can deep-throat my girl cock in one, smooth motion. They remind me immediately of just how fucking good they are at sucking cock as I literally feel their throat open up for me the deeper I go.

I can tell that they want to make me come quickly because of how hard they are sucking me, their tongue pressed against the length of my shaft so that they're stimulating as much of me as they can at all times. Within moments I can feel myself edging close to orgasm. Just as an, "Oh fuck," leaves my mouth, Kate pulls Max firmly to the end of the bed so that their lips slide off of my erection with a loud pop sound.

Once everyone gets a quick laugh out of their system Kate looks me dead in the eyes and points down at the middle of the bed.

"Lie down so we can both ride you."

I do *exactly* as I'm fucking told. Max spreads their legs over my crotch, teasing the head of my girl cock into their dripping wet pussy. Just as I feel myself slide inside of them, Kate giggles and grabs my chin to make me look up so that she can position herself on my face. I can feel myself salivating as I catch a glimpse of a single stream of pussy juice that drips down her thigh. I reach up and grab her ass, then spread her thighs wider. Kate moans, pushing her vulva firmly against my open mouth so that my tongue can explore inside of her.

I can't see a thing. All I can hear is them both moaning and passionately kissing each other. All I can do is feel them both using my body for their pleasure . . . and mine. Kate loses herself in humping my face until her throbbing clit finds my tongue, causing her to stop so that I can focus all of my efforts right there. I clumsily reach for her thigh, then carefully slide my hand up over her hips, her smooth belly, her ribs, before finding her soft, perky breast.

Max grinds down on my girl cock hard; after a few moments I feel their hand slide between their pussy and my pubic mound so that they can stimulate their clit while they fuck me. I'm as deep in them as I possibly can be. The muscles of their pussy tighten and loosen around me with each grind down as the head of my slightly curved girl cock perfectly hits their G-spot.

Suddenly, I feel Kate shudder above me. She stops moving her hips and I know it's because she's close to orgasming so, despite how sore my tongue is, I keep up the pace, hungry to taste her cum.

Max, meanwhile, starts moving their hips even faster. They squeeze their thighs tightly on either side of me, and I know that they are close to orgasming too.

Kate tenses up and falls forward slightly, her hands landing on my chest as I feel her clit throb against my tongue, her cum pouring into my open mouth. Max groans loudly, their body shaking as they squirt all over my pubic mound and thighs.

Then, perfectly on cue, I feel waves of pleasure flow through my body as I ejaculate stream after stream of hot, thick cum inside of Max's pussy.

Falling back into a snuggle pile, Kate lays her head on the right side of my chest while Max lays theirs on the right. They both fall fast asleep.

Just as my eyes begin to close, I catch a glimpse of the light-red glow of the alarm clock sitting next to me on Kate's nightstand, showing 3:43 A.M.

GINA, ACROSS THE TRACKS

Fallen Matthews

The glow from Gina's phone lights up her face. She thumbs the screen, scrolling through a stream of messages. Snippets hasten her breath until the address gives her pause. She hesitates to advance, but her GPS assures her she's on the right path—even though she's on the wrong side of the tracks.

Seated between a condemned strip mall and a railroad, the Treaty Trailer Park blends in with its neighbors. Its name, scripted in mauve, hangs over frosted blue *vacancies* and a peel of periwinkle that promised prospective renters would enjoy all-inclusive air-conditioning and discounted cable.

The park lies in the shadow of the old mall's central tower. It barely stands against the abandoned asphalt, a caved mortar fence, and the parking lot chipped with overgrown weeds. Time wears heavily on the tower; its steeled, cool curvatures are now jagged with rust. Its latticed windows are blown out, but their shards catch light that is visible for miles.

Gina checks her phone again. It sweats between her clammy palms. Her destination blinks brightly. She arrives upon the hum of a radio. Static dots the voice of a man who croons a country song and a woman who sings along. Cigarette butts flood ashtrays along the windowsill. The porch is littered with beer bottles whose necks have lipstick stains.

The yard is thick with limp foliage. Rusty canteens are strewn amidst plastic pails, shovels, and trolleys that were once blue, now muddy and cyan. Gina remembers playing with her own as a child, upturning her buckets to pile sand into castles. At the beach, she would decorate them with sandstones and seashells.

As Gina glances through the lawn, she notices the trailer's curtains flutter. The screen door squeaks open on its hinges. Its panel dislodges as it slams shut. A buxom woman emerges sporting a faded sundress. She stands tall, toned, and unmistakable. She descends the porch stairs and taps a painted fingernail on the railing.

"Gina?"

"Yes, and you're Irene?"

The woman nods and lights a cigarette. She eyes Gina through smoky rivulets. "Are you gonna come in?"

As Gina advances, she realizes this may be the biggest mistake of her life. Everything hits her all at once: the indiscretion of their messages, how the faceless selfies of her intimates can be traced along with their chat logs, how the woman can further place her by her private-school uniform, how easily this secret can be unearthed. Not to mention the leap to skin from cyberspace. The reality unravels every nerve that threads her together. She struggles to breathe, to blink, to do anything.

Gina stands to lose everything: her friends, her family, the prospect of any future afforded by her Catholic school pending graduation. She thinks of the sleepless study sessions and the parties she's missed to augment her grade average; the deadpans she's braved from elders to score references; the good-girl mask she steals behind. Then, she thinks of her competition: the ace students and clique queens; with their delighted whispers comes her downfall.

Gina likes girls.

Irene holds the door for Gina, who musters a small smile as she treads past. The trailer feels smaller inside. Its floor is littered with old flyers and cartons. Every other surface is junked up with chipped dishware and faded figurines. The washroom is clearer, but its counter is crowded with combs and cleansers. At the rear, tiny rooms are separated by thin partitions.

Gina follows Irene to a room marginally larger than the others. Discolored drapes blot out the sun. Lavender pillows pair nicely with the floral bedspread. The rug feels woolly under her toes.

Irene stubs out her smoke. In the afterglow of her last drag, she edges upon the bed. "So, are you gonna show me something, Gina?"

Gina's heart lurches when Irene adjusts the radio. She guides the dial to a local soul station and eases back. "You gonna put on a show for me?"

Gina swallows hard. Her knuckles go white at the hem of her skirt. She shelves her inhibitions. She assumes her sexy persona: Gina4Fun, the profile who prowls for pussy in the personals.

As Irene hikes up her dress, Gina lifts her skirt. The sight of the other woman's sex—pink, porous, pelted with wiry wisps—spurs her own. She writhes to the rhythm, spreads her legs to outstretch her lips.

The good-girl mask comes off.

Irene's gaze never wavers. She starts to stroke her clit. "Show me your tits, Gina."

Gina lets her skirt pool to her ankles, then slides her hands inside the lapels of her blazer. The buttons come undone and split the shirt to bare her breasts. The globes elicit a murmur from

Irene who unclasps the straps of her dress. Gina thinks back to the pictures Irene sent her over the past weeks. They were beautiful, ranging from the friendly, flirty photo to the impish intimates. Her hand strayed between her legs once or twice.

None of those shots compare to the real thing.

"Turn around," Irene rasps. "And spread your cheeks."

Gina turns, then stills to obey. She peers over her shoulder to glimpse Irene, delving within moist musings. Her own arousal trickles down her thighs. She clenches her cheeks.

Furious flicks pass before Irene calls Gina closer. The rustle of fabric and bated breaths encase them. Gina sits beside Irene, soft and slack, as she nudges her knees apart. Irene knows how to touch, how to tease. She claims her mouth, swirls her tongue against hers.

Irene pours herself over Gina and floods her every sense. Gina eyes her body, listens to the squish of her sex, tastes sweetness, feels warmth, and smells musk. Irene lays Gina down, towers over her; makes her feel everything she has on her. Her height, weight, strength: everything of Irene eclipses Gina.

When Irene guides her sex to Gina's face, Gina cows to the unspoken command. She pecks at the pubis, then suckles the petals to flourish. She forgets her inexperience. Irene tells her what to do, how to do it. Clasp her calves, cup her cheeks, put a slick digit in, tongue in tandem, curl it to punctuate each thrust.

Gina's chin is glazed when Irene withdraws to return the favor. The strokes of her tongue startle her, lashing, hastening an unfamiliar heat. She lies paralyzed.

Until: "Move your ass, Gina."

The air holds a crisp, carnal current. Gina straddles the pleasurable palate. Sparks shoot up her spine. Irene cruises her clit, kneads the nub of nerves with a kiss. Her fingers furrow the folds as if reading braille.

She ascends to tower over Gina again. "Play with your tits."

"I . . . I can't," Gina falters. "I . . ."

"Do it, Gina."

Gina turns her head, clenches her eyes shut. Shame floods her cheeks, then her folds; but she does as she's told. Her breasts flush between her fingers. When she thumbs the peaks, Irene tells her to look at her. Gina quivers to meet her eyes. She bites her lip.

Irene spreads Gina's legs wider, hiking her heels behind her waist. She delves deeper, leaning in for a kiss. Her fingers curl within, tender and tight, until the pleasure pitches Gina forth. Wet warmth washes over Irene alongside Gina.

Gina shatters. She wonders if she can recover the pieces. She knows now why they call it *la petit mort*. Every desire and discomfort leaves as the soul soars.

Irene grasps her chin, sweeps her neck, wraps her fingers around her throat to trace her pulse. She watches Gina's chest rise and fall, and lets her hair curtain her cheek.

Gina clings to Irene. She marvels at the strength she feels beneath her palms. Irene is in control. She can fuck her as she pleases. Irene narrows her eyes and urges Gina to raise her hips. Then, she lies astride to slick her sex against the younger woman's. The hiss of heat caresses their cores. The bedcovers bunch beneath their thrusts.

The kiss of their lips drives harder, faster. Their breasts shake with each thrust. Another orgasm builds within Gina like an echo that nears to break the waves. She yelps when Irene shudders. The gush of her heat incites Gina's sex to spasm, then pulse.

Irene eases back and reaches for a cigarette. She recovers her lighter as Gina reels. The radio sputters bits of a ballad laden with a saxophone.

"I got a couple hours before my kids get home," she murmurs. "You need a ride someplace?"

Gina shakes her head. She crosses her arms. She lets her eyes adjust to the bigger picture. The air of the afterglow becomes too thick to bear. A cracked compact on the dresser mars her reflection. She has a marginal mound below a hefty but unremarkable bust.

Then, there's Irene, whose hips swing freely, whose breasts outsize hers; whose sex drips, mouthing aftershocks. Irene and her ramshackle trailer whose phone line is pay as she goes; who leases a burnt-out station wagon she steals into for discrete selfies. The Irene whose husband demands a home-cooked meal, but never thinks to disappear for days on end, like the others; whose smile rivals the sun when she hustles smokes at the legion hall; the woman who always seems to be a day late and a dollar short.

Irene, who can't afford shame.

Gina can spare enough for both of them. She shrinks into the sex that defines her profile. Irene reaches over Gina's chest: mauls her breasts beneath her palm, kneads her nipples into nubs. Gina clasps to counter every caress. Her hands glide over Irene, teasing the tendrils that crown her core, only to ascend and crush her cleavage.

This time, she leers when Irene fucks her. She doesn't need to be told to look her in the eye or broach her breasts. She smirks at Irene, thrust after thrust, then teases her tongue across her lips and tweaks her tits.

Irene smirks. "Are you my little whore?"

Gina nods against her knuckle. Irene swears she's a bitch in heat, a slut. Her heat hisses against the wicked epithets. Their pleasures become less paced than pungent. Irene inhales the musk of their ministrations. She rolls her hips harder, faster. Sounds of flesh and fold squish within the expanse.

Gina rides out another climax and then falls to the foot of the bed. She kneels as Irene eases along the edge. Irene fists her scalp between her legs. Gina laps until Irene gushes her graces.

After Gina dresses, Irene shuts off the radio. She slips back into her sundress and lights another cigarette. The drag she exhales makes her face seem sallow. "Do you want to do this again?"

Gina forces a smile. She shrugs. It would be impolite to decline, so she resolves to lose Irene's number.

"I can get a sitter on Tuesdays," Irene declares. "We can park."

Gina falters, but recovers fast. She reels at the mention of Irene's children. Stalking out of the bedroom, she darts her eyes to the fridge in the kitchenette. Faded magnets pin two little boys with Irene's eyes in creased snapshots.

Before Gina sees herself out, Irene catches her elbow. She corners her by the couch. The scent of smoke suddenly wrinkles her nose.

"I thought you said you were a bad girl."

Gina flushes. "I am."

"I've never fucked a schoolgirl." Irene glares.

"I'm eighteen," Gina says.

Irene laughs. "I never got to see that pussy in that skirt either."

Gina showed her earlier when she danced, but she doesn't correct her. She doesn't want to disillusion Irene. Denial leads to desperation, which leads to an awkward alley of admission.

Quietly, she lifts her skirt. "Do you like what you see?"

Irene hikes the skirt higher and then pops open her blouse. She sinks upon the neighboring cushion and pulls Gina closer, tearing at her tresses. She rains kisses. Her grip inclines Gina's head back, mouth open, so she can have her fill. She only loosens her grasp when Gina is spent, breathless, as satisfaction drips down her legs. One hand strokes Gina's hair while the other rounds her ass.

This Irene is the one Gina carries with her after she leaves the trailer behind. The Irene whose killer curves drew her interest; whose bountiful breasts and fragrant folds she was content to suckle for hours on end; whose voice was curt, clipped with arousal.

That voice rings through Gina as she heads home across the tracks.

ADVENTURE IN PALM SPRINGS

Dorothy Freed

It was a warm October evening at Casa Madrona Country Inn, in Palm Springs, California. The small stucco B&B, built in the 1930s, was located near the center of town—its fenced-in grounds dotted with fruit trees, desert vegetation, and bright-red bougainvillea. The cool tiled floors and Southwestern décor of my studio apartment, with its small modern kitchen, delighted me, as did the swimming pool not twenty steps from my door. A perfect place for a sixty-six-year-old retiree to vacation alone—a good thing since my old standby man-friend whom I'd dated since my divorce three years ago had begged off joining me at the last minute, in favor of closing a real estate deal.

That's what excites Arthur these days: closing deals. Inattentive bastard! I thought, as I unpacked my bags and settled into my room. *I can't remember the last time we had sex that registered above lukewarm for me. Wouldn't it serve him right if I had a fantastic erotic adventure while vacationing alone?*

Wishful fantasies aside, I kept to myself in the week that followed my flight in from rain-drenched Seattle. Except for polite chitchat on the breakfast patio in the mornings, my days were spent in and around the pool, swimming, sunning, reading, and taking long luxurious naps. In the evenings, after dinner, I wandered along touristy Palm Canyon Drive, pondering the nature of relationships, while peering into small shops and galleries, and enjoying the festive energy of people on vacation.

After almost a week of solitude, I felt ready for human contact.

The saleswoman at Luigi's Designer Boutique caught my attention as I entered the shop. I admired the way her short, iron-gray hair was brushed back from her face, spotlighting her deep-set dark eyes and strong, still-firm jaw. She looked about my age, but a statuesque, five-foot-ten or so to my petite, five-foot-one. Her outfit was a stylized version of a man's pinstripe suit—a Luigi original, no doubt—and with her slim hips and broad shoulders, she wore it well. I watched her move purposefully around the store assisting her customers.

Our eyes met. An electric energy flashed between us and we stood observing each other for a moment. Then she headed toward me, smiling, showing even white teeth. "I'm Georgia," she said, in a pleasing contralto. "How may I help you?"

I smiled back, looking up at her. "I'm Belle, and I'm on the lookout for a shawl, deep blue, like the color of this dress I'm wearing. Or green, perhaps, like my eyes."

Georgia leaned in slightly, gazing into my eyes as though to confirm their color. "Belle. A pretty name for a pretty woman," she responded.

To my surprise, I blushed at the compliment.

"Come this way," she said, appearing not to notice, and led me to a display of hand-woven shawls. She selected a lovely deep-green one with accents of indigo, saying, "Here, try this one on," and draping the lightweight garment over my shoulders. I felt a delicious jolt of sensation when she touched me through the thin material of my dress, and I shivered with delight when her long fingers slid slowly down my arms as she adjusted the shawl.

Georgia took me by the shoulders and turned me to the mirror. "Have a look," she said, and I saw us together and felt the energy crackling around us. The look in her eyes told me she felt it too.

I'm not imagining this, I thought, as my pulse quickened and my heart hammered in my chest at the reality of being turned on by a woman. *I never thought of myself as bisexual, but this beautiful woman whom I just met is coming on to me right here in this store—and she attracts me, as well. If she asks to meet with me after closing time tonight—will I dare to say yes?*

"Do you live alone?" Georgia asked. "Is there a jealous husband or wife in the picture?"

"I live alone. There's a man back in Seattle—a friend and occasional lover, but we're not serious about each other. He was too wrapped up in his real estate business to join me here, so I'm on my own."

"How fortunate." Georgia's face crinkled up into a smile. "My wife and I split up five months ago. She moved out. I live alone now. Where are you staying, Belle?"

"At Casa Madrona, a few blocks away." I paused, fiddled with an earring; then brushed a curl back behind my ear. "Why do you ask?"

Georgia raised a sun-tanned wrist to check her watch. "The store closes at nine. I'm free soon after that," she said, and watched me, waiting for my response.

It was my call. *Well, you wanted a fantastic erotic adventure,* I thought. *This must be it.* I took a deep breath, exhaled sharply, and practically stammered, "Why don't you come by at ten . . . for . . . a glass of wine?"

Georgia looked amused. "Is that what you're offering me, Belle? Wine?"

She leaned in closer. Her low, soothing voice was satin smooth. I could feel her body heat radiating out in the air-conditioned store. My nipples began to tingle and stiffen in response. She lifted her brows and half smiled. I flushed again.

The woman was toying with me.

Rising to the occasion, I cleared my throat and smiled up into her eyes. "Why don't we begin with the wine and take it from there."

There was no one else around. Other guests were still at dinner or out on the town. The grounds were enchanting at night, with strings of tiny lights on the trees, and the pool shimmering in the moonlight.

"Belle," Georgia called softly, when she arrived at the gate, and I hurried along the flagstone path to let her in. My face was freshly made up, with my silvery curls still damp from the shower. I'd been waiting on the lounge chair outside my room, sipping wine to steady my nerves, and listening for her footsteps—my senses straining toward the adventure to come.

Trembling with excitement, I took her hand and led her to the warm, low-lit comfort of my apartment. Now that she was really there with me, I felt suddenly insecure, imagining with trepidation how my naked body—with its wrinkles and sags and bulges—might appear to a stranger.

She'd brought along a shopping bag containing the shawl I'd tried on in the shop. I'd been so flustered by our initial encounter, I'd forgotten to buy it.

"This looked so amazing on you. I thought you should have it," Georgia said. Smiling, she draped the shawl over my shoulders, letting her hands slide down my arms again as she smoothed it into place. I grinned up at her. *This lady has style,* I decided.

I poured the wine. We sat on the couch together, chatting and laughing, glasses in hand. A little later, Georgia set hers down on a side table and removed her jacket. Her prominent nipples protruded boldly through the filmy material of her white, short-sleeved shirt. I tried not to stare, but my eyes were drawn to them. My own nipples, already puckered, tingled in response. A sweet heat began to build low in my belly.

Georgia seemed aware of the effect she was having on me. "Have you ever been intimate with a woman, before, Belle?" she inquired.

I shook my head. My voice was soft. "No, not really. Not that the idea hasn't turned up in one or two of my fantasies," I said, meeting her eyes. "I've caressed a few women at swinger's parties back in the seventies, and I was aroused by touching them—but that was mainly to please our male partners with some girl-on-girl action. I've never been...just me and a woman, one on one because we desired each other. That is"—I cleared my throat again—"until right now."

"Come here to me," Georgia said. I drew my breath in sharply at the delicious rush of sensation between my legs at her words. The shawl slid from my shoulders onto the sofa, as I moved into her arms.

We began with the softest of kisses, a nibbling of lips, a teasing of tongues, a nuzzling of necks and ears. I closed my eyes. Breathed her in. She smelled of sandalwood, and female arousal. My senses soared.

But there was no rush to our passionate explorations, no race toward a goal. Our postmenopausal bodies were slower to arouse. Georgia and I took our sweet time together: kissing, stroking, rubbing, fondling, before we even undressed.

"It's warm in here, my dear. You don't need all this clothing," my lover whispered.

"Don't I?" My voice was husky with excitement. "Would you like to undress me?"

She nodded; her eyes hot on mine. I got to my feet, laughing. "All I'm wearing is this dress. Have at it."

Georgia stood up and smiled down at me. She unfastened the tiny round buttons of my dress with maddening slowness, and let it fall to the floor in a heap at my feet. Her entranced expression assured me I was beautiful, as I stood naked before her.

I waited, quivering with anticipation.

"Lovely Belle." Georgia bent and kissed me, gently at first and then with more force. Her large hands cupped my full breasts, and clamped my nipples firmly, twisting them almost painfully between her thumbs and forefingers. I moaned with pleasure and didn't move away. We gazed at each other for a long moment feeling the sexual tension between us mount.

"Now, you undress me," she said.

My heart pounded as I removed her shirt and unzipped her trousers. Her nakedness revealed a lazy little belly and an iron-gray pubic mound. Georgia's small breasts with their huge brownish nipples cried out for touching and I shyly obliged. The heady scent of her arousal filled the room. I felt like I was floating as she took my hand and led me to the queen-sized bed.

We lay down together, I on my back, with my lover beside me, leaning up on an elbow. She bent forward to kiss me. My mouth yielded to the warmth of her lips and teasing thrust of her tongue. Melting into her, I felt lit up, from the inside out—incandescent.

Our eyes locked. Our breathing quickened. Georgia slid a hand between my legs and slipped a finger inside me. My arousal was so intense by then that I was panting, but I no longer lubricated like I once did, with my juices running down between my thighs.

"I'm a bit dry," I whispered, and she laughed when I indicated the bottle of Liquid Silk on the bedside table.

"I like a woman who comes prepared," she said.

And I am a woman prepared to come.

The Liquid Silk worked its magic. Georgia slid two fingers inside my opening, curling them inward behind my pubic bone. My inner muscles clenched down hard on them. I moaned and squirmed, hips bucking—deliciously aware of my swollen labia, and the slow, steady pulsing of my clit.

As she continued to stroke me, I reached for her hard, puckered nipple, rolling it between my thumb and forefingers, squeezing and tugging at it. Georgia groaned, and I shifted position, taking the nipple in my mouth, sucking and nibbling at it, biting down lightly. I reached for her groin, sliding a hand down the smoothness of her skin and wiry pubic curls. Tentatively, I caressed the moistness of her cunt-lips and massaged her rock-hard clit.

"I could come right now from what you're doing," she breathed. "But not yet. I want to taste you first, Belle. I want to make you scream with joy."

I lay back with my legs wide apart. Georgia sat up and reached for a pillow. "Raise up," she said, slipping it under my hips, and then repositioning herself between my knees. I waited, barely breathing, conscious of nothing but the two of us together and the rushing of my blood.

The heat of her breath tickled as she bent to feast between my legs. She licked me lightly first, tasting me, inhaling my intimate perfume. "You smell so good," she whispered huskily. Then, sliding her hands beneath me, she parted the full round cheeks of my rear with knowing fingers. I quivered with delight as her tongue lapped at my labia and probed my delicate inner flesh. I made small mewling sounds of delight when the tight, hot purse of her lips sucked at my clit.

My god, this woman knows exactly what she's doing. No hesitation. No fumbling around unsure of what's where, I thought happily—just before she slipped a finger into my tight little anus, and sent me straight over the edge.

"Yes!" I cried out as an orgasm built and built, until it couldn't be contained and washed over me like an ocean wave. I came hard, with sharp little cries—arms and legs stiff, toes curling, body trembling, and my hands entwined in Georgia's hair.

I felt her kneel up and then mount me, leaning on her elbows like a man would have done. She was taller than me. Her nipples grazed my chest and neck, sending hot little currents of pleasure racing along my skin. Georgia ground her sex against mine with growing abandon, massaging my labia and making my clit come alive again. Her breath was hot in my ear, and the prominence of her clit felt like a mini-cock rubbing and massaging, creating a most delicious friction. I took a nipple in my mouth, sucking and nibbling at it.

"Oh god, oh god, that feels so good," she cried as the nipple play sent her over the edge. She came with a low guttural groan, while continuing the rhythmic movements of her hips. To my surprise a second orgasm rippled through me. I smiled up into her eyes.

"You're one hot woman, Belle," Georgia whispered. "What do you think about that?"

"I think that I rarely come once, let alone twice," I said happily, "and that anyone who thinks postmenopausal women aren't interested in sex, simply isn't thinking."

My lover nodded agreement and, holding me close in her arms, kissed me tenderly. We lay cocooned together, until our breathing returned to normal and we absolutely had to get up to pee.

Georgia got a friend to fill in for her at the shop the next morning. We spent the following three days and nights together—a miniature lifetime, filled with more laughter, communication, passion, and erotic discovery than I'd experienced in years. By the time Georgia drove me to the airport on Tuesday morning, I no longer knew the nature of my sexual orientation—but I did know that since this enchanting woman entered my life, every fiber of my being felt vibrant and alive.

We clung to each other before parting, after making a date to spend two weeks together at Georgia's home two months from now. It was surprisingly difficult to leave the haven of her arms. I knew I'd be counting the days until we were together again.

Arthur texted me earlier to say he'd pick me up at the airport that afternoon. *Miss U. Do U Miss me 2?*

I smiled, considering my relationship with him during my flight to Seattle.

Arthur's history, I thought. *I'll break it to him gently that I've just closed a better deal.*

THE STRIP

J. Mork

We are ladies of the night traveling in the day. I had canceled on my client as his time frame sounded traffic inducing and frankly, the idea of him showing up drunk at five to be physically lifted by me was unacceptable.

At four o'clock, I drive my beloved car, Blue Tiger Love, to pick up my work partner with the large bust, dainty ankles, and shapely legs. We had orbitized ourselves to an Indian gaming casino for an overnight getaway/work-away. We get to the hotel and are checked in as nice ladies. I request a smoking room as I will not be rude and smoke pot in a non-smoking room. They put us on the gusty top floor, facing the freeway, where the parking lot is easily scanned from inside the shoebox room.

We carry luggage up and I smile at our new next-door neighbor, who is, thankfully, more interesting than the multigenerational family at the pool enclosure. She has on clear platform shoes and a skintight, cerulean maxidress that accents the richness of her dark skin. We glance and smile at each other, sniffing for queer-ness, or other.

In the room, Leann and I unpack. I bring blankets from the car: I know what happens on hotel beds, for I am often part of the bodily fluid fray in hotel rooms, for pay. This weekend will be a moneymaking venture we hope. We negotiate ideas and signals and I brush out a Bettie Page black wig that I will wear that night.

The door vibrates with a confident knock. I freeze. Put the chain on the lock and crack it open. The next-door neighbor's clear heels catch the sunlight. I shut the door to unchain it and open it widely. I sense she is checking us out by her knowing eyeful; the pot smoking offers assurance that we are fun friends next door. "I'm Cherin," she says, scanning the wigs and all five pairs of high-heel shoes with the professional eyes of a colleague.

"Hazel," I say, and offer her the joint I'm smoking. She declines. I notice downstairs a cop harassing people poolside. The people of the balcony catwalk recede into their hotel rooms as another cop looks up at us on the second floor.

"Where are you from?"

"San Francisco. Visiting the casino. Going to try our luck."

Our neighbor nods, looking at the spew of makeup against the full-length mirror. "That's my friend Mishi," she says, pointing to a man walking up the stairwell. Mishi is dark skinned and wears a close fade of slants on the nape of his neck. He walks with quick precise steps, a gait that translates easily and with feminine grace to all heels. We watch Mishi ascend the first staircase, move past the closed hotel doors, passing us by, and then head for the second stairwell that will bring him down safely away from police eyes.

A slurp as he finishes a Slurpee, the last sound echoing off the cement motel walls as he crosses into the strip mall across the street. The mall has all the convenience that a person might need: laundromat, Ross Dress for Less, and a dollar store.

"Maybe I'll see you around tonight," Cherin says, as she turns back toward her room. As she reaches the threshold, a gust of wind shuts her door. The other pros facing the freeway melt into their hotel rooms, seeing a cop look up at us and move toward the stairwell.

"Come to our room," I offer, knowing that for people of color, loitering could be seen as prostitution, unlike for us "nice ladies"—real life, hope-to-work-tonight prostitutes. She glances at the cop on the stairwell and silently enters our room.

Once she is safely inside, I observe quietly, "There seem to be a lot of police around here."

"Yes," she nods, still standing near the door, ready to leave if we prove to be a greater threat than the state-paid harassment. I turn the TV volume to high, and motion for her to come away from the door. Leann sits silently on the bed painting her nails. We are on high alert. The cops pass our door, interrupting the sun from the window.

I speak underneath the volume of the TV. "We're here to see what kind of doubles we could get at the casino. I have more of the BDSM slant but I'm open to new adventures. I always like watching people gamble. It seems like risky behavior, which could lend itself to other risky behaviors—like an hour with me." Now I'm rambling nervously, noticing her gold-brown flecked eyes.

Cherin is looking around the room, noticing my plastic bag full of condoms and lube, and the medical marijuana cookies on the mini-fridge. There is enough evidence here to believe the true story; our nice white-lady fade is beginning to crackle.

She sits on a bed, exposing a leg tattoo of a garter that cleverly encompasses the wondrous icon of a Chanel lipstick compact, skeleton keys, and a hundred-dollar bill.

"Mishi is doing laundry at the strip mall and has a hotel key card. He needs to be picked up in a half hour as he can't carry the laundry back, but my car key is locked in the room," Cherin says. I am impressed as she is informational and direct. I whiffed a chaos professional. "He is working the male side of the casino tonight. The heterosexual couple works well around the casino." She is, for the first time, giving information, testing me just a little bit.

Leann, watching all this occur from the bed says, "I can go pick him up. I just need help clicking in the seat belt." She looks at me meaningfully and stands up with jazz hands so as not to muss nails.

"That would be great," Cherin says with emphasis. "Let me get your number in case Mishi can't find an open dryer." I pick up Leann's phone and hold it as Cherin inputs her number, and then grab Leann's backpack and car keys as we exit the room together.

I find Blue Tiger Love in the parking lot and open the door, overtly chivalrously for Leann. Due to my toppish personality I treat all ladies with ladylike deference. I watch the cops in the car watch us. I see on their faces that they judge us to be nice middle-aged white ladies who are no threat to the general sexual populace. They probably assume we are here for the outlet stores right across the freeway. Middle-aged ladies like ourselves get our fulfillment from shopping.

"What do you need to tell me? You've never needed help with your seat belt before."

"I saw her profile on OkCupid." Leann smiles mischievously. "She's from Sacramento and she's into femme-on-femme, BDSM, and switchy masochists. She was a fifty-one-percent match to me. We both know I'm not a masochist."

I look up at the motel window. Cherin is watching us watch her.

"I need to buckle your seat belt." Leann leans back as I smoosh myself over her large, soft breasts to click in the seat belt, saving her still-wet nails. "I swear I just want to motorboat your breasts all the time."

She laughs, "Well, maybe someone will want to double later and we can do that for pay."

The cops cruise slowly by, reconfiguring their nice lady judgments; my skort and thong are in full view as I reach across Leann. Cherin texts Leann's phone that I am still holding. I read the text to Leann: "Mishi's ready to go." I hold up Leann's phone so she can text back that she's on her way.

I return to the room where Cherin is waiting with the synthetic curtains parted. She opens the door covertly so as not to be seen from the street. She has years of experience in an unseen economy. "Your girlfriend is really nice to pick up my friend."

"Yeah. She is. But she's not my girlfriend. We do friendly doubles." Cherin sits down on the other side of the queen-size bed and picks up the clear nail polish. "I have a client at six thirty and I haven't even shaved my legs." I look at the clock on the middle of the bed stand; it says 5:45.

"I've seen him before. A white guy from town. He comes by before his shift starts at the casino. I see him late running the twenty-one table looking like a pompous jackass. The power of money—even if it's someone else's. I'm putting in the extra effort this week."

Her arms spread extravagantly around the room. "My kid wants to go to science camp. She's seven and is passionate about molecules." Cherin looks at the phone and reads aloud a text: "Mishi and I have connected and are on the way to In and Out to get some dinner. What do you want?"

"Monster fries?" I am enthralled watching her fingers glide across the lighted phone screen. Her nails are shellacked dragon green, which resonates against her dark-umber skin. She puts the phone down and leans back on the bed, appraising me at every inch. I go to the parted curtains to see if the cop car has finally left. The cops malinger. "Goddamn, what is going on around here?"

She looks around sarcastically. "Human trafficking." We hear the maid's cart rumble by, knowing that they work for less than $12 an hour at jobs that harm their health with the harsh chemicals of cleaning.

Getting serious, she explains with lots of air quotes: "The cops are waiting for people checking into the motel down the street. As per policy, hotel chains give 'suspicious' IDs to local police as a prevention against trafficking for 'community safety.'" She continues, "That's why I stay at this motel—it's privately owned and doesn't release information to the police."

"I've gone over to that motel over there and no one ever checked my ID," I say breezily.

"No, white girl, they don't," Cherin holds her anger—she is testing me to see if I will be honest in this moment of truthful exchange.

I look at her steadily. "I know the rules are different in how we are treated. I don't know how to ameliorate that within a larger societal context or even in this fucking hotel or at the casino, but tonight if there's anything I can do to create safety for you, I am here." The TV crackles to the 6:00 P.M. news. "Is that why Mishi went alone to do the laundry?"

"Yeah, I am the only one checked in. He has a record of solicitation and if he was driving and the cop stopped us in the parking lot, he would have a pandering or pimping charge. We're family. He's my daughter's friend, and he drives her to school. But he's better than family because we actually like each other."

I think of the easy exchanges my white workplace friends and I have with each other about sharing clients. We never question soliciting clients for each other; we merely know we need to share information for all our safety.

I looked at her dark-rimmed lashes and short blonde shag and reimagine her in a long, black straight wig. "Did you do a workshop at a leather conference on shaving?"

Cherin laughs, exhaling the last of her reservation. "Yes! That was me. You were in a pink LEGALIZE PROSTITUTION shirt, right?"

Having found a real, in-life connection, we sit in tense silence and listen to the freeway.

Cherin carefully touches up the chips in her nail polish with a small green bottle that she finger-fucks from her own breast. Then, she takes the clear coat from Leann's nightstand. She looks to me for permission to use it; I nod yes.

"Your client will be here in twenty-five minutes and you still have to prepare your nails and shave your legs. I went to an excellent workshop. The instructor told me not to rush shaving, to make it a sensual act."

She looks at the clock. "You have a new razor?"

In the bathroom, I notice how thickly muscled Cherin's legs are as she leans down to unbuckle her sandal with the pads of her finger. The counter is cluttered with femme ephemera, so I move quickly to push everything against the baseboard. I set out white towels on which to lay the new razor and a most disgusting raspberry shaving cream, and another one on the side of the tub.

Overly bright lights give me a full view of my blotchy face from the hurried preparation. I look at my dark-blonde hair, shoulder length, with honey highlights, and know that part of my presentation is a conventional, if MILF-y, nice-lady attitude and look. I take off my heels as my back will hurt enough later with them on.

From Cherin's lecture, I had learned that shaving needs to be negotiated just like any other sex. I stand at the doorway of the bathroom with my palms folded in my lap, open toward her. "May I shave your lower leg?"

"You kidding me?" Cherin teases. "I'm going to be shaved

with raspberry sparkle shaving cream? I hope the perfumes in that don't overwhelm me."

"Do I have consent to shave your legs, but not with the raspberry sparkle shaving cream?" I clarify.

"Okay, okay. But if I break out in a rash I will be right back here, expecting you to run out and find some oatmeal chamomile lotion after my work session," she acquiesces, her eyes flirting.

"I think to get the smoothest shave I'm going to have to step into the bathtub, and if you could swing your legs into the tub... I don't want to cause a wet floor hazard." Cherin lowers herself onto the white towels placed on the tub's ledge.

"And since your nails are wet, may I fold your skirt up to your mid-thigh?"

"Yes, you may," Cherin answers. I carefully fold her maxi-dress up to her thigh and, encircling my arms around her soft belly, secure the extra cloth behind her with a hair clasp grabbed from my overnight bag.

"I would not want your linen skort to get wet. Take it off," she says, her dominance building.

"I don't have panties on," I retort.

"I assumed," Cherin laughs. "Why else would you wear a skort?"

I unbutton hurriedly, letting my skort drop.

Cherin sees my paddle in my bag as I lean back over the tub to pack my skort away. "You seem to have supplies that you might enjoy on your back end." I blush at being seen in the light of my desires.

"Yes, please." I hand her my cherrywood paddle, whose tensile strength has been well tested on many other behinds. "I am an experienced masochist and can enjoy a paddling pretty hard right away, and I respect a lady's timeframe." I look up meaningfully at the clock.

"Even better: Get on your knees. I'm not moving from this position," Cherin declared. I place myself over the tub so that my breasts hang against the cool enamel, pulling against my tight pink-stained T-shirt.

"Take off that laundry disaster," Cherin demands. "I can't stand seeing mistakes of inattention."

Her words mock my haphazard packing. I take my shirt off, feeling my knees grind into the hard bathroom floor with my full body weight as I wait for Cherin's next command. "Bend back over the tub." I do as I am told. Cherin takes the paddle into her hand and swings hard with no warm up. I gasp at her hard first hit. "I have to be done in fifteen minutes. The niceties of a warm-up are for other masochists, but you are correct—your endorphin-rivers are well worn." The paddling continues as she skillfully watches my breath, stopping only when I become overwhelmed and begin to pant.

"I think you're in the right space to shave my legs now. Direct your body toward me," she says. My pussy starts stirring from her direct commands. She opens her legs to reveal no underwear. I admire her well-trimmed pubic hair as I carefully wet her lower legs with a washcloth and apply the raspberry shave gel. I unwrap and wet the new razor, and glide it along the inside roundness of her strong calves. I adjust the water to cool and shave her other lower leg as she sits on the tub's edge, holding on with nails wet. A true top femme in bondage.

"I would like a warm-up orgasm before work to get me open and in the mood."

A last drip of water falls to the floor, while I look up at her. "Can I be involved in that?"

"Yes. This is your room. What do you have that might give me pleasure?"

I sit up on my knees running the contents of my suitcase through my mind. "I brought condoms, lube, and a paddle. I didn't expand my brand here."

Cherin looks at the vibrating disposable toothbrush. "Whose is that?"

"Mine. I am an eco-terror," I say feeling the shame of a wasteful lifestyle.

"Get the toothbrush. Put the shower cap over the vibrating head with toothpaste inside. This will give a soft, flowing vibration. My nails are still wet and I want you to control my south-mouth's cleaning and pleasure."

"May I ask how you want your nether region tantalized?" I ask.

"You will use your public mouth."

I blush and squirm in my wetness. I fill the shower cap with toothpaste and insert the vibrating toothbrush head. The $12.95 sensation equals the LoLo vibe found at Good Vibrations for $130. "May I come closer to you?"

"Yes, and use your tongue."

Elated, I dive my tongue into her rich aubergine folds, inhaling her scent. In a flash she squeezes my arms hard, my pussy thumping at the firm physicality of only her finger pads, to avoid her nails being mussed. She is a true professional.

"Give me that toothbrush."

I hand it over carefully as her nails are only three-fourths dry. Cherin leans against the back of the bathtub, squaring her shoulders against the wall. The tub is slippery and the devised vibrator falls in.

"Pick it up. I run the fuck, but I'll use your hands. Put the flat end of the toothbrush on my clitoris." I watch as the pulsing and rotating toothbrush forms perfect, soft circles within the shower cap, rotating with toothpaste grit.

"I never thought of doing this," I say in wonderment, watching her clit grow.

"Well, now you know." Cherin begins moaning as the circles start to bring her closer to the edge.

"Go wash your hands." I disengage from the bathtub area and stand naked in front of the sink. Unwrapping the small hotel soap, I create a frothy bubble as I carefully scrub under my fingernails, creating a slick surface free of germs or miasma. I turn and lower myself back to face the tub, my hands now appropriately clean for any forward action task.

"Put two fingers inside me." I watch as her lower stomach pulls and sucks my fingers in: she is a masterful body communicator. Cherin starts coming. Her writhing body begins slipping off the tub, yet somehow not landing on her wet nails. My hand is still inside her, feeling her pulsating pussy.

I squeeze her breasts softly as she moans. "Pinch my nipple. Let me feel you're there." I respond immediately and watch as she starts licking her lips and grinding her teeth together. Her beautiful, pedicured foot starts arching; I feel her waves begin to plateau into rivers of orgasm.

The small bathroom is fragrant and steamy by now. "I feel work ready," Cherin pants.

"Here to help," I laugh, enjoying her afterglow.

I help Cherin move her legs to the outside of the tub, laying her moonglow-blue toenails on the scratchy hotel towel. The motel door jerks; the chain stops it from completely opening. "We've got dinner!" Leann yells.

I hold Cherin's gaze as the chain jangles back and forth, taut against the wood. "Cover up and answer the door," she exhales.

I grab Leann's terry-cloth bathing suit cover-up and do as Cherin says. Mishi and Leann step inside, looking together at the bathroom filled with steam where no one is taking a shower. Leann steps gingerly over the mess of sex supplies I have left on the ground. She smirks. "I thought you two would be more of a match. At least ninety percent."

"Hazel shaved my legs," Cherin calls from her tub throne. "She took my class when I taught it at Kink Fest."

I go to the vanity outside the bathroom to wash away the last of Cherin's scent. "You know me. A friend to all ladies, all the time." Leann just smiles as she sets out my monster fries and sweet tea, turns on the television and flips through the channels, finally settling on *Naked and Afraid*. We have been hotel comrades for a long time and we have our routines. Emerging from the bathroom clean and fresh for her client, Cherin thanks me for the shave. "I needed the help. I hope to see you at the casino. Maybe we can have a drink there to see how our nights are going?" She hovers near the door looking at me as I blush and press my legs together.

"Main floor women's bathroom? Ten P.M.?"

Cherin nods. She straightens her shoulders, puts on her professional face, and exits.

"Good luck to you!" Leann calls out, as the door quietly shuts behind her.

Mishi has by now completely unpacked his In and Out dinner and is enjoying the femme fluster at the forefront of his view. "Is it okay if I hang out with you while Cherin has her session? This is Santa Rosa. With all these cops I could be arrested for existing while black without government identification."

"I would never throw a friend out before the end of *Naked and Afraid*. Santa Rosa could be worse than the rainforest of Brazil."

Mishi grins between bites of his double-double with cheese. His frame looks smaller, round, and muscle-bound, hulked over the burger.

At 6:30, we hear heavy footsteps outside our door. Then two hard knocks. We sit silently as we hear the door shut and music go on next door to create the sound bubble of privacy. I go over to the Formica round table ripping open my monster fries, finding the salt packet. I devour the mushy, cheesy fries and head back to the bathroom with my sugar-brewed tea. "Diabetes and imprisonment—the dangers of the suburbs," I comment to Leann, gesturing with the sweetened tea toward the window, as we hear another cop signal a car off the freeway.

"Have you had any problems here?" I ask Mishi a while later, after a *Naked and Afraid* recap episode has ended. We hear heavy footsteps exit down the gangway. I look at the clock near the bed, noting that it's 7:35 and Cherin keeps a tight hour.

Mishi chortles, "Yes, I live in the United States. But I have my PhD in code switching. Plus, all holes are paid holes. I'm easygoing, except when it comes to financial arrangements—I'm always the top."

"Yes," I say, "let's be clear. That's never flexible."

THE BUTLER, THE FLAPPER, AND THE STABLE BOY

Gigi Frost

The storeroom door creaked open and a shaft of light illuminated a pair of legs in seamed stockings and heels and another in tweed trousers and riding boots.

"Well, what have we here? Sneaking around stealing kisses from the stable boy, eh? With your face all painted and your knees bare! Slut!" The butler grabbed the flapper by her arm and threw her to the floor as the stable boy recoiled. The flapper started to stand, but a stern look from the butler told her to stay put. The butler turned to address the stable boy who was trying frantically to tuck in hir shirt and adjust hir chest harness. "You ought to know better!" exclaimed the butler, who had adopted *Cockfosters* as her butler drag name for the evening.

The flapper watched, breathless, from her spot on the floor as Cockfosters berated the blushing stable boy for "taking advantage," "shirking hir duties," and "having ideas above hir station," among other despicable things. The stable boy very quickly transformed hirself from voracious lover to abashed servant, shuffling hir feet and mumbling in response.

"Well," Cockfosters was saying, "I am entirely too busy with the running of this fête to deal with you now. If you wish to retain your position, stable boy, you will meet me in the scullery in one hour, where you will submit to whatever punishment I see fit to administer. And if you, miss, would like to avoid word of this little episode getting out to your guardians, you will do the same. Am I understood?"

Cockfosters turned on her heel and slammed the door behind her as the stable boy and the flapper mumbled, "Yessir." As the door closed, they dropped out of character and collapsed into laughter. "Oh my god, her face!" Robin gasped. "Where do you think the scullery is?"

"I don't know, but this night just got even better!" said Amelia.

Four hours earlier

The hallway was lined with tuxedoed butlers who bowed and greeted guests with "Good evening, Sir-Madam." Walking down the tiled hallways in her secondhand silver flapper dress and t-strap heels, Amelia felt like royalty of a decidedly queer variety. A butler with a charming swoop of green hair over her forehead stepped forward. "To the cloakroom, Sir-Madam?" and offered their arm.

"Why yes, thank you." Without even thinking about it, Amelia put on her best *Downton Abbey* voice. *Now what?* she wondered. Was one supposed to make small talk with the butler? Well, this was a queer butler at a queer party, so she was going to chat up this handsome butler if she wanted to.

But before she could ask her escort's name, they were helping hand off her bag to the very ordinary library employees at the coat check and then showing her the party's three areas—a ballroom, a library, and the Gentlemen's Club for All Genders. Amelia decided that the library seemed like the best place for a solo femme bookworm to start her evening.

There she found the gorgeous dark-wood bookshelves and handsome books one would expect. Displays detailing the history of this ball filled the round circulation desk in the middle of the room. Opposite this desk stood velvet ropes on stanchions and a sign that read "Butlers at Rest." Amelia perused the history display, making a mental note to check back in later and see if any butlers were looking for company.

In true queer fashion, the party was slow to start, but that left plenty of time and space to chat with other guests about their costumes, and answer the inevitable questions. Yes, she was American, in London on business, and had extended her stay a few days so she could see London Pride and attend this queer party. Someone with a beard and an exquisite silk gown told her about other historic party reenactments put on by this queer collective.

The room started to fill up. Bartenders in vests and sleeve garters poured champagne and gin-and-tonics with astonishing speed. Amelia ordered a drink and started toward the ballroom, but stopped when she found a recessed corner where she could make a wardrobe adjustment.

Either her garter belt didn't fit like it used to, or it just wasn't meant for long, sweaty walks from the tube. Amelia felt through the thin fabric of her dress to unclip her garters in the front, since the back ones had come undone quite a while ago. Humming "All That Jazz" to herself, Amelia rolled her stockings down to right below the knee and was quite pleased when they seemed likely to stay put.

Amelia stood, smoothed out her skirt, and was startled to make eye contact with a queer dressed in loose-cut trousers, leather boots, and a chest harness over a white buttoned shirt. The voyeur, evidently a little startled hirself, stammered and started to apologize.

"I'm sorry, I didn't mean to be creepy, I just...it's a very good look."

The more flustered ze seemed, the less Amelia minded being watched. This person's visible biceps and their sweet face helped, too. She decided to be bold. What was there to lose, after all?

"That's all right. I'm Amelia, and you can make it up to me by dancing with me or buying me a drink."

"I'm Robin. How about I do both?"

"Can't argue with that."

As they walked into the ballroom, Robin felt torn between utter embarrassment and just a little pride that ze had turned a very awkward moment into something that might be fun.

Hir partner, Sarah, was busy with butler duty and most of their friends who weren't working the event had attended the previous evening. Ze had orders from Sarah to relax, enjoy hirself, and maybe find something fun for them both to do after the party—a challenge for a shy introvert.

Robin guided Amelia to the dance floor, where a few hundred queers dressed as maids, butlers, animals, and mythical creatures danced to the gayest '30s hits mixed with Lady Gaga, Beyoncé, and Kate Bush. Sarah insisted that her boy be able to lead and follow, which came in handy because Amelia clearly expected hir to lead.

After a few dances and several glasses of champagne, they were sweating and ready for a break. Robin kept expecting Amelia to excuse herself politely and disappear, but she seemed content with hir company. After all, Robin thought, these things were hard to attend alone. After a very fast attempt at the Charleston, Amelia did head to the ladies', but promised to meet Robin in the library.

Amelia entered the library and saw Robin sitting on the floor in the "Butlers at Rest" area, leaning against . . . wait a minute, Robin was with her butler from earlier! The butler's hand was in

Robin's hair, and they both looked comfortable, intimate even. "Why do the cute ones always have to be bottoms?" Amelia wondered to herself. Sure, Robin might be a switch but this looked pretty submissive.

The butler whispered in Robin's ear, and the stable boy jumped up to beckon Amelia into their sanctuary.

"This is my partner Sar—uh, Cockfosters." Robin could barely say the name without smirking. Cockfosters brushed blonde and green hair out of her eyes and rose. Amelia barely managed to swallow her gasp as the butler kissed her hand and stood to give Amelia her seat.

The butlers were friendly and easy to talk to. Amelia chatted with them but couldn't help glancing at Cockfosters and her stable boy from time to time.

When the butlers' break was over, Robin took Amelia's arm. "They have to set up for performances; come with me?"

Robin felt nervous, but ze liked Amelia and this idea of Sarah's was enticing. Still, propositioning people and setting up scenes was not really hir thing. Just flirting and dancing with Amelia was a stretch. Ze found Amelia a seat by the bar in the ballroom and took a deep breath.

"Are you interested in a, um, liaison tonight?" The words had sounded so smooth, just ever so slightly ironic, when ze thought them in hir head. Now they seemed ridiculous. Amelia looked a little startled and gulped her drink, but then she nodded for Robin to continue. "Sarah and I have a fantasy about this party. Can I tell you about it?"

Much later
The "scullery" turned out to be a room between the library and the ballroom where cases of drinks were stored. Amelia and Robin snuck in as the party was ending.

They had time to kiss just long enough to smear Amelia's lipstick all over Robin's face. When they heard footsteps approaching, they separated and stood with their hands behind their backs, feet together.

Cockfosters entered and dragged over a crate so she could sit on it and lean against the door. Despite the surroundings, she looked elegant and nonchalant in her tux.

Cockfosters looked her penitent charges up and down. She threw her jacket at her boy, who barely avoided dropping it, but managed to compose hirself and fold it neatly away.

"Well, at least you had the decency to show up for your chastisement. As I said earlier, as you have presented yourselves and are willing to submit to my punishment, I will neither dismiss you, stable boy, nor inform your guardians of your behavior, Miss. Do you both agree?"

The two miscreants nodded and mumbled their responses.

"You shall speak clearly and address me as 'Cockfosters, Sir.'"

"Yes, Cockfosters, Sir!" They tried not to giggle at the ridiculous name.

"Look at me."

Robin and Amelia looked up to see the butler slowly remove her cufflinks and place them in her pocket. Amelia couldn't take her eyes off of the dexterous fingers and strong forearms revealed as the butler rolled up her shirtsleeves with care and precision.

Cockfosters turned to the stable boy.

"As I have been honored with the task of running this house, I am responsible not only for the service we supply the family, but also for the physical and moral health of the staff. When you eschew the tasks you are paid to perform in favor of lewd behavior, you are stealing from your employer. Lustful thoughts and actions will not be permitted in this house, do you understand me?"

"Yes, Cockfosters, Sir!"

"Now you, Miss, should know better than to tempt the lower classes into succumbing to base urges. You are a lady and are expected to act as one. If you choose to act like a common whore, you will be treated like one. I hope this will serve to teach you a lesson."

"Thank you, Cockfosters, Sir," she replied, affecting a demure tone.

"Stable boy, show this slut how I like you to present yourself to be punished."

Robin turned gracefully, undid hir trousers, and bent over from the waist. Ze hooked her thumbs into the waist of hir briefs and slowly slid them down, revealing just a jockstrap that bisected hir asscheeks and held hir cock in place.

Amelia stood, mouth open, watching this display. The butler stood quickly and moved behind Robin, standing so that there were mere centimeters of space between their bodies. Robin moaned as ze felt her heat near. Cockfosters laughed and ran one hand down Robin's spine, raising the hairs on hir back and pressing hir head closer to hir feet.

Then she turned toward Amelia and caught her completely off guard with three quick slaps to her face. Right. Left. Right. "Stupid slut. Get in position, now. Bend over, skirt up, knickers down."

Amelia was delighted. She tried to obey quickly, letting her ass stick out as she bent forward, then slowly lifting her skirt. She felt wetness pulling away from her skin as she slid her silver lace panties down to her ankles. Copying Robin, she stretched her arms forward on the floor until her back arched up slightly and her weight went back into her heels.

Cockfosters stepped back behind Robin as she watched this display. She started on her boy with heavy, stinging slaps, then used two hands to punch right where she had been slapping.

Amelia shivered as she listened to the sound of Robin's punishment. This was one of her favorite fantasies, bent over waiting for her punishment while a fellow transgressor received theirs. Being able to hear, but not see, the blows and Robin's reactions while she waited in this debasing position felt so dirty and right. She let herself sink further into her role, embracing the shame and excitement of the scenario, and listened as Robin counted out fifty blows, thanking hir top each time.

Then it was Amelia's turn for the warm-up, the vicious punches that nearly knocked her off her feet, the fifty strokes. People talked a lot about canes and paddles and all that, but they forgot how difficult it could be to take a hand spanking from a top who really wanted it to hurt. Cockfosters's hands bit and stabbed into her core, made her pussy throb as her thighs trembled with the impact.

The butler stepped back, admiring the juxtaposition of boy and femme, both in a classically humiliating position, both displaying delightfully red asses. She stood between them, teasing, stroking, and punishing their asses as she spoke.

"I'm not finished with you yet."

Robin yelped as ze felt a sharp pinch and a heavy slap under her asscheek.

"I need more from both of you."

Amelia got a slap between the legs.

"I don't believe that you have really learned yet."

The butler grabbed an inner thigh in each hand, twisting and pulling as she spoke.

"If I catch you again, you will find yourselves with an appointment in my office for a good caning."

She grabbed and squeezed both asses right where she had delivered the spankings.

"Since that instrument is not available to us at the moment..."

Both bottoms gasped as Cockfosters pushed her knuckles into their sore flesh.

"You will follow my instructions for additional chastisement. Stand up, please."

"Yes, Sir. Thank you, Cockfosters, Sir!"

"Stable boy, help the lady out of her dress and undergarments, please."

This was quickly accomplished, as Amelia only had to step out of the wet panties around her ankles and raise her arms so Robin could help her out of her dress and historically accurate bralette.

"Kneel and give me your belt, boy." Robin folded hir belt in half and offered it up with hir head bowed and hir eyes down, then followed hir top's signal to get on all fours.

Amelia felt Cockfosters guiding her to her knees so she was lined up with Robin's waist. She did her best to be pliable, but she didn't quite grasp what the butler wanted until she found herself folded over Robin as if ze were a piece of furniture.

The boy was almost, but not quite, the right height to be a perfect spanking bench. On her knees, bent over with her waist across Robin's back, Amelia could only touch the floor with her fingertips for stability, which made the thought of a beating with the belt even more exciting.

"That's right, balance there. How long were you playing the whore with my stablehand?"

"I—I don't know, Cockfosters, Sir. Perhaps ten minutes, Sir?"

The butler checked her pocket watch. "Very well, ten minutes of the belt and whatever else I see fit to give you."

She started with Amelia's thighs, forcing them open wider and wider. Amelia tried to hold her balance, but it was nearly impossible. Robin braced himself against the floor, trying to provide her with a firm platform despite hir sweaty palms and the increasingly distracting warmth between hir legs. Ze felt

Amelia's breath and tried to match it as Cockfosters brought the belt down, hard.

Amelia tried to embrace the burning heat of the belt across the front of her legs and the sharp sting of it on her tender inner thighs. She wanted to learn this top's rhythm, what kind of reactions she wanted, what kind of submission to offer. She waited as the pain and sensation built, letting small gasps and soft thank-yous escape her lips, until she really did need to scream, and kick, and try to close her legs against the intrusion of the belt.

Cockfosters pulled her arm back and gave Amelia six swats on the ass, hard enough that Robin felt like they must have slid at least a few inches across the closet floor.

"Five minutes, slut." She pulled Amelia up by her hair. "Hands above your head." She threw her against the closed door.

"You boy, kneel in the corner and take that dick out. I want you nice and hard by the time I start beating you."

Cockfosters leaned her body weight against Amelia, making the flapper gasp. Then the belt buckle was tap tap tapping against her right nipple while the butler squeezed and twisted the left. Amelia twisted and moaned and said thank you very prettily. Cockfosters switched sides. Amelia thrilled to the feeling of her weight, the smooth cotton of her shirt and its cold metal studs on her skin. But then Cockfosters stepped away.

"Three minutes. Will that be enough punishment for you, slut?"

"Yes, please, Cockfosters, Sir! I've learned my lesson, Sir."

She used the belt like a whip, letting the end of it accelerate and snap against Amelia's bare back. Amelia moaned and arched her back, pressing her hands into the wall and grounding her feet on the floor. As the blows kept coming, though, she couldn't quite stay still as much as she wanted to.

Finally, the butler told the flapper to count ten final blows. *I can't believe this really happened,* Amelia thought as she knelt and kissed the belt.

Sweaty and ecstatic, the flapper was happy to kneel on the floor and watch Robin take a beating over hir partner's knee. Her ass, back, and thighs burned and tingled and she could hardly believe it had been five minutes when Cockfosters announced the time and pulled her to her feet to stand against the door.

The butler positioned Robin so hir head was on Amelia's shoulder and they were embracing, with Robin's feet positioned a little bit away from Amelia's so hir hips jutted out and hir ass was beautifully available. They breathed together, enjoying the bond that came with bottoming together. Amelia reached up to stroke hir hair as the butler began the next five minutes of punishment. Their naked chests together felt so good, even as the final blows were strong enough to knock the breath out of both of them.

When Robin knelt before Cockfosters to kiss the belt, Amelia slid down and knelt next to hir.

The butler surveyed her sweaty charges, the stable boy stripped to harness, boots, and jockstrap, the flapper in her stocking feet, locks of hair escaping from gold pins. Cockfosters signaled to her boy to stand and present hir ass, and stared pointedly at Amelia until she got the hint and did the same. Both asses were bruising nicely, with pink and red welts scattered across their bodies.

Sarah paused a moment, considering. It had been a long night and a long week. She was pleased with Robin, and she wouldn't mind getting off, but she could reward her boy at home, in her pajamas, on her own bed. If this pretty femme flapper wanted to sleep over, so much the better.

She sat back on the crate and directed the two to dress and tidy up, then the three set out together into the twenty-first century evening and hailed a cab.

ALL DOLLED UP

Olivia Dromen

It wasn't a random meeting that brought us together. We didn't run into each other at a club. We knew what we were getting into, what we wanted. She knew of me for months before I noticed her, but that doesn't matter. The only thing that matters is that she made the first move, and it was to beg me to make her cry. It tickled me to say yes.

She really is so adorably, vulnerably cute on her knees with her hands clasped demurely behind her back. A smile breaks across my face as I lean over to whisper in her ear, "You're going to be such a pretty little fuckdoll." My hand reaches to the foundation on the little table next to her.

Her eyes snap open and she nods vigorously. "Yes, goddess! That's all I want."

The way the sunlight is catching her tits almost distracts me for a second. I press my thighs together and continue with my plan. "Well, you also want me to use you after I make you pretty, don't you?"

"Y-yes."

I brush on the powdered foundation. It's a shade lighter than I would normally use on her; I want her to look artificial, plastic.

Maybe she has cold feet. "You're sure?"

"Yes, goddess. I'm sure."

I add a splash of pink blush on her cheeks. "You're just a little bit scared?"

She nods shyly.

My clit is throbbing in my panties. I can't wait to make a mess of her face.

"It's okay to be scared, darling. I like you that way. Just let me know if you want to stop."

"I promise." The way she looks at me is almost as if we've been doing this forever.

"Being a little scared turns you on, doesn't it?"

She blushes a little and nods.

"Good. I promise I won't hurt you for real." I cup her face in my left hand, holding her still. The bright-red lipstick in my right hand slashes across her mouth quickly, making a perfect pout on her well-defined lips. "Oh, that's nice. I like it." I turn to the mirror and touch up my own lips before twisting it back down and capping it.

I reach for the liner pencil. "Now hold still. Remember, you're a good little doll."

"Yes, Mommy." This is very much off script. She knows it. Her face goes bright red under the foundation.

My eyebrows try to claw their way into my hair. Negotiating is hard. Before we came back to my place, we talked for an hour about what we each wanted. We bared our souls as much as you can with someone you don't really know. Now, here we are with her bringing up something else that she wanted—or maybe she didn't even know she wanted it. I'm not ready to decide on that right now.

"Call me goddess, darling." I take a breath and compose my features. "I'm not mad, I just think we should discuss that when you're not in subspace."

She closes her eyes and takes a breath. "Yes, goddess. I'm sorry."

I wasn't really looking for an apology. I just didn't want to go farther down that path. "You didn't do anything wrong. Don't worry about it. Do you want to keep going?"

"Please?" Her face relaxes.

I'm impressed by how quickly she settles back into the scene. "Good girl." The liner pencil gently fills in on her brows. They are so bold they look like they were glued onto her face. Perfect. "You're really coming along." I switch to the eyeliner brush, carefully giving her eyes wings.

The look of contentment on her face distracts me for a moment. I know I need to keep going—after all, I haven't put on the mascara yet—but I just want to lift up my skirt and push her face against my panties.

Her beatific smile breaks me out of my fantasy. "Almost done. I just need to put some mascara on you."

"Thank you, goddess."

The mascara only takes a second. "Stand up, doll. I need to get you dressed."

"Y-yes, goddess." I don't think she realized I had an outfit for her, though it was her suggestion that I dress her up.

I reach into the closet and take out a pastel pink and white dress with a laced-up back. I give it a shake and hold it for her.

She carefully steps in and slips her arms in the sleeves.

"Turn around, sweetheart. I need to tie the back." I tie the laces on the back of the dress and reach in with both hands to adjust her tits into the built-in cups. My fingers brush across her hard nipples as I withdraw my hands. I move in close behind her, and guide her to face the mirror with my fingertips on her shoulders. My clit threatens to come loose in my panties, but I think we'll be okay for now. I know she can feel it against her ass.

As she sees herself in the mirror she lets out a gasp and grins. This may be more than she expected, but judging by her response I'm doing well.

"You are so pretty, doll." My hands run down her arms and slide to her hips. "And, you're all mine to use."

"Yes, goddess."

My right hand slides down her thigh to find the hem of her skirt. I don't know why, but sliding my hand up under her skirt to find her bare cunt is even hotter than if she were naked. It's even hotter than if I had not been the one to dress her. Being in charge is such a turn-on.

My fingers plunge past her labia, into the wetness, then curl up along the length of her hard clit. She shivers against me. "Keep smiling, doll. You're just a piece of plastic."

Rather than tensing up, her whole body responds by relaxing against me. I can feel how much that turned her on; she's dripping now and she's making a low moaning noise that sounds odd since she's trying to keep a fixed smile on her face.

I just want to gloat, but that's not what this scene is about.

My left arm wraps around her, below her breasts, to steady her against me. My fingers start moving faster against her clit and dipping deeper into her. Her thighs relax involuntarily. "That's right, darling. Just go limp. I've got this. You're mine."

Her thighs move apart fractionally. I pull my hand away from her cunt, dragging my wet fingers over her hips so I can grab the back of her thigh. I bend my knees and lift her up, taking most of her weight in my left hand and the rest in my right. I don't have to carry her far—just a few paces—until we're at the bed. I toss her so she lands facedown on the bed. It probably felt careless to her. I hope so.

Her skirt is flipped up, exposing her perfect ass. I feel so lucky. Before I join her on the bed, I slip my lace panties off, freeing my throbbing clit.

I hear a little squeak from her as she pushes her ass up in the air to wiggle it at me. I climb up behind her and give her a playful swat. My knees force her thighs apart as far as they can go. My index and middle fingers plunge into her cunt from behind. I rise up on my knees and press forward with my hips against my wrist, so I can fuck her with my whole body.

My clit lunges sideways, sliding along the crease between her thigh and her ass as I thrust my fingers deep into her. Her cunt tightens around my fingers, begging me for more. I turn my hand so that my thumb can graze her clit as I thrust in and out with my fingers. Her hips are moving, pushing back against me with each thrust.

"That's right. You can take anything I give you."

My left hand clamps down on her shoulder, pulling her back onto my fingers, plunging them deeper into her.

"Fuck!" She seems to have forgotten to keep quiet. That's okay. I'll take it.

I keep thrusting. Her juices drip down on my thumb as it slides across her clit roughly. I curve my fingers down inside her, pressing on her G-spot.

I feel her orgasm before I hear her cry out. Her cunt spasms around my fingers; her hips press up against me and stop. Her whole body tenses, and then the wave crests and she lets go. She screams into the mattress. It's muffled, but it still sends a twinge through my clit.

As her orgasm subsides, I press down a little harder on her G-spot. I don't know if this will work, but it's worth trying. She responds with another wave of pleasure.

I'm grinning as I say, "Turn over darling. I need to see your face."

It takes a moment. She isn't ready to move yet. When she does, she slowly places her left palm on the bed and pushes herself up from the white sheet under her. She's left a clown-mask of makeup on the bed. Smeared lipstick and eyebrows all over her face and all over the sheet.

"Oh my goodness, you are such a mess, fuckdoll. I wish I had a camera." I wish we'd talked about me taking pictures. I push that thought aside and move up to her head. I slide my wet fingers into her mouth, letting her taste herself as I begin slowly fucking her face.

Her tongue caresses my fingers, begging for more and reaching out to lick my palm. I slide deeper into her mouth, feeling her throat open up around my fingertips. Two fingers aren't enough. I pull my hand back and she opens her eyes. I can see the tears welling up. My ring finger joins the other two and I slide them in, fucking her face with them.

She closes her eyes again and the tears run down the side of her face, dragging along her mascara.

"That's right, doll. Take my fingers. This is what you wanted."

Her moan tells me I've hit the mark. This really *is* what she wanted.

"Just let go. I'll do whatever I want with you."

Her tears are coming faster now. She's not trying to stop them.

I rise up on my knees so I can straddle her face. I place my wrist against my hip again, my clit on her cheek. I grind against her slowly, using her.

She's squirming under me.

"You like that so much, don't you, doll?"

"Uh-huh." A pair of grunts.

"You're wondering if you can come like this?"

Her eyes open, letting another wave of mascara-laden tears splash down her cheeks. Her eyes lock with mine. She nods up at me.

"We'll have to see, won't we?" I go back to grinding on her. She wriggles under me, pushing her thighs together.

"You're such a good fuckdoll." I'm moving faster. The rhythm is bringing me closer to orgasm. My clit twitches under me. Her tongue reaches up past my fingers to my palm.

I thrust again and again, each time getting more lost in it, closer to orgasm. My left hand tangles in her hair and I stop worrying about my fingers, letting the motion of my hips maintain what we're doing.

Her hands grab on to my hips, pulling me deeper into her. I am overwhelmed. The orgasm goes on and on as I twitch over her. My clit spasming on her cheek. My own juices washing over the mascara that's made dark feathers down the side of her face.

Her orgasm follows mine immediately. She's moaning around my fingers and wriggling under me as she comes. In that moment, with my come running down her cheek and my fingers filling her face, wedged between my thighs and visible past my tits, she's the most beautiful person I could imagine.

"Fuck! Yes! Good girl." I thrust a few more times to be sure the orgasm has ended, then I tumble down next to her. "Good girl."

She opens and closes her jaw a few times before responding. "Thank you, goddess." She clears her throat.

"You're so welcome, doll." My hand tightens in her hair. "I just want to show you something." I pull her up until she's sitting facing the mirror. I show her what a beautiful mess her face is. "Look how gorgeous you are."

She cries tears of relief and joy.

WHAT I WANT

Laurel Isaac

Casey is hard of hearing. She makes me wince in public by asking me to repeat over and over that I think her ass looks hot. She doesn't mean to give me a crash course in owning my desire, and I know she doesn't want to torture me. She just can't hear very well. With her, I can't get by with whispers, quiet murmurs of *More, harder, please, yes.* I have to use my stage voice, bellow it out, or otherwise the message doesn't get across. And I want the message to get across. I want her to know how hot her ass looks in jeans. I want her to know, with words, how wanted she is.

Casey's only eighteen and I really want to be good for her. I spent my teens pining over older butches who weren't all that gentle with me and I'm loath to repeat the pattern. I've had the alcoholic butch mentors who lost track of how much they meant to me, the flirtatious basketball coaches with terrible boundaries, that pair of leatherdykes who played with me once and then dropped me like a hot potato. Casey's my opportunity to rewrite my own queer history, too. No obnoxious swagger. No condescending bullshit. If I'm going to fuck a teenager—Jesus, am I actually fucking a teenager?—I will follow the campsite rule to a T: leave her in better condition than I found her.

I'm twenty-three and we're both college freshmen, which means Casey's ahead of me in some ways while I'm ahead of her in others. At night we walk around campus and find corners to make out in. Her slim boi body is two-thirds my butch cub size, and the feel of her in my hands makes my whole body relax. When I touch her, she shivers and pulls me closer; we are two clean-cut boys in button-downs wrapped around each other. I want to cushion all of her aliveness, stroke and massage all of the places she doesn't expect to be touched.

The first time I whispered in her ear, "Is this okay?" as I kneaded her ass when we were between the stacks, and she said, "What did you say?" I knew we were going to have to find another communication method. I pulled out my phone and typed out a suggestion for a two-tap code. Two taps to check in, two taps back if everything feels good. She grabbed my butt with her hands and tapped so sweetly I felt like she was sliding a finger into my ass. I opened my mouth to her tongue and tapped her butt back.

I've never had to be so consistently articulate with a lover. Instructing her in how to touch my clit can nearly bring me to tears of frustration. I am so shy and so horny, and the third time I'm asked to repeat, "GET YOUR FINGERS WETTER," or "TO THE LEFT," I want to give up. Each utterance drains me of my precious confidence. I feel more naked than even seems possible for the size of my body. My torso and limbs feel giant, like I've acquired new mass just for the purpose of being stripped.

Sometimes I overdo it, push my words out before they're ready, just to prove I can, just to break my silence, and I end up in shock. The only people who have heard me are me and the imaginary people I believe are around us. But they're not very nice people. With Casey I become aware of how deeply held my beliefs in invisible beings are, despite the atheist button on my backpack. Who are these people I'm convinced can hear my sexual utterances, but I can't see? Who is monitoring my thoughts? With each successive repeat the momentum of my desire wears itself out. Sometimes I hate feeling like I have to be the grown-up with her, owning all of my feelings, demonstrating maturity, when I feel so small. I want to blame her for making me feel clumsy, or run away.

To stop the flood I close my eyes and put a finger up, indicating I need a minute.

Casey looks at me, curious, hungry, receptive, always alert and breathtakingly responsive. She makes me want to be stronger and more open, give back some of what she gives me. Here is this beautiful god of a boi who trembles every time I get something right, who commands me with her body with such sincerity that I almost come in my pants from touching her. The least I can do is open my mouth.

That's when the pads of paper come out, the laptops, the cell phones for texting each other when our faces are an inch apart. I write excessive notes apologizing for my self-consciousness. I affirm how much I like her. When I feel ashen, I ask her to give me a few moments to let me collect myself. To let me regain my voice.

Then I tell her what I want.

She's an eager audience and leans over my pad of paper. We're teenage bois having fun, passing the pen back and forth.

"I want you to fuck me."

"How?" she writes.

My cheeks redden, but my pen is quickly moving.

"On my knees. Your fingers in my front hole while I stroke my clit. Please start slow."

She circles my last sentence and annotates: "Of course."

Her strong hands roll me over.

* * *

On Tuesday night we're sitting in my car outside her dorm. I have my hand on her thigh, tracing patterns, as we take a break from making out. Then we're holding hands, playing with each other's fingers while we talk a little, mostly looking around at the trees and buildings, wondering what's going to happen next. I'm massaging her hand, paying attention to each finger. I've always thought my thumbs looked particularly dykey—masculine, with a sexy scar. Casey blushes when I tell her I think her thumbs look dykey, too. Her hands are smaller than mine, leaner, and wise looking. I wasn't surprised when she told me she knew how cars worked, or that she spent last summer working in a hardware store. I'm a Jewish butch and these are skills that were not passed down to me.

I focus on her right thumb, massaging it between my fingers, stretching out her hand. I wrap my fist around the digit, and become aware I'm stroking it like a cock. We haven't really talked about cocks yet. I slowly jerk her thumb off, up and down. After a few strokes we're entirely focused on this new presence in our relationship.

Casey makes a little murmur. Staring at her thumb, she squeaks, "Looks phallic," like she's unsure if that's what I meant.

My hearing is excellent, though, and I catch every nuance. "I was thinking that, too," I say.

I lengthen and soften my strokes, aware of all the nerve endings. I make each downstroke on her shaft count, and run my thumb over the tip as I pull up, making it clear I want her cock. Here, with me, hard. She tilts her pelvis upward and presses her back against the seat. I feel the warmth of her body through her flannel shirt, her lanky runner's limbs relaxed like after a race.

I continue stroking her thumb as I ask, "Do you identify with having a cock?" The words in my throat are relaxed, resonant, for the first time, effortlessly loud.

"Sometimes," she says quietly. "Do you?"

"Sometimes."

Her eyes are closed. She moves her fist deeper between her legs so she can feel me better. Her cock is jutting out at just the right angle. I stroke her thumb delicately between my thumb and forefinger, causing her to shudder. Her dick is so hard and small. Boi-sized, Casey-sized. I feel myself lengthen in my pants. I think about the first time I got jerked off when I was wearing my cock and how I could barely breathe over the excitement. *Breathe, baby, breathe.* But this isn't about my cock. We can have a circle jerk some other time. This is about Casey's cock. Casey's newborn eighteen-year-old cock, which I quickly realize I want in my mouth.

I bend over the seat. I don't look at her, I just take it in my mouth. Being the older, more experienced one occasionally has its benefits. I know this is what she wants, and she lets out a surprised, relieved, "Oh my god."

I try to remember everything trans boys have ever told me to do to their cocks. At first I'm just caught up in the novel act of cock-sucking, but then I notice myself really tasting her, this thumb, this boi-sized starter cock, which incidentally is more fleshy than any other cock I've had in my mouth in years. It's almost too lifelike, the salt and warmth, the sounds coming out of Casey as I bob my head. I slow down and let myself acclimate to being filled in this way. I listen closely to her breathing and the erection between my legs and what it is I want to communicate with my mouth.

I suck her cock into the back of my throat and notice her other hand furiously digging at the seat. Her hips rock in tiny circles toward my mouth.

"Jerk off. Stroke it for me," I tell her.

I glance at her eyes and see the familiar brow-raise meaning she hasn't heard me. The car is too dark for her to lip-read. Before she can get out a "What?" I lift her right hand and lead it toward her crotch. She squirms and presses the heel against her clit, whimpering. As she's clearly needing more encouragement, I unbutton her pants and slide the zipper down. I guide her hand into her navy boxer briefs. The soft fabric is completely soaked. I lift my hand out, regretfully leaving her swollen cunt, and double-tap the outside of her briefs, pressing her fingers up against her clit. My head is still near her lap and she firmly taps the back of my neck twice in response. I wrap my lips back around her thumb and she lets out a grateful sigh.

We relax into a comfortable rhythm, Casey jerking herself off while I tease and lavish attention on her stiff cock. We're in sync, stroke for stroke, her hand sweetly rubbing her clit while I dive up and down on her hardness. When she's clearly about to come I slow down and move my mouth lower to the base to cup and nibble the flesh between thumb and pointer finger. Automatically, Casey slows her stroke as well, and lets out a high-pitched whine as she holds off her orgasm, waiting for me to return to her cock.

"Good boi," I say, loud enough so I'm certain she can hear me. I feel her smile. "Such a good boi."

I mouth what feels like her balls, kissing her palm, and let her regain control before traveling back up, tonguing the tip. I replace my mouth with my hand and sit up to look at her.

The car smells like sex and Casey's college-boy cologne. It's late but not that late and I pray that someone doesn't decide to park next to us. The lone light from the edge of the lot illuminates Casey's handsome face. She kisses my mouth, my lips soft and puffy. I groan, my own cock aching.

"Can I come in your mouth?" she asks. I nod, in love with the sound of her voice. In this moment, there is nothing I want more than to feel her shooting down my throat.

She guides my head back toward her thumb and I feel her

cock slip between my lips. I suck her hard, giving her the firm strokes she needs to get off. I hear the smooth tick-tick of Casey's fingers running over her clit. It only takes a few strokes before she explodes, shoving her cock into my mouth as I hold my head down to pull each jolt out of her system. I swallow every drop.

We sit in the dark a long time like that with my head resting in her lap. Glassy-eyed, Casey strokes my short hair with her cock. I breathe her in, deep into my chest. After a while, I reach into my pocket for my phone. The bright light of the screen warms the car like a fireplace. I start to type her a note.

BRUNCH SERVICE

Tobi Hill-Meyer

I stood on the doorstep, my finger hovering over the doorbell. It was a gray Seattle day, not yet raining, but it could start at any moment. The air smelled clean and crisp, and all the shades on the house windows were drawn. I rang the bell.

I could hear footsteps. The door swung open. Addyson welcomed me inside. It was bright and much cleaner than her place had been on the handful of previous visits I'd made. Angela was setting down a bowl of fruit on the coffee table to join a spread of cheese and crackers, deviled eggs, and muffins—home-made, by the smell that hung in the air. She was naked. I hadn't seen Angela naked before. I tried not to stare.

When Addyson invited me to a brunch and afternoon sex party, I was incredibly nervous and also intrigued. Being there now, I still had no idea what to expect. When she'd asked me, I'd mumbled something about not being sure, and it took two weeks for her to convince me. Only then did she let slip that she had an agenda. A certain fantasy that she was hoping to make reality. Well, not her fantasy; it was Angela's. I hadn't even realized they were lovers until they invited me to this gathering. At least all the times I'd seen them in public they hadn't acted couple-y, but apparently they've been hooking up for . . . well, I'm not sure how long, but awhile.

Addyson wrapped me in an enthusiastic hug. "Celia, I'm so glad you chose to come." She directed me to sit and then disappeared into the kitchen. Angela was kneeling on a pillow by the table. Her eyes were downcast, and without anyone to notice me staring, I found myself doing so.

I'd always envied Angela's body and her connection to it. Her short stature, her curves, even her fat rolls are placed well and look good on her, unlike mine. Her confidence is always clear, but not absolute. It was hard won. It's different because she's cis, but the way she's dealt with taunts, and fatphobic street harassment, and the whole world telling her that she isn't supposed to be sexy reminds me of the transphobia I have to deal with. I hope to someday feel as at home in my body as she appears to be in hers.

I heard Addyson returning from the kitchen and forced myself to look at the deviled eggs instead of Angela's body. "So, am I supposed to be all bossy?" I asked her.

"You're welcome to if you want," Addyson laughed, "but no, you don't have to. We'll just hang out like we always do. I've been cooking all morning, and you can enjoy the food and drinks. Angela will serve us, it'll be sexually charged, and at some point some kind of sex will happen. But if you'd rather simply be catered to and pampered, get a foot massage, and enjoy the company, you're welcome to." She turned to Angela. "Speaking of which, you should probably set the table."

While Angela was bringing out the dishes, the doorbell rang, and Addyson went to answer it. A moment later she came back with Katherine and Rachel. I hadn't seen them in over a year, but they had always been draped over each other at our meetings.

Rachel works for one of those large tech companies. She's always bringing snacks raided from their employee pantry. Sure enough, she had a six-pack of ginger beer and an assortment of snack bars that Addyson took to the kitchen.

Angela came out with a carafe of orange juice and glasses. "The main dishes are warming in the oven as we await our other guests," she said. "Did you squeeze this yourself?" Katherine asked teasingly.

"No." Angela bent slightly, playfully presenting her ass. "But there's plenty else available for squeezing if you're so inclined." Katherine took her up on her offer, grasping firmly. "Is it to your liking?"

"Very much so," Katherine said, and smiled up at her, gave one last squeeze, and let go.

"Do you have any coffee?" Rachel interjected.

"Certainly."

"Thanks, beautiful."

"You're welcome, ma'am." She turned to me. "Would you like anything else? Coffee? Tea? Hot chocolate?"

"Oh, wow. Hot chocolate sounds really nice right now." She disappeared into the kitchen. Addyson struck up a conversation with Rachel and Katherine about downtown development and rising housing costs, and I tuned out. When Angela came back with our drinks, she noticed I was left out of the conversation, and she sat on the floor by me and asked if there was anything else she could do for me. There was nothing I could think of.

"I just want you to relax and enjoy yourself, and it—" She paused to find the right words. "It would make me very happy to be a part of that for you and to attend to any desires or whims you have this afternoon. Like Addyson said, I'm pretty good at foot rubs. Would you like one?"

My feet had been pretty tired all week. I told her that I would and thanked her. She pulled off my shoes and slid off my socks. I was somewhat embarrassed about the lint, but she simply brushed it away. Her touch was soft and heavenly, and I found myself letting go of a breath I hadn't realized I was holding. I heard the doorbell, but I wasn't really paying attention. She found some kind of pressure point, and I couldn't help but let out a moan.

I heard laughter and sat up. Monica, Evelyn, and Lora had arrived. Apparently the sounds I was making had led them to believe something else was going on in here.

"I'm going to have to get one of those later," Monica said.

Angela ran her hands over my skin a few more times and then kissed one of my feet before putting my socks back on and going to wash her hands and serve the food.

Everything was delicious. Addyson had apparently worked at a brunch place years ago. It was nice getting to see everyone. We'd all been pretty close during the summer when we were organizing all those trans lady picnics, but since then, we hadn't spent much time together. Over food we caught up about new jobs, new relationships, and such.

Monica told us about some fucked-up street harassment she had gotten. I mentioned a new coworker who was incredibly condescending to me and incessantly called me darling and sweetheart. Lora had been struggling to get the bank to deposit a check because it wasn't made out to her deadname. It was really good to have people to talk with about that kind of stuff, people who don't need explanations and who give instant feedback about how fucked up it all is.

"So Angela," Evelyn said. As soon as Evelyn addressed her, Angela got up on her knees from the sitting position she had been in on the floor. "I want to thank you for being the impetus to getting us all together, but can you explain more about this fantasy of yours? You get to be the one cis woman serving a group of trans women. What's that about?"

"I have great admiration for the trans women in my life. I know so many who are incredible powerhouses doing really amazing things. When transmisogyny affects my friends and lovers, I'm impacted by it too. Especially when it's done in women's spaces, ostensibly for my benefit, it just makes me sick. I wanted to flip the script and create a women's space that centers trans women, where I can be the cis woman who is at your service, and in doing so, show you all my appreciation."

"That explanation makes a bunch of sense," Monica chimed in. "At first I thought the whole scenario felt a bit exoticizing. But I'm not getting that feeling now that I'm here."

"But it's more than just flipping the script," added Rachel. "There's the sexual aspect, of course. And it has an odd feeling of cis guilt, or something."

Angela grinned and looked away for a moment.

"I'm never going to claim to be perfect," she said. "Maybe cis guilt is part of it. But being a service submissive is my fetish. So more directly, this is my fantasy, and I'm grateful to you all for allowing me to indulge. But that's the basic logic of why this particular service dynamic is something I specifically wanted."

Breaking the tension, Katherine crassly interrupted, "In that case, I'm up for being serviced."

She lifted the edge of her long skirt and beckoned. Angela went to her and placed her lips on Katherine's calf. She slowly worked her way up until her head disappeared under Katherine's skirt.

I was surprised how the casual conversation returned, despite Katherine's occasional sighs. After a while, though, Monica summoned Angela back to the table. Grabbing a cookie from the tray, she wagged it in the air.

"You've been such a good ally," she said. "I've got something for you."

Angela's embarrassment took her over and her cheeks flushed

red, but dutifully she crawled over to Monica and received a bite of the cookie from her hands.

"I know you've got a thing for feet," Monica said. "How would you like to suck on mine?"

The view I had was quite a thing to behold: Angela on her knees, head bent to the floor, her pussy peeking out just underneath her ass. Apparently I wasn't the only one enticed. Rachel was the first to move over and began feeling up the inside of her leg. Katherine joined in, positioning herself behind Angela, gently pressing her hips into Angela's.

"Ma'am, I don't want to presume your preferences for kinds of sex," Angela said. "But if you so desired, I'd be honored for you to fuck me however you like. There's condoms, gloves, dams, and lube tucked under the table next to you."

Rachel and Katherine had their arms around each other and were kissing. Monica moaned loudly from the attention she was getting. Evelyn had leaned back and was enjoying the show. Addyson was caressing Angela's back and quietly speaking. "That's right, that's a good girl. I'm so happy with you. You're doing so well right now."

When I saw Katherine fucking Angela that way—I mean using her, uh, junk to penetrate her—I was struck with amazement, and perhaps a bit of confusion. All these messages were running through my head. I closed my eyes and tried to shut them out.

Then I looked again. She didn't actually look like anything but herself. Despite the internalized messaging still playing on a loop in my head, I couldn't actually imagine her as a guy even when I tried. Sure I'd seen that motion in movies and in porn, but come to think of it I'd seen images of women thrusting their hips in the same way just as often—sometimes with strap-ons, sometimes just dry-humping.

I wondered: how did that work for her? Did she feel dysphoria about it? I mean, how could she not? Did she just do it anyway? Did she hide from it or dissociate from that part?

It kinda made me wonder if I could ever—no.

No, I didn't think I could. When I thought of what she was doing, I alternated between a half-dozen feelings. There was disgust at the thought of it. There was admiration: I was impressed that she was capable of it; it made me see her as strong in a way I hadn't considered. There was a sense of amazement at how much pleasure they both seemed to be having. There was a feeling of shame at the thought of enjoying something like that. There was shame at the idea that I'd been caught in the same room as it. And maybe, just maybe, there might have been a bit of jealousy.

There was a hand on my shoulder. It was Lora. "So, um, I wasn't sure if I was going to come to this or not, but then I heard you would be here." She smiled and cast her eyes down, stealing glances up at me. Was that . . . flirting? "But I was wondering if you might be up for—" Lora was blushing now. "Can I give you a kiss?"

She was so cute—how embarrassed she was getting. Suddenly all the times she hung out after meetings were done or the note of excitement in her voice when she said hi to me made a lot more sense. How could I not have noticed? I leaned in and gave her a kiss, and then I pulled away to look at her face. A wide grin was plastered over it. She laughed slightly, and then she leaned over and kissed me again, more deeply, and then she pushed me back onto the arm of the couch.

Coming to this party was definitely a good idea.

Her kisses were tentative at first, but as it became clear that I was into it, she got more forceful. There was almost desperation in it, as if she knew there were only five minutes left in the world and wanted to get in all the kisses she could. Or more likely, she had been afraid of admitting her crush and now she was finally giving herself permission to believe it wasn't all going to blow up in her face. Her passion was intoxicating and I found myself pressing against her body just as hard.

Eventually, she stopped to catch her breath. Her eyes were checking in with me and she said, "Wow, this is so good."

I was panting, "Gods, yes!"

She kissed me again, pressing her knee between my legs and working her way up. I squeezed my thighs against her as she kissed my neck. She was squeezing back with her thighs. We ground against each other, and she moaned softly into my ear.

She pushed herself up, and without unlocking our legs she took off her shirt. A pink sports bra covered her small breasts. I reached up to feel her, stopping short when I remembered I hadn't checked in about it. But she grabbed my hand and pressed it to her breast. I could feel a small lump behind her nipple, and remembering how tender I was when my breasts were still growing, I tenderly squeezed and was rewarded with a gasp.

In the moment she paused to react, I pushed her onto her back and leaned over her. One hand moved her bra aside to tease her nipple while the other reached down to caress her side, moving down toward her hip.

She reached under the hem of my shirt. "Do you feel good about removing some clothes?"

I stopped to look around. No one else was fully clothed and several people were completely naked. The scene centering on Angela had expanded now. Addyson, Rachel, and Evelyn all had their fingers in her while she was going down on Katherine. Our fun on the couch was not going unnoticed. As I looked around, Addyson caught my eye and smiled at me, clearly glad I was having a good time.

Even being semi-naked in front of other people was intimidating. I'm so self-conscious around my body that I removed all the mirrors from my apartment. But here it felt different. I was surrounded by girls with bodies like mine. We all deeply cared for each other. Things felt more than safe. Like I didn't even have to think about it.

I turned back to Lora and smiled. "Yes."

She quickly pulled my shirt over my head and planted a line of kisses down to my waist. Then she took her time with my skirt. I reflexively held my breath as my underwear was revealed. She smiled up at me and kissed my thigh. "Your body is beautiful."

I breathed out a sigh.

We explored each other for a while. After our underwear came off, her tentative touches turned into a palm pressing into my junk. But when I began to get erect, my embarrassment came back. It made me upset at my own anxieties. I wanted more than this—so much more. I reminded myself that this was a safe group of close friends, but it was getting to the point where I couldn't force myself to relax.

My breathing became sharper and the look on my face must have changed. Lora stopped and asked, "You doing okay? You know we could go to another room if you want some privacy."

"Yeah, I think I need that."

I tried not to think of it as a defeat. I had pushed myself a lot so far. If anyone saw us heading down the hallway, they were too caught up in their own activities to care about it. When the door closed behind us, the noise from the living room quieted to a muffled murmur. It emphasized that we were alone.

Lora looked up at me with devious intent. I backed up until I felt the bed behind me. She pushed me onto it and pounced on top of me. I reached down to touch her. She was very hard. I paused for a second, not sure what touches she would like and what might be a problem.

"What do you like to call your . . . um . . . this?"

"I like *girl cock* pretty well."

I had heard the term before and it had always felt a bit dysphoric, like it was too masculinizing. But the way she said it, she was unabashedly taking ownership of her own body. In this context it felt powerful and confident. Still, the brazen language caused me to flush for a moment.

She started thrusting herself into my hand. I gripped more firmly. Leaning over me, she brought her head down for a kiss. Her pace quickened. She used one hand to grab my breast, and as she struggled to hold herself up with the other, she dropped closer and closer to my body. I could feel her girl cock brushing against my thigh and hips with each stroke. She was panting.

Suddenly she slowed and rolled over. "I don't want to come just yet." She pointed to the nightstand that held lube and safe-sex supplies in a highly visible display. "We've got a lot of options here, is there anything you'd like me to do for you?"

"I like everything you're doing." I paused. Talking about this was difficult.

"Can I do more? Would you like me to go down on you?"

"I do enjoy the touches to my girl...junk. But I don't get as much out of it. When I'm by myself I mostly play with my ass."

She grabbed a glove and applied some lube to it. "That sounds really fun."

Lora leaned over me and placed her non-gloved hand on my chest, letting her weight sink into me. Her gloved hand probed downward to find my ass. The cold lube made me shiver for a moment as my body acclimated to it, then it felt warm as she circled around my opening.

I stretched my neck upward to kiss her. She started tapping on me and the pressure made me want more. I arched my hips upward, craving the feeling of her opening me up. She kissed me harder and thrust in.

Everything felt amazing and there wasn't a moment I didn't want more. She reached in deeper and brushed against my prostate. I reached down to touch myself as she sped up to match the rhythm of my hips.

"The way your body is responding, demanding more, it's so fucking hot and makes me want to give you even more."

I struggled to get words out, "Yesss. Soooo. Gooooood!"

"I wanna fuck you with my girlcock. How's that sound to you?"

She noticed me thinking and slowed, then paused her motion. It brought on a wave of all the feelings I was having watching Katherine and Angela. But I hadn't considered myself on the other end of things. There was still a shock of fear that ran through my body telling me it's not an okay thing for a trans woman to do. But it wasn't like I would be the one doing it. And when I imagined her fucking me I realized—I really did want it. I wanted to feel her thrusting into me the way she had been thrusting into my hand. I wanted to feel her pleasure and her enjoyment of my body. I wanted her desire and urgency to set the pace. And, oh my god, did I want to feel her come inside me.

"Yes, I want that."

Reaching to the bedside table, she put some lube inside a condom and rolled it on. Poised over me, she made eye contact again, checking in one last time. I nodded, and then she used her gloved hand to guide herself to my opening. I felt the slow buildup of pressure until she suddenly pushed through and was inside me.

She pulled off her glove and dropped it to the side of the bed. I could tell she was trying to take it slow for me, but with every push she was so vocal I could tell how much she wanted more. I pushed my hips upward and she couldn't hold herself back anymore. I touched myself furiously. Looking up, I saw her panting, eyes closed in concentration. She opened her eyes and looked down at me. Something about the intensity of her desire set me off in that moment. Everything felt so incredible. I lost my focus and as much as I wanted to maintain eye contact, I couldn't. I realized I was coming and shouted out.

She realized what was happening and hurried to catch up. I could feel myself tightening. As my muscles convulsed around her, each thrust into me felt euphoric and caused my orgasm to keep going longer. It was finally fading when I could tell she was very close to her own orgasm. I dug my fingernails into her back and she immediately came. I wrapped my arms and legs around her body and she groaned and shivered.

Lora rolled over and snuggled into my arm. I gave her a squeeze and she made a contented purr. We took a few moments to talk. I was finally able to set aside my anxiety about everything now that it had all turned out so well. I realized I was fine with what happened. It was great. As long as Lora felt comfortable topping me, then I didn't have to worry.

Eventually we decided to rejoin everyone in the living room. They were all in a naked pile.

Monica was sipping coffee. She saw us walking in. "Wow, that sounded like a really good 'foot rub' Lora was giving you."

I blushed, but didn't shy away from the innuendo this time. "The best."

PAY ME NO MIND

R. Magdalen

The commute was a difficult one. I was surrounded by too many people, too close, looking and touching and so unbearably loud. Sometimes I can handle it. I actually like riding the train. I'll listen to my headphones or wear earplugs. At this moment, though, I was exhausted from working, from masking my autism, from trying to decipher the feelings and metaphors of the neurotypical all day long. The train jostled along, and I lost my footing a few times, touched on all sides by strangers. An alarming number of people were engrossed in loud conversations. It was too hot and there was a smell. My jaw was clenched and my fists were tight balls in my pockets. My eyes stung as tears formed. Knowing that crying was a socially unacceptable response for an adult on a crowded train just worsened my anxiety. I already look weird. I leaned against a pole for stability and closed my eyes, even though I knew that looked weird, too. I counted down the stops. I started to sweat. The ride lasted for thirty minutes.

I reached my stop and it was like a weight had lifted. The panic attack was gone, but I was tired and tense. Now it was just a short walk home, to her. I thought about picking up dinner, and decided against it. I was out of spoons and I needed to get home. Dinner was another decision I could put off.

When I got there, she was sitting naked in an armchair, reading a book. It was a book of queer short stories I'd bought for her ages ago. I put down my bag, making unsubtle noise. I knew she'd heard me, but she didn't look up. She just remained there, fully concentrated on her reading. I am not always sure of how to interpret the things she does, but I took it as a cue to stay quiet, not ask her how her day went or tell her how hellish it had been on the train. I can't always talk right away when I get home, even on my best days. This day had been bright and harsh, with all the forced eye contact and complicated pleasantries that a job out in the world entails. Home was simple and quiet and dark, except for the light she read by.

Her thick, dimpled legs were crossed at the ankle and they dangled over the arm of the chair. Only a fraction of her giant round ass was visible. It was enough, though, to make my mouth water. The way she curled her body in the chair compressed her sides and belly into rolls that looked, if you'll forgive me, buttery in the lamplight. She put her fingers through her dark, short hair and squinted at the text, as if she'd reached a tense scene or a turning point in the plot. She was utterly beautiful. She paid me absolutely no attention and it made my clit hard.

I hung up my jacket, took off my shoes, and walked toward her, noting the coolness of the wooden floor beneath my bare feet. There was a chair next to hers, and a small table where the lamp stood. She didn't even look up when I reached her. I tentatively touched her smooth round knee with one finger, distracted by the hairs there. They picked up the light and sparkled. I drew circles around her knee, mesmerized by the smooth texture of her skin. When she didn't react, I ran the finger slowly up the ripples on her thigh, finding a bruise I'd left there a few days ago when we last played. It was already fading. I traced a circle around it and then pressed my finger into the blue flesh, hard. No reaction. I moved my finger over a bit of her belly, touching each roll ever so lightly. Then I moved up to the delicious fat on the back of her arm, one of my favorite places on her body; it is as soft and round as a breast, but easier to grab in public, where holding her there brings calm and reassurance. I dug my nails into it, squeezed it, trying to mark it. She turned a page.

I moved my finger to her shoulder, across her chest, tracing the intricate tattoos that swirl around her body. She didn't look up, but she adjusted herself slightly to give me access to her breasts. They are round and soft, with large pink nipples, which were already hard from the cool of the apartment. I moved my finger down, drew a circle around a nipple, and then shifted to the other breast. She ignored me, and I could feel myself getting wet. I bent slightly and put both hands on those beautifully soft tits, just holding them gently at first and then squeezing a little harder. Just touching them was joy enough to erase the stress of the day. Her breathing became audibly heavier as I pinched her nipples, softly and then more brutally, trying to make her squeal. Her breath caught for a second or two and she just turned another page.

I got to my knees and put my mouth to her thigh. I kissed, I licked, and I sucked until I had worked my way up that thick, luscious thigh to where it met her ass, and then I bit her. If she reacted at all, I couldn't perceive it. She flipped the page of her book and I put my tongue between the rolls of fat on her side. I am quite particular about flavors and textures, but she is the most delicious thing. I bit the back of her arm and put my tongue in her armpit. Returning to her breasts, I teased with my tongue until I had a nipple in my mouth and then I bit down hard, testing to see if I'd get a reaction. Nothing. I kept biting, lightly, enjoying her body in my mouth until I found my way back to that thigh and bit down hard, right on the bruise. I was rewarded with a tiny moan from her throat, but she didn't stop reading.

Then, she shifted. Without looking up from the book even once, she turned and opened her legs, her fat cunt so close to my face I could breathe it in. I went back to her knee, and bit a line up her inner thigh. Not hard enough to bruise this time. I needed the feeling of that soft flesh between my teeth, the taste of her skin. When I reached the crease at the top of her thigh I could feel her wet cunt, its hair scratchy, tickling my cheek. She turned another page. I inhaled deeply and chose patience and symmetry, moving back to her other knee, biting another line up her leg and delighting in her fat flesh between my teeth. Another page.

I reached the top of her other thigh and I couldn't take it anymore. I plunged my face into her cunt. She reacted, but only by scooting forward in the chair to give me a better angle. I kissed her labia, took a few bites of her fat round mons, and then tasted her. She was wet and lovely and I felt my own clit start to throb. My boxer briefs were getting soaked by now. I took my time, working my way inside in slow measure, not wanting to get to her clit too soon. There is so much to enjoy there, so many folds, each secret place with its own unique flavor. She tastes like sex and citrus and heaven. I could stay there forever. I had finally reached her clit with my tongue and teased it just a little, when I heard the page flip again.

I pushed my mouth in harder now, finding a rhythm with my tongue, now flat against her clit. She opened her legs wider and I put three fingers in her. It was awkward, but I fucked her and pushed on her clit with my tongue, trying to find the beat again. Her wet smoothness sent waves of quiet bliss through my fingers, up my arm, into my brain. This was as much for me as it was for her, probably more. I grew overstimulated and I had to close my eyes, but I smiled involuntarily into her pussy. I felt her muscles clenching, felt her come, but she didn't stop reading and I wanted to keep going. She paid me no mind. I straightened up, stopped licking her clit, and focused on the fucking. She was still deep into her book, but I could see her face was flushed and had taken on that beautiful expression she wears when she comes. That is an expression I can always read, out of all the inscrutability of human faces, and that fact makes it all the more addictive. I love to see that face. I put in a fourth finger and started making circles around her clit with my thumb. I kept fucking her, adding more and more pressure with my thumb, until her muscles let me know she was about to come again. I started rubbing her clit directly with my thumb. This time she moaned out her orgasm and closed her eyes and it was gorgeous, but then she turned another page.

I slipped my thumb inside her, fucking her with all five fingers. Her pussy was still wet and open, so I pushed my whole hand in and curled it into a fist. My heart swells every time, the way her cunt accepts my hand, like it's hungry. I needed this. Again, the sensation almost became too much for me and I had to close my eyes. Before I got completely overwhelmed, I paused, took a few breaths, and tried to block out everything in the world except for that warm, wet, wonderful feeling in my hand, her cunt around my wrist, and how it made my heart feel so light and sweet. As I pulled myself together, she closed her legs around my body and compressed me, calming me, and I put my other arm around her belly and my head on her thigh. I fucked her slowly, and then faster, my eyes closed, my mind focused entirely on her body. My cunt's muscles were pulsing to the same rhythm, and I could feel myself on the verge of an orgasm.

It seemed to only take a minute of this before I heard her drop the book. It might've been longer, but I'd lost all sense of time. I looked up at her lovely round face. When her eyes met mine, the intensity of it made me come hard. Waves of that beautiful high traveled up through my arm and I felt like I might pass out. I held her gaze until her faced clenched and her cunt gripped my wrist so hard, for a moment I thought she might break it. Her face was sweaty, strained perfection. Her pelvis thrust toward my hand three times, she cried out, and then she finished. She closed her eyes and lay back in the chair, her legs limp. I waited a few beats and slowly pulled my hand out of her and rested my head in her lap.

My mind had quieted. Every muscle in my body was relaxed and warm. I did not mind the pain in my knees from kneeling, nor did I regret the decision not to get dinner despite my belly starting to complain. I thought I might sleep like this, hungry, still on my knees, my hand wet and smelling like cunt.

This is peace.

After a time, she sat up. She put her fingers in my hair, pulling it to force my head up and back so she could look me in the eye. Then, smiling, she looked at me and said, "Hey, you. I got us takeout. How was your day?"

MODERN LOVERS (YOU PROBABLY HAVEN'T HEARD OF THEM)

T.R. Verten

"Whoa, whoa," the doorman barks, as she holds out a crumpled five. "Let me check that."

Martha doesn't care about getting a wristband but she forks it over. Meaty hands covered in knuckle tats fondle her out-of-state driver's license. She stands straighter, transforms her face into the photograph's smile, coaxed from her by the cheerful lady at the Portland DMV. Smiling, like so many things (ska, pockets on T-shirts, clove cigarettes, patches from the mall, too-sharp eyeliner, automatic gears, new Chucks), isn't punk.

He hands it back. "Don't get many of those here," he remarks with a smirk. Does he know? He takes the door money, though, wraps a pink band around her wrist—too goddamned tight— Martha tries to wriggle a finger in while the seal's fresh. He holds the metal door and says, "Happy birthday, *sweetheart.*"

Martha flushes despite the cold, his knowing chuckle swallowed by the rising sound of distortion as she pushes inside and scans the room. It's familiar. The scene is the scene. Skate rats monopolizing the pool table. Made-up girls with Bettie bangs sipping carefully at long-necked beers so as not to smudge their lipstick. Andrew behind the bar making cow-eyes at a brunette rockabilly bitch with razor-blade cheekbones. She catches sight of a black T-shirt, grungy blond hair, and her mouth goes dry in anticipation. It's not her, though—just a skinny dude in an Op Ivy T-shirt, who gives her a once-over as he walks past with his pack of Old Golds. Charlie's there, running sound from the back, chubby cheeks obscured by a winter beard. Spring break brought her home, but Lake Michigan failed to receive the memo. It is fucking freezing, and she'd huddled next to the outdoor heater waiting for the train. Even now her fingers are still numb.

Julie's onstage, screeching into the mic, red hair incandescent in the spotlight shining down from above. The distortion is heavy, the air thick with smoke. The mosh pit calls to her, and she elbows her way to the front, edging carefully past a guy with a blue Mohawk and spikes on his army surplus jacket. There's a stomp on her boots, she kicks the fuck back, and then she's there at the edge surging forward with the cascading guitar riffs. The pit: a swirling mass of skinheads, hardliners, angry girls like her, and anarchists working out their ideological differences. All that rage has to go somewhere. She holds back instead of diving in herself, using her arms to push back on the people who break free from the spinning churn. By the time the set's almost over she's drenched with sweat, grateful for the decision to leave her coat at home.

The sound cuts out. Julie calls for more vocals, though it doesn't matter. Like everything, the club's system is on its last legs. Propped up by alcoholics who come for cheap beer and suburban kids subsidizing all-ages nights. Kids like Martha used to be, and might be still. The guitarist pulls a riff out of his ass, a cheesy doo-wop line, and the crowd groans, in unison. She makes for the bar.

It's odd to drink, legally, and she plunks down a ten for an

Old Style. A tip goes into Andrew's jar, but he's too busy with his brunette to notice. Julie's band breaks down and the next one sets up. Rufus is front man, which explains Izzy's absence. Rumors have grown up around their feud's mysterious origins, tangled up like an overgrown rosebush: Rufus totaled Izzy's Tercel, Rufus puked in the office, Izzy punched Rufus for trying to con her out of her door cut, Rufus let Izzy's brother OD in Minneapolis.

Martha asks if she's planning on making an appearance tonight, and Andrew gives her a shrewd look.

"Go grab me another case," he says. "I've got my hands full."

The rockabilly girl glares when he smiles at Martha, and she doesn't have time to consider if it's a bad idea. If she should stay put and drink her beer and head home like a good suburban girl. She doesn't question the way her legs push her onto her feet in the direction of the basement. The door scrapes against the cinder blocks and the smell at once overwhelms her: rank smoke, stale beer, mildew.

Rufus is running sound check but down here it's church quiet. She tiptoes down the stairs and goes straight into the back room, where she hefts another case of Old Style onto her hip. A familiar profile is visible through the cracked door. Boots on her desk, nose buried in *Punk Planet*. She's got a longstanding feud with Larry Livermore. Dislikes the publication, reads it anyway. A full ashtray at her elbow, a space heater in the corner.

At the first sight of her mentor, Martha makes a strangled whine in her throat. The case shifts against her body.

Izzy hears the glass clink and says, "Andrew?" Martha curses beneath her breath. "Who's watching the bar?"

Martha shoulders the plywood divider that separates the office from the stock. It creaks inward with barely a push. "He is," she says, "I'm just doing the beer run." If she's surprised to see her, it doesn't show. Implacable as ever, that's Izzy.

"Hmm," is the response. She looks back at her magazine. Martha sees the faded lines of old scars, the distinctive burn on her left thumb from a long-ago bar fight. She licks her lips. She wants to scream, to throw herself at Izzy's feet. She wants to beg for hurt in a thousand different ways. But she's quiet. It's not punk to be fucking desperate.

"How's Julie's crew?" she asks.

"Good," Martha answers enthusiastically, before remembering to rein it in. When she speaks again her tone is cooler, voice lowered. "The new bassist sounds better."

Izzy snorts, nostrils flaring. "That's not saying much." She scopes out the case in Martha's hands. It's getting stupid heavy. She'd like to put it down. She'd like to pound a couple and let Izzy mark up her upper thighs. She'd like to hide out down here all night.

"You want?" Her tone's pleasant, but the question sounds unbelievably dirty. Won't matter. She's already buzzed. Her hands twitch, itching to touch. She wonders if she should mention that it's her birthday.

Instead she says, "It's room temperature," but puts the case down and hauls two out.

The folding chair creaks as she sits. Izzy takes one and rests the cap against her desk. With a karate smack, the top goes sailing off. It rattles against the hard floor and she passes it back.

"College spoiling you?" asks Izzy as the second cap clatters to the concrete. Martha takes a long swallow, to prove that it hasn't. The beer's bitter and warm, but drinking it gives her something to do with her restless hands.

Martha watches Izzy's throat move as she drinks, too rock-and-roll to be fazed by tepid beer. She tips back her head and the movement lifts her collar enough to show a faint curlicue of a tattoo, snaking its way up her neck. The T-shirt is black—

only plain, only ever black. Martha'd listened, but bought band T-shirts when she could scrape up the money. Hell, she's wearing one now.

They sit there for a while, listening to Rufus start in on a political tirade. They're too insulated to make out the words, but the gist of it is always the same. Fuck the man. *Fuck the police. Fuck the system.*

Izzy leans back in her chair and tucks her hands behind her head. She gives Martha the once-over. It burns to be looked at, to be really fucking seen.

Stay cool, she tells herself. *Be fucking cool, or she'll scoff you right up those stairs.*

"It's all right." She picks the label with her thumb. "We get kegs after rugby games." The space heater grinds out a noise that sounds potentially fatal.

"You're still into that?" Izzy asks, voice strange and rough. "Huh." There's a pause while she considers this information.

Damp paper peels up beneath Martha's nail. Maybe it's the heater, or that she hasn't eaten since noon, or the fact that she can't stop thinking about Izzy's fingers, with their scars and chipped black polish, covering her mouth so she can't make noise.

She's about to answer, to goad Izzy into a follow-through, when there's a scrape of wood and cinder block. A voice echoes down. "Babe, you coming back?" Andrew, antsy for his delivery.

Martha pounds her drink quickly, and stands up. Too fast. Her head fucking spins.

She sets down the bottle, empty now, on Izzy's desk. "There's an after-party," she says, quietly.

Izzy answers, even more quietly, "I'll be sure to miss it." Then she calls out, to Martha's retreating figure, "Shut the door, kid." Martha pulls the plywood to. A shiver runs up her neck as she trudges upstairs.

When the set's finished some head for the diner, others the after-party, still others the suburbs. Martha stays put and feeds quarters into the jukebox, opting for the Buzzcocks and Jonathan Richman over the horrible rockabilly Andrew's groupies prefer.

Close to closing time, Izzy makes an appearance. A hush falls over the room as she emerges from her lair, and everyone watches her go into the bathroom, wiping hands on her jeans as she swings over to the bar.

"Pack of smokes," she says, acknowledging the Luckies Andrew hands her with a curt grunt.

He's sucking face with the brunette by the end of the night, so when Martha suggests that she lock up, that's all the encouragement he needs to count his tips, close out his register, and do the drop.

She locks up quickly, thinking only of what awaits. She pulls a couple more beers from the cooler and goes back into the basement. Izzy's there, smoking, hunched over a stack of flyers, using a black Sharpie to add the missing umlauts over the ö in the name of next Friday's headliner. "They're not actually from Sweden," Martha says, by way of greeting.

"It's the principle of the thing." Izzy glowers at the neon green pages. Black smudges stain her fingertips from the toner.

Martha giggles, because it's so fucking stupid.

"What's so funny, kid?" Izzy asks, and Martha laughs aloud before she can stop herself.

Better to deflect. "It's my birthday," she says, and has to think on this. "Okay, wait. Yesterday was my birthday. Like, before midnight. Is it still the same day?"

"It's the same day until you go to bed." Izzy lays down the marker and scrutinizes Martha. Her gaze burns her up inside. She wants, she *wants*. "Well, well," she says, and then pauses. "You don't look any different to me."

"No?" Martha asks, coyly. She swigs her beer, lowers her eyelashes demurely, playing up the innocent thing. "You haven't seen me since, what? December?"

"You still look like a fucking poser," Izzy says, dismissively, and presses her thin lips together. Then almost as if she realizes she's being mean, rubs the bridge of her nose. "Sorry. I didn't get you anything."

Martha feels audacious calling Izzy out. Her head swims to contradict this woman she worships so. "Why? If I'd told you, you would've?"

The chair scrapes against the floor. Izzy stands back from her desk and rests her fingertips on the wood. Martha looks at them, at her, the rise and fall of Izzy's chest. Want swells in her own so bad she can hardly breathe.

It's mutual, that want. Izzy meets her halfway. Fuck kissing, though—kissing is for the kind of people who believe in romance, in fairy tales. *Punks don't kiss.*

Martha's on the floor before she can think to contradict herself. Concrete coldness seeps up through her jeans. Izzy widens her stance so she can snuggle up between her legs, where the real heat is.

Driven by overwhelming impulse, she ducks her head, brushing her bangs back from her face, and touches her lips to Izzy's cracked leather combat boot. There's a sharp inhale above her. Pride swells in her stomach. *Izzy* wants her. Izzy *wants* her. Izzy wants *her.* Her tongue darts out. The steel caps beneath provide no give, their taste metallic. Then the other boot is kissed, licked in turn, the smell of leather thick in her nostrils. Martha could stay here all night. Breathing in the scent, worshipping at her feet.

Izzy gives Martha's hair—and she can almost hear her *Too long, what is this Trixie bullshit?*—a tug. "Up with you."

Martha leans her cheek against Izzy's upper thigh. Together

they pull her three-row studded belt from its buckle. She unfastens it, reverently. It jangles. She turns her face up with silent entreaty in the look, asking for that which only Izzy can provide. The pit helps, kind of. Women's rugby fills the space. She's even tried pinching herself, or smacking her own ass while she humps a pillow. It feels fucking stupid. Hardly the same.

"No way, kid," says Izzy, and thumbs her bottom lip with a fond shake of her head. "You'll end up in the fucking ER if I take that thing to you." But her voice is proud. Martha could take it, if Izzy wanted to dish it out. Hell, take that and then some.

Martha pulls open the button and notices, then, that the zipper isn't fully closed. Maybe it's shitty, or she forgot when she went to the bathroom or maybe, Martha thinks with a hot rush as she lowers it, one achingly slow tooth at a time, she's had a hand down her pants. Waiting for her to get on her knees where she belongs.

The jeans are worked down past her thick thighs. Izzy's breathing is labored. She cups Martha's head in one calloused hand, groans when her underwear are slid down. She lets her hands find familiar places. Izzy's damp, swollen, and she curses when Martha runs a fingernail down the ridges of her cunt. God, she's missed this.

Martha licks—back and forth, side to side—until the other woman's thighs shake. When she's pulled away with a yank on her hair her vision is blurred.

"Haven't forgotten what you're about, huh?" Izzy breathes. Spit runs out the sides of Martha's mouth, her fingers flexing against the seams of Izzy's jeans. "Fuck," says Izzy, and lifts her T-shirt up. Her stomach is littered with black ink. Gothic letters shift and ripple as her muscles tense, grinding slow and deliberate against Martha's mouth.

It's bliss, even with the hard floor cold beneath her knees, or maybe because of it. The position comforts in its familiarity.

Izzy's thumb on her pulse point, Martha's blood thick in her ears as she slobbers for a while. How long it lasts she can't tell. Her own arousal is a distant echo, thrumming faint between her legs. It doesn't matter if she comes; that's beside the point. She might have to stay here for hours. Martha's own cunt twitches shamefully as she imagines herself. The veins on her neck standing out, face red, smeared with hot saliva. Ice crystals forming in her eyelashes, mascara wet and running.

Izzy comes again, with a lazy groan. She pushes Martha back onto her heels and with a quick motion peels her shirt off, revealing muscled pecs, a tattered white sports bra obscuring her chest tattoos.

It happens fast, then, like she'd been angling for all along. She's on her feet and a second later she's splayed out on the desk, facedown, her forehead on the pile of fliers, a heavy hand on her neck. Izzy strips her, opens her up, front, back, front again. It takes every shred of self-control not to fuck back onto her.

"Hold yourself open," she prompts, bringing Martha's hands up. There's a wet slurping sound. Knowing what's coming, Martha recoils as a gob of spit hits her. Izzy rubs against her tailbone, dips into the wetness. With a quiet, considered noise, she spits again. One rough finger sinks in. Martha lets out a ragged sigh. "Good girl," Izzy coos, and gives her more. With a squelch a second one slides in, then a third.

It's awful. It's excruciating.

It's rock and roll and smoking a cigarette down to the filter. It's reverb and being kicked in the shins. It's watching the sunrise from the lake, a blizzard that whites out the skyline.

It's perfect.

"You fuck a lot last semester?" Izzy asks, conversational. She pulls her fingers out, drags them down the crack of Martha's ass while she waits for an answer. It sets her teeth on edge. Martha twists her head as best she can with that firm hand pressing her down. Paper rustles beneath her body.

"No," she lies. Why lie? Course she fucked. College girls playing at rebellion. They had coffee, went on dates that weren't. They told her about their radio shows. They wanted to make out, go thrifting, write love letters. She lied because it gets Izzy off, to play like it's their first time. It makes Martha remember other firsts. The first time they'd dry-humped behind the bar, Izzy's leg in black leather between her thighs. The first time they'd kissed, over the car's gearbox during a January snowstorm, the tape whirring after the songs ran out, blank like the wind. The first time Izzy put her hands on Martha's throat and Martha made her do it again, again, again.

So Martha lies, because what's a lie between friends?

"I haven't been fucked since Christmas," she says, and shifts to accommodate the stretch. Her hands slip away but Izzy growls, so Martha puts them back. It pulls the skin taut. She's wet between her legs, but it will wait.

"That's a goddamn shame," Izzy purrs, pulling her hand out again. "Although I'd like to see those girls make you whine like I do," she says, and thumbs at the tender skin near her asshole.

Lower half prickling with sensation, Martha's thoughts race wildly. It's a challenge presented as truth. Her forehead lists against the stack of fliers. On an outward groan she says, "Not as much as you would."

Izzy's hands still. Powerful thighs rest against Martha's own, sticky now, pinning her down. The ashtray is gently overflowing, hovering just beyond her field of vision. The space heater whines out another angry sob. "Going to pretend I didn't hear that," Izzy grits out, and smacks her on the ass.

Martha leans into the hurt, arching her back so the sting ripples outward. She hears a click. Her belt? A cigarette lighter?

No, a Sharpie being uncapped, the harsh chemical scent of permanent marker wafting down to her nostrils.

"Remember," Izzy says. "Remember who this belongs to."

There's a tickle on her lower back. The marker skids across pooled sweat. Izzy takes her sweet time, Martha split open on her fingers as she scratches out an obscene message only she can see.

"There," she proclaims, tossing the marker aside. It clatters down next to Martha's cheek.

"That'll do. Wear that for me."

"It'll wash off." Martha bows her head low. She's so fucking full, Izzy's fingers sliding hot and merciless inside of her, hitting every good spot. She knows Martha's body through and through. Her ass, her cunt. Izzy made her realize that she'd always needed more. She'd simply tapped into what was there. *Your true nature*, she'd said, and Martha had never forgotten it.

"Then don't fucking wash," Izzy growls and drapes her body over hers. Her free hand reaches beneath Martha's T-shirt to twist at her piercings, exactly what she needs to get there.

"I need," she gasps, limbs flailing against the desk. "Please, Izzy, fuck."

"Gonna fuck you into next week, you hear me?" she says low into Martha's ear. She's cold, she's hot. She's breathing too much; she can't get enough goddamn air.

"Give it," Martha stammers back, senseless. "Give it to me, you fucking asshole."

"Dirty little bitch," comes the reply. Martha whines, collapses onto her forehead.

Izzy's hands leave her hips smarting with bruises. Her chest is hollow. Every fiber in her body burns with the need to finish. But Izzy hates weakness so she clamps her want down tight, silently begging to be allowed to come.

Izzy smacks her ass, again, but there's no real heat to it this time. "Turn over then," she says, and Martha scrambles to obey. Despite the screaming pain in her legs she manages to get her back against the desk. The ink from the topmost flier has transferred onto her chest, she sees, as she peels it off and it flutters to the floor. A Xerox smudge remains on her skin that rubbing does nothing to remove.

Izzy reaches across Martha's prone body for a cigarette. She lights up. Smoke wreathes her face. She nonchalantly picks a shred of tobacco from her tongue. Martha wriggles against the hard surface, watching as if she's outside her body. She tries to replace her needy pout with a sneer. Cigarette ash threatens to flake off and join the ink on her chest, but Izzy leans over just in time to tap into the full glass ashtray. The movement presses her thigh against Martha.

Not enough, not *enough*.

"I can't," she says, as denim scrapes against the puffy rim of her hole. "Izzy, I can't."

"Like fucking hell you can't," she gruffs. Izzy's leg jostles against her, a staccato rhythm that sets her teeth on edge.

Martha hooks both her legs around Izzy's thigh. "Fucking touch me."

"This way," says Izzy, and grinds against her. "If you can't then you don't. You hear me, sweetheart?"

"Kiss me then," Martha snarls back, and at last, Izzy blessedly complies, holding the cigarette a few inches away. She might get singed but that's all part of the appeal. Izzy's mouth is hot, pressure stinging against Martha's wind-chapped lips. She rocks her body along the length of Martha's, each slide against her ass sending a shiver across her. Her nipples are drawn up tight, the silver barbells pinching on their own accord. Izzy's zipper catches in her pubic hair. Martha flings her head to the side, inhaling a harsh lungful of smoke.

Her neck tightens as it washes over her, and then the room isn't there, the city isn't there, it's just the two of them, in this freezing room that reeks of beer.

When she comes to, her teeth are chattering. How long has it been? Twenty seconds? An hour?

Martha slides a tentative finger down her body, hisses at the touch. It's raw from the rough fabric, but the hurt holds promises of its own.

Izzy isn't having it. She laughs good-naturedly and says, "You're on your own for round two, kid."

Martha sits up. She takes the drag that Izzy offers, and rubs her eyes. She examines the damage: a bite mark on her side, ash and printer ink smeared across her stomach. What it says on her back she can only imagine. She swallows down a hot wave of shame—Izzy *claimed* her; Izzy claimed *her*—and covers herself up. She'll get the hand mirror when she goes home. Izzy always gives her something to remember her by.

She is unruffled, save two spots of red, high on her cheeks. "You need me to run you to the train?"

Martha lowers herself down from the desk and winces. There's no clock, but it can't be much past two. Izzy watches her, lights another cigarette as she laces up her Chucks.

She's shocked to hear, "I heard there's an after-party?"

"What?" she replies, shocked. Izzy doesn't *do* after-parties, unless there's a band involved, and even then they'd better be from the UK.

"Yeah, you're right," Izzy says, and rubs her stomach. "Golden Nugget? I'm fucking starving."

BECAUSE TODAY HAS BEEN THE MOST BEAUTIFUL DAY

BD Swain

I walked out onto the sidewalk into the brightest white light, as if scores of paparazzi had shot their flashbulbs all at once, right at my face. I saw a blinding light and the world turned blue, tinged with highlighter yellow. I froze in place, my hand still open behind me in a half grasp where the door handle had just slipped off my fingers. I heard the door to her building close with a click and a sigh before it hit me that the night was gone and this was daylight. Everything was new.

I was in Minneapolis doing tech on a show and had flown in a few days before. It was my second day in this town and I was already in the doghouse for not going out with the local crew the night before. It's not done. When you blow in and out of towns like smoke and work side by side with people, there are rules. You're supposed to go out, get drunk, stumble back into work with everyone hungover and laugh about it. Back at work, you go hard and get it all done. Over and over, you repeat this for each little dot on the map. I never seemed to fall in line.

Theaters can be freezing during the day and this one was

especially so. We all blew on our cupped hands making little smokestacks from our breath to keep stiff fingers limber enough to be useful. Hanging lights is not my regular job but someone on the tour was sick or still drunk and they had asked me to lend a hand. I don't mind ladders or the catwalks and the work is nice. Your fingers wrap around and tighten the screws. You check and double-check and adjust the angles. The lights can be heavy and make you work for it. I respect that I enjoy the work. My hands feel good. My feet are grounded. Maybe you know what I mean or maybe you don't, but when I'm doing a job like this and the work feels good, my dick gets harder and I pick my head up to look around.

Who's that over there? I wonder. This is a very real question in my head because I cannot remember faces. It's not distraction; it's something in my brain. I can pick up clues but I'm always in a new town before I can put them together, so people assume I'm an asshole. The truth is too hard to explain so I tend to wear my rudeness strapped tight. On the one hand, it's easier that way, and on the other, it's served me pretty well. When you're a quiet stranger passing through town and people think you're a little cold, a little mean, some of them want to be the ones to crack into you.

Now I've come to expect as much. More than that—I want it. And in the smaller towns, it's easy to get. Those small-town bars where they tell me they're straight and they've never even thought about being with a dyke. They tell me they don't know what to do and they would die if anyone found out. They see my thick knuckles and something shimmers and moves through them like a ghost. They might not want anyone to find out, but it's a lie that they don't know what to do. They know, every one of them. They know to get just drunk enough. They know how to grab the back of my head when I lean over to kiss them. They know how to wriggle those hips so I can slide their jeans off easy. They know how to roll over on their bellies and tease me, lifting up off the couch, the bed, the cramped car seat, the dirty floor, pushing away from the sink. They know how to pout and open their mouths just enough for my tongue, my fingers, my dick. How to tilt their head back keeping their eyes on me when I grab their thighs and ease them apart.

They know what to do, but if they wish they didn't, I'm not going to judge that. We all build our walls and plaster our lies thick across the slats until we have our retreat. I feel my own thick clay packed with every fucking falsehood and devil I've trapped inside my skin. I am thick with it. There are stories buried inside me. Here's the archetype:

I licked her lips before I touched her and I tasted the olives she had chewed on all night like a rat. I bit the inside of her lower lip and she gave herself to me. We moved from our spot at the bar to a booth in the corner and I pushed my hand under her shirt. My cold fingers and calloused skin snagged against her bra. She pushed me away and undid the next two buttons on her shirt. I leaned in a little more roughly with less feeling and more need. "Don't do that again," I said. "Don't stop me." I could have said, "I need to do this so just shut up right now." I could have asked her something, one question. I should have told her that I was her reckoning and she was mine. I thought about the fact that back in our collective past, we lived like every bar we went in could get raided that night and we'd be lined up and humiliated and dragged to jail. I thought this explained everything. I could have said that but never did.

We fucked in her car in winter—a cold, hard metal box with a skinny, hard bench seat. I pressed her down, pinning her shoulders while I kissed her. I moved her face side to side with my thumb digging into the meat of her jaw. I undid more buttons.

Her body steamed when I breathed on her skin. She watched me yank her belt loose and dig inside her jeans. She told me that was her favorite song and I thought she meant my fingers inside her, but later I realized we could hear the music seeping out of the bar and she just meant some tune. I used my forearm to hold her down. I watched her belly quiver as she squeezed and pushed herself against my hand.

I told her a story while we fucked. I told her how I loved Westerns as a kid; watching the cowboy in his tight jeans and his brown leather vest. How I liked the stiff ropes and the horses and was drawn to the whores, the whiskey, and the sex. It felt important that the cowboy wouldn't stop even when she begged. I stopped short of telling her how this is how I learned to jerk off, holding an imaginary woman down trying to stop her from struggling while I fucked her.

That is the first story, the amalgam of the first stories. It's important that I tell you the background to this day and what came before I met her and before I walked out into that bright and unexpected light. Who I was before I went to Minneapolis.

She blew by me when she showed up. The seamstress hired at the last minute, she swooped in and sat down on the stage. She sewed by hand, sitting on a low stool that was part of the set. I could see sweat seeping through her shirt under her armpits. Her knees were together and her feet wide apart. I was busy taping the stage, working late after hanging lights most of the day. I'd been with this show for months and knew where to mark the stage without thinking. The table goes here—rub the floor with a rag, stick the tape. The stack of newspapers goes here. The final scene in a spotlight goes here, the one where the lead actress wears a fake bird on her head and I cringe every time at how dumb it is.

She sewed with a fever, her arm weaving in and out. Someone asked her if she wanted to join us at the bar and I stopped what

I was doing to look up. I watched the curls at the back of her neck sway as she nodded her head, yes. She would go. I would go after heading to my room and finding the only decent-looking shirt I had with me. I saw her right away, sitting with the director who was already bombed. I didn't want that drama and stayed at the bar drinking vodka on the rocks, playing with the twist of lemon. I didn't notice her next to me until she'd already ordered. I expected her to say something, but she grabbed the drinks, paid, and stepped away leaving me staring at her until I felt stupid.

I turned back around and decided to leave after one more, but before I had time, she was back and ordered two shots of something. She held one to my lips. "Not many bars have this," she said. "Enjoy." She tilted the glass and I let my mouth open. The liquid was ice cold and I couldn't name the spirit. "Do you taste caraway?" she asked and I looked at her with my dumb, wide eyes not knowing what caraway even was. She watched me. Her face was bright and warm. We were silent for longer than felt comfortable and then a look passed on her face as if she had decided something. She leaned over and whispered, "I don't want you to speak." A wave washed over me and I felt drenched in a tangle of relief, confusion, curiosity, and twinge of unease. I shook my head, *no,* to mean, *yes, okay.*

I felt like I was suddenly at the wheel in the middle of a slow-motion spin. The evening switched to a new gear, and something broke. I was aware of a sudden tempo change all around me. My brain was moving at the same speed, while everything around me slowed to an unreal pace. Even more jarring was the fact that the music in the bar was now filtered out of my hearing altogether. The loud, beating rhythm had evaporated leaving all other noise heightened and crisp. Every sound that evening at the bar, everything she said, the sounds of ice, laughter, beer spurting out of taps, footsteps, whispers, glasses being picked up or set down—I heard them all with distinct clarity. I observed, watching from inside the eye of it.

Inside my head, I kept thinking, *Who are you?* And each time, she would cock her head, frown at me, and say in the gentlest way, as if she heard me, "You don't need to worry." She said this and it seemed clear that she knew something deep down about me— that worrying is my waking state. She said these words over and over and each time I experienced genuine relief. "You don't need to worry." I had been wrapped tight in something with no give, struggling against the pressure of it until I gave up and relaxed. Letting go allowed more space, room to breathe. Her words released me for a small moment before my instinct would ratchet tight again and we'd start all over.

She told me stories. When she left home for college, she skipped all her classes and worked as a waitress. She wanted to be in the world. I reveled at the way she didn't seem to judge her actions. She told me her stories as a matter of fact. Her decisions and choices made sense to me, and I listened in silence. I drank when she brought me a drink. I listened without judgment, taking her cue, when she talked about letting some guy fuck her because it was easier than the other options. I admired a story about leaving her girlfriend mid-trip and taking a Greyhound home with all the cash she had left once she realized things were no good and wouldn't get better.

We held what looked like a normal conversation and would have sounded like one if I'd spoken a word. I felt deeply known by her and grateful that somehow she knew I never would have found the space for her if she hadn't asked me not to speak. When she stood up and walked behind me, taking my chin in her hands and pulling my head back against her belly, I stayed still and let her move me where she would. She rubbed my cheeks and slid a finger just inside my mouth, feeling the edges of my teeth. I tasted orange peel and the bright falseness of a maraschino cherry. My heart started racing.

I followed her out of my chair, out of the bar, staring at the hand she held slightly behind her as if holding my leash. She didn't have to say anything as she walked out the door. She didn't turn around because she knew I was behind her. We walked for several blocks, crunching over the icy snow that had fallen in the afternoon, melted in the sun, and frozen again in the cold night until eventually she leaned over a car door. She moved a bag stuffed with fabric to the backseat and gestured for me. Her car smelled like licorice, like comfort. I rode in her car staring out at Minneapolis. Snow was falling. She said, "I want to see your hands on your jeans," and I obeyed. "I want you to rub your thighs," she said, and I rubbed my thighs through my jeans. Time still moved slower outside of me than inside. I began to believe she was showing me something so important that my brain had slowed down to follow each individual thread as if this were an intricate tapestry I had to study.

After driving around thirty minutes, with me rubbing my thighs the whole time, she pulled up in front of a brick building. I followed as she walked through the front door and down the hallway. She shoved my hand under her skirt the moment her apartment door closed behind us and I felt her soft thigh before she pushed my fingers inside her. "I like warm hands," she said and bit my shoulder. When she eased my fingers inside her, I moved slowly, wanting to take time to read her. I thought I knew what was happening. I thought, *Here we go. A quick fuck and she's sending me off.* But even as my mind found that easy route, the thought that I knew what was happening here, my heart picked up speed acknowledging how different everything about this was.

My fingers were wet. My fingers stayed with her when her teeth slid across the thick, ropy muscles in my neck. She held on tight. When I slid my free arm up to the back of her head, she whipped into motion, reaching her arm back to grab my wrist and from a distance it would have looked like we were locked in a strange dance as she dragged me back into the dark room. As we walked, I could feel things under my boots. Light, little things like clothes or maybe some rags. Our dance, her control and pull, led me deeper through her apartment until she spun me around and I crashed halfway on, halfway off something hard. I thought it was a bench at first, but it was a small and nearly cushionless couch. In the storm that blew us across the room, her teeth managed to stay locked on tight to my neck, but now she let go. Taking both of my wrists in her hands, she brought them up and held them in front of her face. I had a hard time visually because the lights were still off, but I made out the edges of her movements and felt her delicately flatten my palms, pull each finger straight, and watched her open mouth hover over each movement.

When she was done positioning my hands, her eyes looked straight at mine. "Don't speak," she said as if I needed a reminder. It was already a rule I wouldn't dare break. "Don't move unless I move you," she said. "When I move your hands, you should know what to do, but if you don't, just leave them still and I'll make everything clear." With her words, she moved first one and then the other of my hands casually behind my head and propped me up on a pillow on the arm of the sofa. She pulled my legs onto the couch and crossed one ankle over the over. I was the picture of relaxation but with a pounding heart. She stood at the end of the couch looking over my posed body and lifted her skirt. "Are you getting hard already?" she asked, watching me struggle not to move. I watched her hand move closer to her cunt. She eased the hem of her skirt higher, looked down and then back at me. Her hand disappeared under her sweater. Watching it move, imagining her skin, I shifted my hips.

* * *

"Hey," she said, bending over me. "You need some self-control." She followed my eyes and pulled her sweater over her head. I stayed stock-still watching her. Like an animal desperately waiting for a treat it was never exactly promised, I held as still as I could while she rubbed her neck and shoulders with her hands. She played with her tits, sometimes holding the lace of her bra and rubbing it against her, sometimes teasing herself with her fingers. She bent over and delicately undid my belt, sliding it out of the loops. She slid her bra down and pulled my belt tight between her hands to rub the rougher side of its leather against her tits. I licked my lips and burned with shame hoping she hadn't seen this gesture. *I am not your dog,* I thought and then immediately knew that I was acting just like I was her dog. The realization stiffened me. I knew I would sit still, wait, let her prod and pose me, and that I would enjoy all of it with pure abandon.

She teased me until my pleasure and suffering were so inter-mixed, it felt unholy. Her simple pattern repeated itself: she touched herself, rubbed her clit until she nearly got off, stopped with a sudden real or feigned disinterest, looked at me with her head tilted to one side or the other, took a step closer, and started over. How long this lasted, I couldn't say. I went from raw desire to a different, desperate interest before my emotions finally geared down like a purring engine. She charmed me in the original sense of that word, using this scene as her incantation, my belt now hanging loosely around her neck. When she bent down and unbut-toned my jeans, I had to blink hard to surface out of my dream state. With one hand snaking down each thigh and up, across my belly, back and around, she reached her other hand up to take my wrists from behind my head. I don't move as easily as I used to, but even stiff with pain I let her position me how she wanted.

She settled on top of me, straddling my hips, and moved my

hands so I held the curve of her ass. She leaned back just enough to show me her cunt before grabbing my hand and moving it beneath her. I felt my fingers slide inside her. She moved slowly at first, steadily building until she leaned over and with her fingers splayed out against my chest watching me closely, she came. She asked me to run my hands all over her, and the shift in her tone signaled a change. I got up and positioned myself behind her. "Wait," she said and grabbed my jeans pocket, pulling me toward a door and then her bed. She stopped at the foot of it, saying, "Okay, go."

I ran my hands from her thighs to her shoulders before pushing her face down on the bed and shoving her up toward the pillows. I crawled on top of her feeling grubby when I pushed my sweaty briefs down enough to touch the tip of my swollen clit against her ass. Her skin felt cooler than mine and it slowed me. I rocked against her, laying the full weight of me on top of her shoulders, her back, her ass, her legs. My hands held her head and I buried my mouth in the hair falling behind her ear. She only moved once to pull my arm so it wrapped under and around her, otherwise she let me do what I wanted with no distractions. I came with my clit shoved hard against her ass. I came and felt a shudder run through me. I came and wrapped both arms under her, holding her to me while I let my breath out in one long moan against her neck.

We were silent and still for several minutes before she stood up quickly and left the bedroom, coming back with a cold tea, something herbal by the smell. Whatever it was, it immediately helped me feel more sober and awake. She told me that she liked the way I came against her ass and invited me to see her the next day. She took my number. I told her when I'd be off work and she reminded me she would be there too. She kissed my cheek. As I stood looking at her close like that, with more light in the room, I realized I couldn't tell if she was older or younger or about my same age. I smiled at that. She patted my shoulder and turned me away. It was time for me to go and I left without turning around or saying good-bye.

Only when I hit the sunlight on the sidewalk did I realize I had never said a word to her—not a single word. I planned to say hello to her when I saw her later, but I didn't need to say a lot. I walked in a single direction, fully aware that I didn't know where I was or how to get back to the room where I was staying. I didn't know much. I didn't know her name. She didn't know mine. There was time for that later. I wondered at this new feeling of space all around me. There was more room to breathe. There was time waiting out there ahead of me and it was more than I had ever realized.

CRAVE

Xan West

With particular thanks to A.

I pull on my gloves and you know I'm about to begin. You know what's coming. You are ready. You will never be ready.

I want you to crave the intimacy of my gloves on your skin. So I begin by not touching you with them. I move you into the chair with my body instead, nudge you into position with my boot, my hip, my shoulder, a nod of my head, the knife in my hand. You're in the chair against the wall, eyes trained on my face. I'm standing close, blocking your view of the room, but you know people are watching us, because you are the one who suggested we do this scene in public, and you are the one who arranged for our friends to be here tonight.

One of the joys of public play is sharing our kink with friends, having them hold space for us. Xóchi and her girl Lina are here, doing just that, as you arranged, along with Rain, Gray, and Wendy. There are a smattering of other watchers, too, but they stay farther back. It's our friends that I'm aware of. I can feel them as a calm presence at my back, forming a circle around us, keeping us safe. This scene is different from most of ours. It's primarily about my pleasure, my control, what I need. And their support makes it feel more possible, eases the knot inside my chest a bit.

If it were ten years ago we'd both be standing. Now we save your knees and your spoons for getting down to the floor later in the scene, and back up again afterward. I'm actually slightly taller than you in this position, which is a rarity; at six-two you generally have half a foot on me. The banquet chair is sturdy, has no arms, and puts you at exactly the right height so I don't need to bend much at all. My back is grateful for that.

Unlike me, you're a butch who doesn't mind being naked in public, you just want me to call it your chest and not those other words that make your skin itch and have you locating the nearest exit. I enjoy having you naked, staying still exactly where I put you, while I stand fully clothed and make you wait for what comes next. Wait for the moment I decide to let you feel my gloves.

Rain gave me these leather gloves, one of my most treasured pieces of gear. Rain is a trans leatherdyke and was my first submissive. She taught me so much about being a dominant, so much about being in leatherdyke community. (She still does; she's one of my best friends.) I carry those early lessons into every scene I do, twenty-five years later, right along with these gloves.

I've told you the story behind them. You know what they mean to me. I know that's one of the core reasons you crave their softness on your skin. Not just because they feel amazing. Not just because you think about me touching you with them every time you care for my leathers. But because for me, they embody my dominance.

I'm a simple stone butch leatherdyke who likes to do things a certain way. I wear boots every day. I go to the same barber every other Thursday. And when I play, I'm wearing these gloves. Every single time. Pulling them on is the final step of settling into my dominant headspace. They feel like a second skin, the soft buttery leather gripping my hands just right.

This summer afternoon, I'm wearing a soft, faded-red muscle shirt and my favorite vest, the one that hugs my torso tight and keeps me grounded like nothing else. (Autistic doms have our tricks.) I'm in my Corcoran jump boots and cutoffs, because I wear boots regardless of the weather, dammit, and I wanted ones with treads today. I pack hard when I play. It feels right, that pressure in my jeans. It has very little to do with whether sex is going to happen. And it's not.

Sex isn't allowed at this play party. Carter Hall, our local accessible dungeon run by a wonderful group of queers, holds play parties that don't include sex at least twice a month, and I've found that I really enjoy them. Enjoy being in a space that intentionally creates welcome for ace-spectrum leather queers who don't do sexualized kink. Enjoy being in a space surrounded by folks doing nonsexual kink, and the energy that creates. Enjoy the opportunity for public play without sexual pressure, because I'm almost never up for public sex.

We can fuck when we get home. Or I might make you wait for it until tomorrow, because I'm just that kind of dominant, who enjoys the control and the delay and the tease of *not* having sex as much as I enjoy fucking. Sometimes even more. Yes, waiting for tomorrow sounds very good. Now is about other intimacies, other cravings, for I have you cornered against the wall in a chair, my gloves so close but not touching you. The only thing touching you right now is my knife. It's my favorite knife, one long piece of matte black steel, the wide blade close to six inches, the handle wrapped in cord. I'm a bit of a size queen about knives. I like them wide and long, and this one fits in my hand just right, cord pressing into my palm. It's been my favorite for over fifteen years, and we both know it well.

I stroke your throat with the blade, and I slide into the hyper-focus I always find with a knife, all my attention on our play. I can trust my friends to keep people far enough away that no one will bump me while I'm holding a knife. I get to hone in on you. I'm close enough to hear the hitch in your breath as the blade moves along your throat.

You are larger than me in every way, and I'm always awed by the experience of dominating someone who is substantially bigger, taller, and physically stronger. It feels like you are big enough—physically, energetically—to hold all of me. All of my dominance, all of my sadism, all of my yearning for connection. I'm not tiny myself, and for the first half of my life I was constantly told that I was too much, too butch, too fat, too stone, too loud, too picky about how I needed things to be. I still carry that sense of self with me, still bring that fear that I am more than anyone can or wants to hold, even after years of knowing different. When we play, it truly feels like your tall, supersized, powerful, strong self has no problem at all holding all of my midsize self with my enormous needs and desires. It's a tremendous gift. Especially in scenes like this.

It's delicious to slide into the hugeness of my dominance and really take up room in your space, corner you, intrude upon you, assert control that way first. The matte black blade is particularly gorgeous when it's menacing your soft lips. I love the extra touch of stillness that comes from you when I do this, the way it makes me feel powerful, a bit like a leopard who has cornered prey. I lean in to bite your lower lip, delighting in your gasp, before pulling back to meet your eyes. Eye contact in scene is the only time eye contact makes sense to me, with all the intensity it brings, and I hold your gaze as I growl, enjoying the slight flinch in your eyes, and the way your eyes lower in deference. Yes.

I hold the point of the blade against your throat, digging it in just gently enough to not break the skin while still evoking the delectable bursts of fear we both want. This is one of my favorite things in the world, to be devouring your fear as my knife threatens your throat, making you completely still. I stand there enjoying it for several long minutes before lifting the large flat blade, and turning it, so I can use it to hit you in the chest. The shock of that has you digging your boots into the ground and gripping the sides of your thighs so you remain still for me.

There's nothing quite like using a blade as a paddle, and you always clench your muscles when I do it. The fact that you still manage to offer your chest to me is one of the best things about it. Your chin is lifted so as not to impede me, and you're gripping high enough on your thighs that it opens your chest up instead of you curling in on it. Submission is an act of will, and you have one of the strongest wills of anyone I've had the pleasure to know. This is a concrete manifestation of that strong will, offering your chest, making sure you are still and open to the blade. The steel makes a dull, thuddy, metallic sound against your skin, and leaves a slight redness behind in its wake. I know how intrusive and relentless the sensation is, because I've made you describe it to me. You called it "cold fiery invasive thud."

Your chest is begging for me to punch it. I consider whether that's the first way I want to touch you with my gloves tonight, as I put away my knife, scanning your face. You are licking your lips, and perhaps it's nerves, but it might be thirst, and you're notoriously bad at noticing when you need to hydrate, so I decide to make you drink water, regardless. You take more than an obligatory drink, and as I watch your throat while you swallow I realize where I want to touch you first.

After I put down the water and know I have your attention, I take a slow breath, concentrating on taking in the air all the way through the soles of my boots. I flex my hands, drawing your gaze to them, and smile, thinking about what I want to do, waiting for you to ask me to touch you.

"Please, Sir," you whisper.

"Tell me exactly what you are begging for."

"Please. I want to feel your gloves, Sir."

I lean toward you, my hands outstretched, moving oh so slowly...and place my gloves on the wall on either side of your head. My face is very close to yours, and I feel your exhale whisper along my cheek as you give me the tiniest whimper. I stroke my cheek against yours like a cat, scent marking you. Your skin is one of my favorite things to rub my cheek against, softer than my most treasured stim as a kid, a blanket with a satin edge that was the most soothing thing in the universe. But your cheek against mine in this particular moment isn't just so wondrously soft I want to roll around in the sensation of it. It has this deliciously tender scent of my sweat mixed with yours: salty, sweet, with just a hint of metal underneath.

"Mine," I whisper in your ear.

"Yours, Sir," you say softly, renewing the promise whose symbol you wear on your wrist. That you belong to me, and in my own way, I belong to you. It's been true for over a dozen years.

I smile and kiss you. It starts out sweet, then gets possessive and claiming, finishing with a long torturous bite on your lip because those things wrapped together are all in my love for you. We cannot tease them apart, and really why would we even try when the way they intertwine is precisely what we both desire?

"I love you," I whisper as I lift my head, stepping back. You begin to mouth the words back to me when my gloved hand wraps around the front of your throat, making you still again, your eyes full of dreamy pleasure. This is your most favorite thing, and you moan when my hand tightens. This is about the threat for you, and the feel of it, not about actual breath play, which we don't do because of your asthma. About the way your adrenaline surges, your body knows it's a threat even as you trust me not to actually constrict your airflow, just to tease you with the possibility of pressure on your carotid artery. About the leather at your neck, where you cannot wear a collar, but wish you could. About giving yourself over to my will. Nothing drops you into subspace like this, a cool round stone dropping into that deep dark well, letting yourself sink far and fast.

I lift my hand to stroke your cheek, the leather scent surrounding you. My thumb traces your bottom lip, and your mouth opens for me, in case I want it. Just a tease for now, I decide. I grip your hair to hold you still for me, and thrust my thumb into your warm wet mouth, letting you taste the leather. Your mouth feels amazing, and I'm teasing myself as much as you as I take several long moments to enjoy your tongue caressing the leather. Then I pull it out again and stroke your chest, slapping a few times to build warmth, before I begin to punch you.

You are a pleasure to punch, offering your wide chest to me as a target, glee on your face that matches my own. I feel so free, able to sink into my body, to let the punches be as hard as I want them to be, knowing you will welcome them, stay steadily there for me, taking my blows. Because I need you to, and this is for me. I love how solid you feel, as the thud reverberates back up through my arm each time I punch you. This is the kind of sensation I only get from punching, kicking, and body slams, this level of contact and reverb, and it feeds me, calms me, fills me with a tremendous joy that's unmatchable.

In kink community, we talk a lot about how tops ride the sensations they give to bottoms, making them fly together as one. With *our* rough body play, it's more like you're riding the sensations that I'm feeling, as I strap you to my back and we rocket into space together. The more I punch you, the more I find this dreamy happy space that I can float in, where we're in our own bubble, and I'm getting exactly what I need. When I'm sated, and pause, you grin up at me, and I match your grin with my own.

"Thank you, Sir," you murmur.

"What are you thanking me for?"

"For letting me be your stim toy, of course," you joke.

I chuckle. It's a joke we have traded back and forth for years, as comforting as a heavy blanket, funny because of the truth at its heart. Today it is particularly true.

"I'm not done with you," I promise. "I need you on the mat on your stomach."

"Yes, Sir."

You make your way to the wrestling mats nearby, taking your time to get down. I sit in the chair you were in, watching, as I drink my water. The folks who were watching us play have begun to ring the mats, while keeping a respectful distance. If they're hoping for wrestling, they will be disappointed. That's not what we'll use this play space for. Our friends holding space certainly won't be expecting us to wrestle. While we were playing, I was focused on you, but now that we have paused I am much more aware of having an audience, and a swirl of adrenaline winds into my calm, certain dominance. Good. I can use that now.

I love looming over you and just looking down at you, devouring you with my eyes, your full wide back with all its curves and folds, your fat muscular arms, your gloriously large meaty ass, your thighs thick as tree trunks. It still awes me, even after all these years, to dominate someone so strong and big and fucking powerful. I rejoice in the certainty that you can take all of me, as I begin to circle you slowly, kicking your arms, your thighs, your ass. Enjoying the reverb through my boots. I am a thunderstorm, my boots raining down on you, swirling around you, building the energy between us. This is why our friends are here holding space for this part of the scene, because I feel so huge and full of destructive potential, and they help me concentrate all of that just on you. You can take it, you want to take it for me, love doing that more than anything, and I don't need to worry that it's too big for you, too much. I pour everything I have into you through my boots, and you soak it up for me, groaning.

I pause, letting the storm of energy grow inside me as I brace myself on the wall, placing the sole of one boot on your thigh, then the other boot, and I am standing, my full weight balanced on you. Your moan is beautiful. I continue to hold the storm back, just savoring how gigantic and powerful I feel to be literally standing on the mountain of you.

Then I bend my knees, thrust my weight downward, into you, letting the energy follow it, a lightning burst of pain in your thighs. The wall is there to help me balance as I need to, but this is the moment when I begin to dance my weight up and down on you, driving it into the soles of my boots, enjoying the knowledge that you are going to have tread-mark-shaped-bruises by the time I'm through. I concentrate my weight on one boot so I can grind the treads deep into you with the other, and you scream. Your screams continue as I enjoy the soaring power of the storm I am trampling into you, and the sound of them brings out answering growls from me, as a maelstrom of energy roars through us both, wrapping us together.

And then I feel too far away from you, too high and tall and floating, so I step down, and lay my weight on top of yours, watching out for your knees, and rest my face against your back, panting. You feel amazing under me, still and grounded and mine. That storm of energy continues to whip around inside me, so I remind you to protect your head, and lever myself up with my arms, then drop my weight onto yours. You take it beautifully, I can feel the energy slamming into you and then into the ground, and revel in the reverb driving back up through you into me, reminding me the ground is there, to let this go, the ground can take it. I do several more body slams, each one filling me with increasing calm, until all I want to do is rest my weight on yours and wrap myself in the familiar scent of you, that warm sweetness that endorphins bring out, combined with the salty tang of sweat. So I do. Vaguely, I can sense the people around the mats leaving, and then it's just our friends, holding space until we are done. We are, so I lift my head and mouth my thanks to them. Xóchi points to the bottles of cold water her girl has brought for us, nods her head, and our friends leave us to ourselves.

And so we gather ourselves up to sit. The cold water is amazing, and fills me up in this way I really needed. As if being that energetic thunderstorm had drained me of all moisture until I was bone dry. After I drink it all, I smile at you, stroking your hair, your cheeks, my eyes full of wetness I don't want to acknowledge.

"Thank you," I manage to say, a bit more gruffly than I intended. "I really needed that."

"It's okay to need things, Sir. I'm glad you asked. You know how much I love giving you what you need."

You gather me into a hug, and it's full of all the love and pride and care and tenderness that I couldn't bear for you to express out loud, but can take in this way, so that's how you give it to me.

"You were wonderful. I'm so glad that you're mine," I whisper in your ear. I can feel your smile against my neck, and relish it, letting you hold me for as long as you want, knowing that it helps you come down from a scene, and feeling safe with your arms wrapped tightly around me.

We eventually move over to one of the couches and cuddle up close, eating the dark chocolate you brought. My gloves are off, and I'm stroking your hair with my bare hands, wrapping my fingers into the curl of it, knowing that as soon as we finish after-care you will head to the bathroom to repair it. You cannot tolerate it when your hair isn't perfect unless we're actually playing.

My cheek is slowly rubbing against your bare arm, and we are lazily watching Gray and Wendy do their thing. It always seems to involve Wendy doing things to herself on Gray's command, as she sits a couple of feet away, watching. Tonight, Wendy has put herself in a gorgeous purple rope harness and is waiting for Gray to tell her exactly where to start applying the rainbow of clothespins that are sitting on the table next to her. I can feel the energy arcing between them, can see how Wendy preens under Gray's praise as she follows her orders. Gray is so intense and deliberate, it's clear she's hyperfocusing. There is something so affirming about watching other autistic people play in public. It makes me feel held.

Just as our scene made me feel held. Not just by you, but also by our friends, and by this space, the only public dungeon I know that's not too loud for me, that doesn't have lights that hurt me, that is accessible for us both. I am filled with a dreamy calm as I relax into you, glad to be cuddling with you. Glad that you were able to give me what I craved tonight. Glad to be your dominant, to belong to you in this way.

LOVE REMEMBERS

Angora Shade

Janice rocked in her favorite porch chair, the southern wind blowing her gray locks free from under her hat and pressing warm breath over her sun-kissed skin.

"Mama?"

Kendra's face was careful when she handed over the photo album. Although her mother had never spoken on why it remained untouched on the study bookshelf, Kendra understood the book was a precious thing.

"You've got me worried, Mama."

Janice chuckled and exchanged the newspaper in her lap for the album, running her thumb along the dusty spine. "You've got nothing to be worried about, sugar. There's just something I yearn for."

"What's in there?"

Janice opened the book and flipped to the first page. "Living," she sighed.

The first image presented a much younger version of herself holding a dark-skinned beauty around the waist, Janice's chin resting upon a bare shoulder, her face half obscured by her companion's naturally untamed hair. The beach had been packed with bodies evading the heat on the gentle ocean shoreline that day. She still remembered the humid weight of the air and the sweet smell of Annette's skin.

Kendra turned her attention to the paper in her hands. "That looks just like this woman here in the paper, Mama."

Janice hummed an affirmation while she glanced at her two grandbabies chasing one another in the garden. Her heart held no regrets for loving Kendra's father, having his children, or caring for her husband until the day he died, she only wished she hadn't waited so long. Regret was more a wretched beast than the cancer. There was no ignoring the deep, desperate ache still in her heart.

"It says here she's organizing floats in the Atlanta Pride Parade this afternoon."

Kendra looked at her mother as her wrinkled hands flipped more pages, revealing slightly faded images of the same black woman running through a field, another shot of Janice pointing at the sky while holding her hand, both sporting matching bell-bottomed jeans, their bare feet molded together like yin and yang in the sand. There was even one where Janice kissed the thick joyful lips of her companion.

Kendra sidestepped and shook her head. "Mama, this woman is a lesbian."

"Back then we just said 'gay,' sugar," Janice corrected her.

"Mama . . ." Kendra swallowed hard and crouched down next to where the old woman continued to rock, her fat-knuckled fingers outlining her memories. She hesitated, fearing the question on her lips could offend, but what was more grave, the answer could change everything, and change was a hard thing. But despite her anxiety, Kendra felt the need to understand. "Mama, are you a lesbian?"

Janice cackled and slapped the arm of her chair. She turned to her daughter with tears cresting her eyes. Kendra couldn't tell if they'd been caused by amusement, wind, or memory.

"Oh, sugar. It's not all so cut and dry." She wiped her face and went back to her photos. "I loved your father. I loved Annette too. Still do. But the world was different forty-odd years ago." She eyed her pale daughter's arm—sleeved in colorful tattoos of birds and butterflies—and the shiny piercing of rebellion in her nose. "We weren't all so free back then."

Kendra drew a melancholy smile and paused, then furrowed her brow. Her mother knew the look; it usually preceded some kind of mischief. Kendra stood abruptly while she fished her keys from her jeans. "Let's go, Mama."

The chair stopped suddenly. "Go?" The startle in her voice was genuine.

Kendra called out across the yard to her children. "Get in the car, Patrick! Help your brother with his buckle."

Janice began rocking again, though her movement betrayed a hint of agitation as her gaze wandered dreamily toward the sweet-smelling fields. "Annette won't know me, child. This was back in the '70s. Some of the world might be free to do as they please now, but I'm existing on numbered days." She closed her book and shut her eyes. "This community won't bury a godless old soul."

Kendra lifted her mother's arm and handed her a faded cane. "God loves us all. You don't got nothing to prove to no one but Him." She'd set her hands on her hips and speak in her no-nonsense way whenever she spoke her truth. Janice was proud. "And so far as this Annette woman goes . . ." She helped her mother down the porch steps, at a snail's pace to the car. "Love remembers, Mama."

Janice hobbled into the open passenger seat with her bible of memories clutched under her arm, wondering what her daughter could be thinking. It was the young folks campaigning for societal failure, not the withered, life-beaten ghosts who'd endured the inner shame in being unable to follow their hearts, or so Janice told herself. Maybe if she'd stood up little higher, her life would've taken another direction. A newspaper article, an old volume of sunshine, cheering on a bunch of rainbowed liberals—nothing could make up for choosing the easier way. The coward's way. She'd had that option; Annette didn't.

Kendra picked up the county highway north toward Atlanta, turning her rusty pickup's stiff steering wheel with a firm grip. "How'd you know her, Mama?"

Janice glanced in the backseat, hearing the excited voices of young people playing their portable video games. She cracked the window with a slow crank of the handle, waiting for a fresh breeze to carry her back to what she could still recall.

"We met on the beach." Janice's voice broke with the brutal hack of her typical deep cough, but she cleared her throat and went on. "We were friends immediately, talked about everything, existing in a bubble of our own despite glances we got, words shot at us." She caught her daughter's eye as she shifted gears, and reiterated the firm lessons she'd always tried to impose. "We never saw color. We never thought it strange to hold the hand of a friend."

Janice didn't push when her mother went quiet. She wasn't really in the moment. Although spry in her mind, each passing day took the old woman further into her thoughts and quiet solitude, the way an absence of joy shucked the spirit out of many. This had been a secret all her life; better to let her process through it with the time she had left. Kendra turned the radio on instead, and was greeted by the loud rhythms of modern rock. She adjusted the volume the same time a tire hit a pothole.

Janice caught her book as it jerked on her lap, but not before a photo shook loose and lodged in the folds of her long dress. She scooped it up, her hand grasping it to her heart on impulse, her eyes tearing up again. The day between her fingers came back to her with a recollection so sharp it made her frail hands shake.

Annette's laughter roared over the breaking tide, the threat of sunset chasing her with a speed to match the tight press of her clothes to her body. The shoreline was just how they liked it— empty—with only a few indifferent birds on wing or pecking in the sand. "Come on, Janice!"

The girl loved to run and she won every race. By the time Janice caught up, the water had already reclaimed Annette's bare footprints. She'd sprawled out against their favorite flat outcrop upon her belly, hands supporting her chin, grinning like a wild thing while Janice huffed for breath and climbed up after her. The rock still retained heat from the scorching day despite the cooling ocean spray, and only the scent of fresh nature hung in the breeze.

"You could outrun the world, Netty." She took her seat in an exhausted heap, half sprawled over her companion.

Annette bit her lip with excitement as she rolled Janice around, positioning her limbs more comfortably, and straddling her beneath her crouching form. "I'm not outrunnin' anything. I'm a-runnin' to you." She leaned close to kiss her, but dodged sideways, making Janice laugh and wrestle her immobile. Their bodies were a mass of tight tangles, pressed together like sand and water, only falling still when their giggles ran out with the ebbing tide.

Annette's lips found the shape of Janice's ear as her hand caressed the smooth, round muscle of her upper thigh under layers of skit. "Tell me it'll always be this way."

Janice whispered back, reaching for fistfuls of soft textured hair. The world and morality, or what she'd learned as right and wrong, was tucked safely away under shells or gobs of seaweed, making every word she spoke a simple confession of the heart. "It's the only way I wanna be."

She found Annette's lips, pressing and folding into her mouth, her tongue twisting with unrestrained passion. Their hands began to wander in unison, postures changing from lying to semi-sitting, clothing shucked between a kiss on the neck, shoulder, and jaw, peeling away the layers of propriety until only raw, radiant beauty remained. The stark contrast of their skin color meandered like their quickening breath, shifting their bodies again so they lay opposite each other with heads to knees. Janice slowed only to crawl deeper still, and to taste the tangy open sea between her lover's thighs while Annette engulfed Janice's committed need.

She'd felt pressure in her soul as her rear and center were explored, sliding in unison to demand her explosion. An internal connection was made between the thin layers of her skin, shooting dots of heat and stoking the fire higher with every added lick and point of pressure of Annette's tongue against her pleasure switch. Sweet, agonizing pulls and glides quickened her breath. The rock had felt too hard then, or perhaps it was the squeeze of Annette's strong calves crushing Janice's eager head to her drenched pleasure.

Janice was the first to cry out as she unraveled like a sand castle, losing herself in a flash of near panic and her uncontrolled inward tumble. Her roar set off her lover, pulsing vibrations gripping Janice's fingers, pairing with Annette's unintelligible mumbles. The flavor on Janice's lips, the scent of woman and salty ocean water clung to her as fast as Annette's desperate, sated hold. And it lasted until the final gull gave up his call; the ocean lulled, and the evening sky drew a blanket of dotted crystals.

"Mama?"

She'd been dozing, but Janice suddenly began to cough. Her hand clenched the armrest and the worn seat lurched with every heave. Only her arm waving her daughter's concern away kept the truck from pulling over. "Just my lungs thanking me for quittin' smokin', sugar."

They'd popped onto Interstate 75 while she slept and were an hour from the city. Multiple lanes, car horns, and high-rise signs for gas and food replaced lush fields and spots of housing. Kendra pulled off to refuel, returning with snacks for her kids and her mother's request for sweet tea. The blatant sign for Adult Warehouse stared them down from across the street, sending Janice back into a daydream.

"I'm so glad you made it." Annette had closed the door after a proper look around her shadow-filled stoop.

Janice took her waist and kissed her high cheekbone. "I wasn't gonna miss my Netty's birthday. You only turn nineteen once."

"My daddy's out awhile. Come have some tea."

Annette led Janice to the kitchen where remnants of a meal still scattered the stove and table. She poured a drink but the beverage never exchanged hands. Janice pushed it away still in Annette's grip, the clank of the container assuring her it had contacted the counter.

Janice's smile was wicked. "I'm not thirsty for tea. Netty's gotta get her birthday present."

Annette giggled and hid her mouth fearing someone might hear her. The house was empty but the thin-walled structures of her community betrayed many secrets. They didn't often meet at home. Their friendship wasn't unheard of, but suspicions had grown and negativity hounded them. "What kind of present?"

Janice spun Annette around to face the counter and pushed her thick hair to the side to expose her dark, slender neck. Her lips brushed her friend's skin, followed by a gentle suck. "Tell me you trust me."

Annette didn't hesitate. "With my life."

Janice's right hand stuck a plug into a socket on the wall before moving to her friend's waist and planting sweet rows of kisses up her neck to her jaw. She was engulfed by the rich scent of hair oil and skin. Her other hand slipped down over a hip to a thigh, clicking on the button of a small device no larger than a middle finger. She drew the buzzing toy to Annette's front below the counter while her right hand reached for hidden cleavage inside the top of her dress.

Annette sighed when she felt the vibrations pass her groin. "What is that?"

Janice slid her hands down in unison to hike the hem of Annette's skirt into a ball behind her back. She held it there while her mouth trailed to the other side of Annette's neck and her left hand pushed her object over the crest of her friend's thin panties.

"That's amazing," Annette moaned. She'd reached behind her to feel any bit of Janice she could manage, but she'd had to catch herself when the vibrator hit her sweet spot. She'd called out larger than a giggle; it had been a divine squeal.

Janice could feel the flash of heat between them and the growing damp rolling over her fingers and the toy. Every tap she made caused Annette to squirm, to search it out when she moved it to the side, and push her rear toward Janice's stomach when the pressure became too much. The control had been as intoxicating as the aroma of sex and need that quickly filled the air, and Janice only wanted to give Annette more.

Annette's body was pressed against her, leaving little space for her hand. Janice left the skirt pinned between them and switched her tired wrist for the other. She licked the cream on her fingers before reaching back into the top folds of Annette's dress and returning her gift down below.

A slick entrance and a soft moan a moment later had Janice's thumb and forefinger pinching Annette's large nipple while she partially inserted the wiggling thing inside her body. She held it at an angle against Annette's throbbing clit, rotating it in her hand while she nipped at her ear. Annette ground into Janice's hand and shook, her face pressed hard against the forearm she used to brace herself against the counter to muffle her cry. Warm heat pooled around Janice's fingers as she whispered, "Happy birthday, Netty."

"Let's go, Mama!" a child screeched.

"I got a game level upgrade, Gramma!"

"I want a cookie."

The engine sputtered and turned while the traffic grew thick. Every mile exposed more bumper stickers and colorful streamers flying like taut kite strings from secured windows. And when the skyline of Atlanta was in view, Janice's heart skipped beats. She might really find Annette within the throng. She swallowed hard and wondered if she'd find forgiveness too; thinking back on their final moments together had forever left a sour taste within her mouth.

They'd heard only footsteps and not the telltale squeak of the door or the powerful arm guiding it closed. Annette's dress had come down, the toy was pocketed away again, but their bodies had come to face forward, their arms around each other, their lips locked in a fierce kiss they hadn't expected to be ripped away.

An enraged black face threw Janice to the floor. She'd slid a ways but was too shocked by witnessing the blow that struck Annette across the mouth to hear the dishes on the upended table crash to the floor.

"My daughter." There was no inflection in the voice of Annette's father, just a straight, teeth-gritting rush of syllables.

But Annette's eyes had become saucers, wincing tight before the second blow spun her off her feet. "Not. My. Daughter."

Janice watched the blood drip from a swelling lip and nose, and the growing rouge on Annette's cheek the same moment two heavy hands lifted Janice out of the kitchen and shoved her tripping out the front door. A neighbor stuck his head out of a window, and a head turned to look from a passing car. The night had been dark; no one would've seen the scrapes on her palms or the fresh hole in her jeans.

"If you see her again, I will kill you," she'd heard. "And her!"

Janice began to cough hard. She leaned her weight against her cane, but the hack continued and Kendra had to hold her upright until it passed. The hot air and heavy memories felt like a crushing wall. Even the brilliant shocks of color painted on the faces and bodies around them as they made their way through the crowds felt more like a swarm of gnats than the jubilant celebrations of diverse people. The singing of free voices sliced at Janice's heart.

"Over there, Mama." Kendra pointed and began to lead her mother and children toward a group of bright-pink people. They stood before a parade float in the shape of a heart near a large sign reading Float Gathering. "That looks promising."

Janice gripped her cane as she hobbled, mentally pushing back her fears. It had been decades; children were born, world leaders died, medical breakthroughs were made. She was just a woman out of time, both in action and in years. She'd stayed away out of love and respect for the principles of yesteryear, going on to make her way, never knowing how things had gone for her friend. She'd left her safe. Better safe than together.

But she was there, a stunning large African woman in a royal blue, sleeveless, skirt-sweeping dress, giving directions to joyful faces; young and old, light and dark; black, tan, and those more pale than the starlight. Strings of gray appeared like highlights from the sunshine in her hair, but time had been kind; she was older but still every bit of what Janice remembered. She froze; in that moment she could barely breathe; her heart thundered away in her chest.

"Go on, Mama."

Janice turned to see a screen of people block her from her family. A few feet ahead stood the only woman she'd ever loved.

"Excuse me, Ma'am," a tall man said as he bumped into her. Janice hesitated. She could turn back. She didn't have to do this. Forgiveness, or whatever it was she sought for lost time or confusion, was as hard to ask for as it was to comprehend why she'd waited so long.

The crowd grew thicker still, and royal blue blurred in a soup of pink and gold as music erupted and feet began to move. Her nagging cough hit her hard again. There was no more time to waste; she didn't have any. Shoving one unstable foot in front of the other supported by her cane, Janice shouted with her small, raspy voice above the din. "Netty!"

A little white boy tugged on his mother's shirt hem. "Mama, why's Gramma huggin' that woman?"

Kendra looked down on him and smiled. "Because love remembers."

ABOUT THE AUTHORS

MARIE CARLSON lives in the Midwest US with her partner and an Australian cattle dog/beagle mix who is a complete cuddle monster. She's been published by Circlet Press, Storm Moon Press, Xcite Books, Total E-Bound, and Torquere Press. Marie writes about hunger and power in all their forms and spends far too long making the perfect playlist for even the shortest project.

AVERY CASSELL is a writer and artist living in San Francisco, whose historical books include Lambda finalist, *Resistance: The LGBT Fight Against Fascism in WWII*, *Butch Lesbians of the 20s, 30s, and 40s Coloring Book*, and *Butch Lesbians of the 50s, 60s, and 70s Coloring Book*; the erotic romance *Behrouz Gets Lucky*; and short stories in several anthologies, including this one, *Best Lesbian Erotica 2015*, *Unspeakably Erotic: Lesbian Kink*, and *Sex Still Spoken Here*.

CATHERINE COLLINSWORTH (catherinecollinsworth704@ gmail.com) lives in New York City with her partner, a retired teacher. When not writing, she is . . . writing, because after breaking a twenty-year writer's block, she doesn't want to do anything else. Except see her therapist once a week. She is currently working on the catalyst that broke the block, a coming-of-age story set in the city during the AIDS era. She thanks her Monday Night Brilliant Writers' Group for their love and support as she wrote nothing for years, and for their unerring guidance and constructive criticism when she finally did.

OLIVIA DROMEN (wordscanbesexy.com) writes realistic, kinky, queer, trans erotica. She is nonmonogamous, trans, kinky, and magnetically attracted to awkward queers with cats. She lives near the fabled lesbian-centric town of Northampton, Massachusetts, with her cats and her partners. She enjoys hiking, listening to klezmer music, and having lots of sex. She has been writing her Queer Quickies series since 2011.

MARIA CHIARA FERRO (mch.ferro@gmail.com) is a goth queer femme living in Naples, Italy, with her partner and their cat.

DOROTHY FREED (DorothyFreedWrites.com) is the pseudonym of a San Francisco Bay Area writer, who began writing smut because art imitates life. She is the author of *Perfect Strangers: A Memoir of the Swinging '70s*, and a contributor to the anthologies *Best Women's Erotica of the Year, Vol 1*, and *Dirty 30, Vol 2*.

GIGI FROST is the nom de plume of a mild-mannered East Coast femme who has travelled the US touring with The Femme Show and Body Heat: the Femme Porn Tour. Her erotica writing has been published in *Say Please, Girl Crazy*, and *Me and My Boi*.

MX NILLIN FUCHS (mxnillin.com) is a renowned queer sexuality blogger, an accomplished speaker who has provided

LGBTQIA+ diversity training around the province of Saskatchewan, and a growing queer sexual pleasure and wellness advocate whose work has been featured worldwide, including in the *Bedfellows: Porn as Pedagogy* exhibit at the Tate Modern Museum of London in October 2016. They can be found collaborating with other writers and doing queer advocacy work. Mx Nillin recently spoke about the struggles faced by polyamorous and nonmonogamous folks at the 2018 Interpride World Conference and AGM in Saskatoon, Saskatchewan.

TOBI HILL-MEYER is an indigenous Chicana transwoman with fifteen years' experience working in nonprofits, serving on boards, and consulting in nonprofit management. She is editor of the Lambda Literary Finalist anthology *Nerve Endings: The New Trans Erotic*, author of children's books *A Princess of Great Daring* and *Super Power Baby Shower*, and director of the erotic documentary series *Doing it Online,* which won Most Dazzling Docu-Porn at the Feminist Porn Awards. Currently, she serves as Co-Executive Director for Gender Justice League.

FOSTER JOY (fosterjoywrites@gmail.com) is the pen name of a published poet, events writer, and researcher most recently featured in the *Journal of GLBT Family Studies.* She/they identifies as a bisexual/pansexual, white, cisgender native San Franciscan. With a degree in English and a minor in creative writing, Foster has also written numerous short stories, flash fiction, and a screenplay. This is her/their first published piece of erotica.

LAUREL ISAAC is a queer memoirist living in the Pacific Northwest. More of her sex writing can be found in *Shameless Behavior: Brazen Stories of Overcoming Shame, The Big Book of Submission,* and *The V-Word: True Stories of First-Time Sex.*

ADA LOWELL (twitter@untonuggan) is a chronically ill and neurodivergent disability rights activist and writer. They live on their couch on stolen Pamunkey land in the DC metro area.

R. MAGDALEN is a queer single mother on the autism spectrum who loves to write smut of all kinds. She started out an artist, became a linguist, then a textbook writer, and now she works with spreadsheets. In addition to her day job, she does freelance writing and editing, and is working on a novel that will likely feature lesbian aliens. She has enjoyed the *Best Lesbian Erotica* series for many years.

FALLEN MATTHEWS (fallenkittie.com) is an Afro-L'nu scholar who studies existentialism and supernatural folklore. Although she's always liked to write, she only thought to pursue publication during her undergraduate years after one of her professors inspired her to critically consider the realms of cinema and the senses. She holds degrees in sociology and gender studies, and hopes to promptly finish her interdisciplinary doctorate further down the line—in between movie marathons and indie reviews on her website.

J. MORK is a longtime resident of San Francisco. She has written and performed in the Bay Area focusing around issues of disability and sexuality. She has been a sex worker for eighteen years, starting with a stint in phone sex at age twenty. Normally she parcels little bits of information about what she does, so she always finds it a real pleasure to reveal all the sticky and gory details.

JUNE AMELIA ROSE (Twitter and Instagram @anarcho_slut) is an anarchist leatherdyke fiction writer and submissive transsexual femme living in Brooklyn. Her stories "Bootlicker" and "Porngirl, The Illustrious" were self-released as zines to cult praise. Her writing has also been featured in *FIST: A Zine for Leatherdykes*. She has edited four books so far, ranging from memoirs about underground punk music to novels about lesbian teenage sexuality. She is currently at work on her first novel, as well as a collection of essays.

ANGORA SHADE (angorashade.blogspot.com) is an American erotic romance author living in Europe. She enjoys creating stories that surprise, amuse, or tease the reader, providing an alternative outlook to the monotony of someone's usual day.

BD SWAIN (bdswain.com) is a butch dyke who writes queer smut because of a deep need to do so. You'll find BD's stories on her site and in anthologies like *Best Lesbian Erotica 2013, Best Lesbian Erotica 2015*, and *Unspeakably Erotic: Lesbian Kink*. One of BD's favorite hobbies is taking dirty pictures and you'll find fifty-two of them in her custom deck of playing cards and a lot more on her Instagram stream @bdswain.

Unbeknownst to her dissertation committee, **T.R. VERTEN** (Twitter @trepverten) is a spy in the house of academia, creating an aesthetic manifesto in disguise. Her erotica appears in anthologies from Cleis, New Smut Project, Republica, Burning Book, and Ravenous Romance, and the recently reissued novella *Confessions of Rentboy*.

XAN WEST (xanwest.wordpress.com) is an autistic queer fat white Jewish genderqueer writer with multiple disabilities who spends a lot of time on Twitter. Their erotica has been published widely, including in the *Best S/M Erotica* series, the *Best Gay*

Erotica series, and the *Best Lesbian Erotica* series. Xan's "First Time Since" won honorable mention for the 2008 NLA John Preston Short Fiction Award. Xan's queer kink erotica collection *Show Yourself to Me* was described by M. Christian as "a book that changes what erotica can and should be." They recently published *Their Troublesome Crush*, a polyamorous queer kink romance.

SINCLAIR SEXSMITH (they/them) is "the best-known butch erotica writer whose kinky, groundbreaking stories have turned on countless queer women" (AfterEllen), who "is in all the books, wins all the awards, speaks at all the panels and readings, knows all the stuff, and writes for all the places" (Autostraddle).

They have written at sugarbutch.net since 2006, recognized by numerous places as one of the top sex blogs. Sinclair's gender theory and queer erotica is widely published online and in more than thirty anthologies, including *Best Lesbian Erotica 2006, 2007, 2009, 2011, 2014, and 2016, Sometimes She Lets Me: Best Butch/Femme Erotica, Take Me There: Trans and Gender-queer Erotica, The Harder She Comes: Butch/Femme Erotica, The Big Book of Orgasms: 69 Sexy Stories, The Sexy Librarian's Dirty 30, Me & My Boi: Queer Erotic Stories, Paradigms of Power: Styles of Master/slave Relationships, Queer: A Reader for Writers, The Remedy: Trans and Queer Healthcare, Queering Sexual Violence: Radical Voices from Within the Anti-Violence Movement, Persistence: All Ways Butch and Femme, Nonbinary: Memoirs of Gender and Identity,* and others.

ABOUT THE EDITOR

Sinclair has edited *Erotix: Literary Journal of Somatics*, *Best Lesbian Erotica 2012*, and *Say Please: Lesbian BDSM Erotica*. In 2015, they published a six-novella series, which included *Bois Will Be Bois: Butch/Butch Erotica* and *The Dyke In Psych Class: Butch/Femme Erotica*. Their short-story collection, *Sweet & Rough: Queer Kink Erotica*, was a 2015 finalist for the Lambda Literary Award, and they were awarded the National Leather Association Cynthia Slater Nonfiction Article Award in 2015 and the National Leather Association John Preston short story award for 2016.

They have taught kink, gender, sexuality, relationship, and writing workshops online and throughout the US and Canada. Sinclair is also a facilitator and cofounder of Body Trust, a somatic arts collective. All of their work centers around studies of power and the body—individual, interpersonal, and institutional. They identify as a white nonbinary butch dominant, a survivor, and an introvert, and they live on Ohlone land in Oakland, California, with their boy. Follow all their writings at patreon.com/mrsexsmith.

Printed in the USA
CPSIA information can be obtained
at www.ICGtesting.com
LVHW031634281123
765190LV00046B/1156

9 781627 782951